"You were made t[...] he murmured against her hair. "Let me show you how loving's meant to be. Let me give you the pleasure you deserve."

Ruby's throat tightened. She struggled to reply, but no words would come.

"What is it? Are you afraid of me?"

She shook her head, finding her voice. "It's not you I'm afraid of. It's me. All those years of steeling myself against the things he did, the nights of lying there, wondering how he was to use me next..."

She exhaled raggedly. "What if I'm broken, Ethan? What if I can't— ?"

His kiss lasted just long enough to block her words. "Hush," he breathed.

* * *

The Widowed Bride
Harlequin® Historical #1031—March 2011

Praise for
Elizabeth Lane

The Horseman's Bride

"The Gustavson family has won the hearts of Americana fans seeking a realistic love story. Lane wisely continues in this vein with the latest in her series, in which a fiery young woman meets her match in a mysterious drifter."
—*RT Book Reviews*

The Borrowed Bride

"Lane's pleasing love story brims over with tender touches."
—*RT Book Reviews*

His Substitute Bride

"This tender and loving story, spinning off from Lane's previous Western, showcases her talent for drawing three-dimensional characters and placing them in an exciting time and place."
—*RT Book Reviews*

Wyoming Woman

"This credible, now-or-never romance moves with reckless speed through a highly engrossing and compact plot to the kind of happy ending we read romances to enjoy."
—*RT Book Reviews*

the Widowed Bride

ELIZABETH LANE

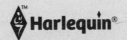

TORONTO NEW YORK LONDON
AMSTERDAM PARIS SYDNEY HAMBURG
STOCKHOLM ATHENS TOKYO MILAN MADRID
PRAGUE WARSAW BUDAPEST AUCKLAND

If you purchased this book without a cover you should be aware that this book is stolen property. It was reported as "unsold and destroyed" to the publisher, and neither the author nor the publisher has received any payment for this "stripped book."

Recycling programs
for this product may
not exist in your area.

ISBN-13: 978-0-373-29631-6

THE WIDOWED BRIDE

Copyright © 2011 by Elizabeth Lane

All rights reserved. Except for use in any review, the reproduction or utilization of this work in whole or in part in any form by any electronic, mechanical or other means, now known or hereafter invented, including xerography, photocopying and recording, or in any information storage or retrieval system, is forbidden without the written permission of the publisher, Harlequin Enterprises Limited, 225 Duncan Mill Road, Don Mills, Ontario, Canada M3B 3K9.

This is a work of fiction. Names, characters, places and incidents are either the product of the author's imagination or are used fictitiously, and any resemblance to actual persons, living or dead, business establishments, events or locales is entirely coincidental.

This edition published by arrangement with Harlequin Books S.A.

For questions and comments about the quality of this book please contact us at Customer_eCare@Harlequin.ca.

® and TM are trademarks of the publisher. Trademarks indicated with ® are registered in the United States Patent and Trademark Office, the Canadian Trade Marks Office and in other countries.

www.eHarlequin.com

Printed in U.S.A.

For my girls
Tanya, Teresa, Tiffany and Olivia

Chapter One

Dutchman's Creek, Colorado
May 1920

The sooty cobweb stretched from the chandelier to the high ceiling, a good four feet out of reach. Lurking near its center was a spider—a monster with long, prickly legs and a body as big as a copper penny.

Ruby Denby Rumford glared up at her adversary. She'd always had a mortal dread of spiders, but she couldn't let this one get the best of her. If she wanted to attract good tenants for her boardinghouse, the place would have to be spotless from floor to ceiling. The spider had to go.

Circling warily, she plotted her attack. She might be able to reach the web with the broom. But if she knocked the spider loose, it could end up anywhere—in her hair, in her face, down her blouse… Ruby shuddered as she weighed her options. The only way to make sure the creature didn't land on her would be to capture it first.

A dusty Mason jar with a lid sat on the kitchen counter. That would do for a trap. But she'd need something to climb on. Ruby sighed as she surveyed the rickety cane chairs that had come with the old boardinghouse. Maybe she should have paid four-fifty for that stepladder at the hardware store. But buying the property had taken almost all her money. Until the rents started coming in, she would need to hoard every cent she had left.

Moving a chair to the center of the room, she tried standing on the seat; but the spider was still out of reach. She needed something more—that wooden crate in the corner might do. Placed on the chair, it would raise her a good eighteen inches.

With the crate in place, Ruby retrieved the jar and prepared for battle. She could do this, she lectured herself. A woman who'd fired three bullets into her raging, two-hundred-pound husband at point-blank range should have no trouble facing down a creature the size of her thumb.

Hollis Rumford had deserved to die. Even the jurors had agreed after they'd heard how Hollis had abused her and threatened worse to their two young daughters. At the urging of the best lawyer in the state, they'd acquitted Ruby on grounds of self-defense. But her wealthy friends—mostly Hollis's friends—had been less forgiving. The Springfield, Missouri, social set had cut her off cold.

Exhausted and needing a change of scene, she'd fled to Europe with her little girls. A few months later she'd returned to discover that her late husband's estate had been gobbled up by creditors, leaving her with little more than a pittance.

There was nothing to do but pull up stakes and make a new start.

Dutchman's Creek had been a natural choice. Ruby's brother Jace, her only close kin, had settled on a nearby ranch. He and his spirited young bride, Clara, were expecting their first baby. They'd urged Ruby to come to Colorado so their children could grow up together.

Ruby had welcomed the invitation. She'd seen the town on an earlier visit and been captivated by its peaceful mountain setting. She'd always been close to Jace, and Clara was like a sister to her. But she had no intention of becoming a burden to them. Whatever it took, she'd vowed, she would find a way to provide for herself and her children.

The vacant boarding house at the south end of Main Street had looked like an answer to her prayers. She and her daughters could live on the main floor and rent the four upstairs rooms for a steady income.

Only now was she beginning to realize how much she'd taken on.

She was glad she'd accepted Clara's invitation to take the girls for the week. Mandy and Caro were having the time of their lives on the ranch, riding horses, climbing trees, bottle-feeding orphaned calves and gathering eggs in the chicken coop.

Meanwhile, their mother had a spider to dispose of.

Clutching the jar in one hand, she hitched up her narrow skirt and hoisted herself onto the edge of the chair. Her brother had offered to come and help her get the place in shape. Ruby had turned him down out of stubborn pride. Jace had already done enough for her, risking his life and freedom to protect her after Hollis's death. It was time she learned to manage on her own.

Holding her breath, Ruby mounted the crate. Her knees quivered as she steadied her balance on the wooden slats. Seconds, that was all she'd need to do the job.

Close up, the spider looked bigger and nastier than ever. Steeling herself, Ruby twisted the lid off the Mason jar and positioned it below the creature. A little more stretch and she could use the lid to maneuver it inside. Heart pounding, she eased onto her tiptoes…

A wooden slat splintered beneath her weight. Thrown off balance, Ruby lurched upward. The jar shattered against the floor as she grabbed for the chain that suspended the small chandelier. Miraculously, the chain held. But her thrashing feet had toppled the crate and chair, leaving her to dangle above the wreckage. The distance to the floor wasn't all that far, but falling could land her on a splintered board, a jutting chair leg or shards of broken glass.

The web was empty now. The spider, she realized, could be anywhere. Panic clenched Ruby's stomach. Her grip was getting weaker, and she had no safe place to fall. There was only one thing she could do.

Scream bloody murder.

U.S. Deputy Marshal Ethan Beaudry had been assigned to weed out bootleggers, not rescue females

in distress. But the shrieks coming from the old boarding house were too urgent to ignore. Vaulting the picket
fence, he charged up the steps and burst through the
front door.

His breath caught in his throat.

The woman had stopped screaming. She hung by
her arms, staring down at him from beneath a tumble
of red-gold hair. Her eyes were as blue as the heart of a
mountain columbine.

She did make a fetching sight, dangling like an acro-
bat from the chandelier chain, with her white blouse
pulled loose and her skirt hiked over her shapely calves.
Ethan was tempted to spend a few more seconds admir-
ing the view. But then she spoke.

"What are you staring at, you fool? Stop gawking
and get me down from here!"

Her voice was low, with a taut, gravelly edge that
roused Ethan's senses. "Do you trust me to catch you?"
he teased.

"Are you sure you're strong enough?" she retorted.
"I'm not what you'd call a little woman."

No, she certainly wasn't, Ethan observed. At five foot
eight or nine with a body that could grace the bow of a
frigate, she'd make an armful for any man.

He wouldn't mind being that man.

Kicking aside the debris, Ethan stood beneath her
and held out his arms. "Come on," he said.

She hesitated, her eyes taking the measure of his
broad shoulders and six-foot-two-inch height. One by
one, her fingers peeled away from the chain.

With a little yelp, she dropped straight down, feet

first. Ethan caught her awkwardly around the knees. From there she slid down the front of him, delicious curves gliding intimately down his face, over his chest, down his belly to—

Lord have mercy, he was in trouble now. His erection had sprung up with coiled-spring efficiency, ready for playtime. She would have felt it all the way down.

Feet touching the floor, she pushed away from him. Her face was flushed, her full lips parted. Ethan fought the temptation to fling caution to the wind, seize her in his arms and kiss her till she burned. The lady would probably slap him hard enough to dislocate his jaw. And she *was* a lady. Ethan made a practice of reading people, and he was certain of that. Her clothes were simple but expensively made. The Irish-linen blouse, smudged with dust and edged with the barest touch of lace, looked European, as did the daintily pointed kidskin oxfords. And he would bet money that the pearl studs in her earlobes were as genuine as her upper-class Midwestern accent.

So what was such a woman doing in this run-down boardinghouse, a rumored delivery point for the bootlegging trade? He didn't want to believe she was involved. But he'd known stranger things to happen.

A flick of her tongue moistened her lower lip. Her complexion was like a porcelain doll's, but close up, Ethan could see the careworn shadows beneath her eyes. He estimated her age at about thirty, and something told him she'd had her share of troubles. He'd noticed right off she wasn't wearing a wedding ring. But she was far too stunning not to have married. A widow, Ethan surmised. A luscious redheaded widow who'd been around the block and knew every step of the way.

Intriguing. And damn tempting...

Ethan brought himself up with a mental slap. He'd come here to do a risky job. As long as he was working undercover, he'd be crazy to get personally involved—even with a female as enticing as this one.

But that didn't mean he couldn't have a little fun.

The silence between them had begun to crackle like the air before a summer storm. Ethan cleared his throat.

"Are you all right?" he asked her.

She hesitated, as if examining herself for inner wounds. "Yes, but I think I...*oh!*"

Her body stiffened, eyes jerking wide. With urgent gasps, she began yanking at the front of her blouse, popping the tiny shell buttons in her haste. Ethan made a gentlemanly show of averting his eyes, but continued to steal furtive glances desire warring with dismay. Either the woman was in genuine danger or her nerves had snapped.

As the last button gave way, she ripped the blouse off her body, shook it furiously at arm's length and flung it to the floor. Ethan felt a touch on his arm. Turning, he met her frozen gaze. "If you please." Her voice was a husky breath. "I need you to look..."

Her lacy camisole and gently cinched corset covered her modestly. Still, the woman looked good enough to lick like a strawberry ice-cream cone. Ethan feasted his eyes as she slowly turned.

Damnation!

There, clinging to the back of her pink satin corset was a Texas-size brown spider. It didn't strike him as a venomous sort, but he couldn't blame the lady for being spooked. He wasn't crazy about spiders himself.

"Hold still," he muttered, raising his hand.

A quick brush sent the spider flying toward the floor. Ethan would have crushed it with his boot, but it skittered down a crack in the planking and disappeared.

The woman's knees sagged. Ethan readied his arms to catch her in a faint, but she righted herself as if by force of will. Snatching up the discarded blouse, she thrust her arms into the sleeves, pushed the remaining buttons through their holes and tucked the hem into the waist of her skirt. Only when she was as presentable as she could make herself did she turn back to face him. Her face was pale, but her ripe lips managed a smile.

"We haven't been properly introduced," she said, offering her hand. "I'm Ruby Rumford. I just bought this place, and I'm very much in your debt."

"Ethan Beaudry. Happy I could be of help, ma'am." Ethan accepted her handshake. Her fingers were strong and smooth, her manner so genuine that it made him want to cringe in self-disgust. Only a low-down snake would lie to such a woman. But that was exactly what he was about to do.

Starting now.

Ethan Beaudry.
Ruby turned the name over in her mind like a child examining a pebble. She liked the sound of it, and the way it suited everything about him—dark, rugged

features, a rangy body and a drawl you could cut with a butter knife.

She remembered how he'd caught her in his arms and lowered her to the floor, paying no heed to the sparks their bodies had ignited on the way down. Ruby understood men well enough to know that some things couldn't be helped. But she'd been surprised at her own response to that brief contact. It had been so many years since she'd experienced anything good with a man, she'd forgotten what it felt like.

Sliding down the front of Ethan Beaudry had sent a shock of pleasure all the way to her toes.

But what was she thinking? With Hollis gone barely a year, the last thing she needed was another man in her life. She had a future to forge and two daughters to raise. And she had her own shattered sense of self to rebuild. After what she'd been through, she was no longer fit to be any man's sweetheart, lover or wife. Maybe she never would be.

She was damaged goods—damaged to the roots of her soul.

"I'm sorry I can't offer you something to drink." She glanced toward the front door. Ethan realized it was his cue to leave. But he wasn't ready to walk out on what might be his best chance to learn more about her.

"You say you just bought this property?" He righted the chair, inviting her to sit.

"Yes. I signed the papers two days ago." She sat on the edge of the seat, clasping her fingers in her lap. "I'll be open for boarders as soon as I get the place cleaned up—if the spiders will let me." Her edgy little laugh deepened the dimples in her cheeks. Ethan swore silently. Why did she have to be so damn appealing?

"Don't you have anyone to help you?" he asked.

"Nobody that I can afford to pay. My brother offered to come, but I didn't want to impose on him." She glanced down at her hands, then met his eyes again. Her long lashes were the color of molasses taffy. "How was it you were able to hear me and rush right in, Mr. Beaudry? You must have been close by."

"Please call me Ethan. And yes, I was out for some morning air, just passing this place when I heard you. It was pure luck."

Lie number one. Ethan had been keeping an eye on the vacant boarding house since his arrival a week ago. The recent passage of the Eighteenth Amendment, outlawing the manufacture, transportation and selling of alcohol for consumption, had spawned an epidemic of illegal whiskey stills and a network of criminal activity. The U.S. Marshals Service had been assigned the job of law enforcement in this matter.

The back cellar of the hitherto-empty boardinghouse was a suspected drop-off spot for illegal moonshine whiskey, to be loaded onto trucks and hauled away for clandestine sale in places like Denver, Omaha and Kansas City. Ethan had seen tire tracks and boot prints leading around the building though he had yet to catch anyone in the act. But identifying the deliverymen wasn't why he'd come to Dutchman's Creek. He was after the boss who was running the operation, not his errand boys.

Which led to the question of the scrumptious widow Rumford. If she'd been placed here to provide a safe link between buyers and sellers, then she was as dangerous as a spitting cobra. But if she'd bought the old boardinghouse in complete innocence, heaven help her, she could be in more peril than she knew.

"So, what is it you do?" she asked.

Ethan's cover story, devised by some pencil pusher in the head office, was well rehearsed. "I'm a history professor, taking a year's leave to write a book about Colorado. This town struck me as a peaceful place to settle down for a few months and concentrate on my work."

Lie number two. Blatant, but necessary.

She studied him, one delicate eyebrow arching upward. "So you're new in town? I must say, you don't look like a professor."

"I'll take that as a compliment." Ethan leaned against a dusty sideboard, his mind working. Having stumbled into this situation, he'd be a fool not to put it to use.

"I have a business proposition for you," he said. "Right now I'm staying at the hotel. But it's expensive and noisier than I'd like. I know you need help and that you can't afford to pay for it. Would you be open to my moving in here and lending you a hand—say, in exchange for my first week's room and board?"

Emotions played across her face as she weighed his offer. Ethan could pretty well guess what was going on in that lovely head. He was a stranger, and they'd be spending time alone together. Would she be safe with him? Would her reputation suffer from his presence?

Then again, he could be wrong. Ruby Rumford could have dark motives of her own. If she suspected he was lying and wanted to trap him, he might already be in trouble. But that was a chance he'd have to take.

"I'd be happy to work for the pleasure of helping a lady," he added. "But something tells me, if you wouldn't accept free help from your brother you wouldn't accept it from me. This arrangement would be fair, and it could work well for both of us. So, do we have a deal?"

Hesitation flickered in her eyes. Her amply curved bosom strained the fabric of her blouse as she took a deep breath. "You could have your choice of the rooms. But your meals would be a problem at first. I won't be able to cook until the kitchen's set up."

"I can make do until then. The food at the hotel is all right, but I'll confess I've been hankering for some good old-fashioned home cooking."

"Then I suppose we have a deal, as you say." Her smile wavered as she stood. "Come on, I'll show you the rooms."

She led the way up the wooden stairs, giving him the pleasure of following behind. With each step, the fabric of her narrow khaki skirt molded to her buttocks, setting his fantasies ablaze. He imagined his hands cupping those rounded moons as he thrust deep between her legs into her tight, wet warmth, pushing toward that instant of blessed release.

Would she be willing to play by his rules—no messy emotions, no promises, no tears when he walked away for good? A man could never be sure of such things. But a woman like Ruby, delectable, mature and unattached, would certainly know the game. At the very least, he could have a hell of a good time teaching her.

Damn!

Ethan brought himself up with a mental slap. He was here to break up a bootlegging ring, not seduce his luscious landlady. If Ruby proved to be involved with the smugglers, he could end up hauling her pretty ass to jail. He'd be smart to remember that when his mind strayed below his belt.

But meanwhile, there was nothing wrong with enjoying the view.

The four upstairs rooms were of equal size, with a common bathroom off the central hallway. The plumbing had been added after the house was built and was crude at best. But at least the place had a flush toilet and a tub with running water for the tenants. Downstairs, there was only a toilet and basin for Ruby and the girls. They would have to make do with a washtub or wait their turn to bathe on the second floor.

It was a far cry from the grand mansion she'd shared with Hollis in Missouri. But at least their lives here would be safe and peaceful. Ruby could only hope her daughters would adjust to their reduced circumstances.

Ethan Beaudry was prowling from room to room, pausing to check the view from each of the windows. He moved like a panther, lithe, alert and powerful, his presence filling every space he entered.

Watching from the hallway, Ruby tried to imagine him lecturing to a gallery of students. The picture refused to come together. But then, what did she know?

She'd married at nineteen and never attended college. Her only idea of a professor was the aging, bespectacled stereotype she'd read about in books. There was no reason a professor couldn't be tall and darkly handsome, was there?

A flash of memory brought back that brief instant in Ethan's arms. Her senses reveled in the clean, leathery smell of him and the manly contours of his body. Her legs heated and softened beneath her skirt. Oh, this wasn't good. Not good at all.

With a deep breath, she willed the memory away. She was a businesswoman and the man was her tenant, nothing more. She would remember that even if she had to remind herself every ten minutes.

Ethan seemed more interested in the back rooms than the two in front. Again, he checked the windows, pressing close enough to see the muddy backyard below. Not that there was anything down there to see—just rutted tracks where people had left their cars and wagons when they came into town; maybe teenagers as well, who might have used the secluded spot as a late-night lovers' lane.

According to the real estate agent, the place had been vacant for nearly a year. The bank had taken it over when its previous owner, an elderly woman, had passed away, leaving an unpaid mortgage. Ruby was just beginning to discover the old boardinghouse's secrets. But then, she had secrets of her own. Maybe in time she'd begin to feel a sort of kinship with the old place. Maybe in time it would even become home.

Ethan was bending over the single bed in the south

room, scowling as he tested the worn cotton mattress with his fist. The springs squeaked as he pushed up and down. Heaven save her, was he planning on having lady friends up? Maybe she should have asked more questions before agreeing to have him as a tenant.

"The beds are old, but you can have your choice of them," she said, stepping into the room. "I don't mind your moving things around."

"This one will do fine." He straightened. The sunlight pouring into the room heightened the gold flecks in his dark brown eyes.

"The room hasn't been cleaned yet." Ruby focused on brushing a speck of lint off her skirt. She was alone with a compellingly attractive man in what had just become his bedroom. Maybe this arrangement was a mistake.

"It'll be no trouble for me to clean it," he said. "But I'll need a desk or a table for my work. Do you have anything I can use?"

"Not that I can spare." Ruby had already taken an inventory of the sparse furnishings. "But the agent told me there was some older furniture stored in the cellar. Maybe there's something useful down there."

"You haven't looked?"

"Not yet."

"Spiders?" A knowing twinkle lit his eyes.

She feigned a shrug. "Actually, I haven't had time."

"Then what do you say we go down there now, together? If you see anything you want, I'll haul it up the stairs for you."

His suggestion struck Ruby as a sensible idea. Loath as she was to admit it, the thought of entering that dark, spider-infested cellar alone made her skin crawl. She'd plumbed a well of excuses to put off going down there. But with Ethan leading the way, the prospect didn't seem so daunting.

She followed him downstairs to the kitchen, her eyes lingering on the muscular outline of his shoulders. His black hair grew low on the back of his sun-bronzed neck. Ruby suppressed the urge to reach out and brush the curls clear of his collar. How would he react if she touched him? Would he take it as an invitation?

As a stranger, Ethan would have no idea what she'd done to her husband. Here in Dutchman's Creek, only a few people did—Jace and Clara, of course, as well as Clara's family and Sam Farley, the elderly town marshal. None of those good people would reveal her secret on purpose. But scandal had a way of oozing into the open. Sooner or later word was bound to get out. What would the people in town—like her new tenant—think of her when the truth was revealed? For her own sake, Ruby no longer cared. But for the sake of her innocent young daughters…

Maybe she should have settled someplace else—a place where no one knew about her past.

But she would cross that bridge when she came to it. Right now she had more urgent concerns—and one of them was walking right in front of her.

Ethan had said he was looking forward to some good home cooking, a reasonable expectation for any boarder. With no money to hire a cook, Ruby would have to run the kitchen herself.

Unfortunately, she'd grown up in a home where meals

were prepared by a housekeeper. Upon her marriage to Hollis Rumford, she had moved into a mansion with a full staff of servants, including a chef.

Heaven help her, she didn't know the first thing about cooking. She barely knew how to boil water.

What had she gotten herself into? Right now the thought of finding tenants, cooking meals, maintaining the house, laundering a mountain of sheets, collecting rent and managing expenses was more than she could wrap her mind around.

She'd dreamed of having a steady income and a place to live with her girls. The reality was more like a nightmare. But she'd sunk her money into this old house and moved from Springfield with all her possessions. She was here to stay, and she had no choice except to make it work.

Chapter Two

The entrance to the cellar lay at the back of the house, next to the kitchen stoop. Its slanted door was the kind that children might have used for a slide in happier times when the house was new. Now the wood was warped and weathered to a splintery gray.

There was no padlock, Ethan noted as he twisted out the stick that fastened the rusted hasp. Anyone, including bootleggers, could have gotten into the cellar. Until now he'd kept his distance from the door, not wanting to raise suspicion by getting too close. But Ruby had given him a perfect excuse to investigate.

Maybe too perfect.

"I don't suppose you carry an electric torch with you." She leaned past his shoulder, teasing his nostrils with a sensual whiff of perfume. Ethan recognized the scent as a pricey one. Clearly, the lady had money, or, more likely, knew some man who did. So what was she doing in a place like this? He'd be a fool not to watch his every step.

"With the door open, we should be able to see well enough." He glanced back at her. "Ready?"

She nodded, all wide-eyed innocence. "Lead the way."

Gripping the handle, he raised the cellar door. It came up easily, swinging outward on hinges so silent that they must have been recently oiled. Instincts prickling, Ethan started down the rough-cut plank steps. Ruby followed so close behind him that he could hear her shallow breathing. Maybe this wasn't a good idea. For all he knew, the woman could be scheming to shoot him in the back and leave his carcass down here to rot. Or maybe she had cohorts waiting in the shadows to jump him and drag him away.

He cursed the oversight of leaving his .38 Smith & Wesson revolver locked in his suitcase at the hotel. There was no reason for a man posing as a scholar to carry a gun in a small town, especially on a sunny spring day, or so he'd thought. But that was before he'd encountered a seductively mysterious redhead, who appeared to be in the wrong place for the wrong reasons.

"Watch your head." He ducked under the bottom edge of the rough concrete foundation and stepped into the low cavern of the cellar. Overhead, cobwebs festooned the timbers that supported the floor of the house. But there'd been no web strands across the entrance, Ethan noted. Someone had been down here, probably within the past couple of weeks.

A jumble of dusty furniture was piled against the

far wall, as if it had been pushed there to make room for something else. The rest of the floor, covered in loose clay tiles over bare earth, was empty. If a stash of bootleg whiskey had been stored here, someone must have already hauled it away.

That might explain why Ruby had been so willing to bring him down here.

As he crossed the floor, Ethan suddenly realized she was no longer following him. Glancing back, he saw her hesitating at the foot of the steps.

A vision flashed through Ethan's mind—Ruby racing up the stairs to slam the cellar door and lock him in. Odds were she hadn't bought his inane story about being a professor. Hellfire, he probably wouldn't have bought it himself. He should have insisted on a more convincing cover.

"What's the matter?" he demanded, turning back to face her.

Her gaze shifted upward to the spiderwebs drooping from the beams. Suspicion crackled along his nerves. Was it an act? He'd be damned if he was going to find out the hard way.

"For Pete's sake, if we don't bother the spiders, they won't bother us! Come on!" He grabbed her wrist and jerked her toward him more roughly than he'd meant to.

"No! Don't—"

Suddenly she was fighting his grip, thrashing like a trapped animal. Ethan struggled to bring her under control. His free hand captured her flailing arm. With an expert twist, he whipped her against him, pinioning her hand against the small of her back. Even then she resisted, straining backward, gasping with effort.

"Listen, damn it," he began. "There's no need to—"

He broke off as her eyes met his. In their blue depths, Ethan recognized the look of stark terror.

This woman, he sensed, had been hurt by a man. Not just hurt, brutalized.

He let her go. She staggered backward, lost her balance and fell to the floor. Stunned, she struggled to raise herself onto her elbows. Her eyes smoldered up at him through a tumble of fiery hair.

Ethan stood over her, feeling like a monster. "I'm sorry, Ruby." He spoke softly, hoping to soothe her. "I'll confess I got impatient, but I wouldn't have hurt you. So help me, I'd never hurt any woman."

She glared at him, her gaze flashing defiance. "Don't you *ever* do that again," she breathed. "After my husband died, I swore I'd never let another man raise a hand to me. That includes you, *Professor!*"

She flung the title at him like an epithet. Ethan willed himself not to react. With a long exhalation, he forced the tension from his body. "My apologies. Believe me, you've nothing to worry about," he said, extending his open hand toward her. "Now, will you please allow me to help you up?"

She hesitated, then raised her hand. Tentatively at first, then with growing confidence, her fingers locked between his. Her grip tightened as he pulled her to her feet. She was quivering, her eyes wide, her lips parted. Ethan resisted the urge to gather her into his arms and comfort her. He was certain she'd prefer him to keep his distance for now. Besides, the fact that she'd been abused didn't mean the woman was harmless.

"Are you all right?" he asked.

"I will be." Her chin took on a determined thrust. She withdrew her hand and turned away from him, her spine as rigid as a poker. "Now, as I remember, we came down here to look at the furniture," she said.

Ruby's eyes had grown accustomed to the dim light. She focused her gaze on the jumble of broken chairs, torn cushions and detached bed parts, doing her best to ignore the powerful man beside her.

Ethan had insisted he hadn't meant to hurt her. She wanted to believe him. But when he'd seized her wrist and yanked her toward him, all the old instincts had kicked in. She'd fought him—fought him like she'd tried to fight Hollis until the night her husband had fractured her jaw. After that, she'd simply clenched her teeth and taken her punishment...up until the night he'd gone too far.

Those ten years of abuse were branded on her brain and seared along her nerves. The memories came back as violent dreams that jolted her awake in the night, leaving her shaken and drenched with sweat. The physical and emotional reflexes were, if anything, even worse. For a time, Ruby had hoped they would heal. Now she feared they would never go away.

"How did your husband die, Ruby?"

Her throat jerked tight. She willed herself to breathe before she spoke. "Are you in the habit of asking such personal questions?"

"Not usually. But you're an intriguing woman. I'm curious about you."

"Well, take your curiosity someplace else," she said. "I prefer to keep private matters private."

One dark eyebrow slithered upward. Ruby gave herself a mental kick. She should have lied, told him that Hollis had died of something ordinary, like influenza or heart failure. That would have been the end of it. Now the man would be more curious than ever.

Dutchman's Creek was a small town. Sooner or later, she knew, word of her scandalous past was bound to spread. But Ruby had resolved to keep the secret for as long as she could. She needed time to establish a good reputation. Her daughters needed time to make friends. She wasn't about to reveal her story to a man she'd just met.

"Look!" she exclaimed, seizing on a distraction. "Could that be a table behind that old bed frame?"

"Where?" He leaned close to follow the line of her pointing finger. "I don't—"

"Right over there. I could be wrong. It's hard to tell from here. If you could move a few things out of the way…"

Striding forward, he lifted a chair off the top of the stack, wiped away the dust and set it upright, next to her. "Have a seat. We might as well spread everything out. Then you can choose whatever strikes your fancy, and I'll earn my keep by hauling it upstairs."

"Fine." Ruby moved back out of the way before settling with her hands in her lap.

"Speak up if you see something you can use." Ethan

set to work, lifting the lighter pieces—stools, kitchen chairs and empty wooden crates—off the stack and setting them on the floor. Many of the items were broken. The best of them needed a good scrubbing and a fresh coat of paint. But never mind that. As the minutes passed, Ruby found herself paying less attention to the furniture and more to the man.

Ethan moved with a healthy animal power. Muscles rippled beneath his shirt as he freed each piece of furniture and moved it effortlessly onto the floor. Even the heavier items—solid armchairs, bulky chests, metal bedsprings—caused him little strain. He had the body of a man who'd led a vigorous life, not a scholar who'd devoted his days to research and teaching.

His face was weathered by sun and wind. His big hands were strong, the skin lightly mottled, as if something had scarred them. Ruby had never claimed to be a keen judge of men, but even she could surmise that he hadn't told her the truth.

If Ethan Beaudry was a college history professor, she was the queen of Sheba!

So who was he? What was he really doing here? Maybe it was time she found out.

She rose and sauntered toward him, pausing to inspect a rocking chair with a missing arm. "So you're on leave from your job, Professor. Where did you say you teach?"

"I didn't say." He righted a tilting chiffonier and moved it away from the wall. "But since you asked, it's Oberlin College, in Ohio. Maybe you've heard of it."

"Is that where you're from? Ohio? I must say, you don't sound like it."

He shot her a scowl. "For a woman who likes to keep private things private, you ask a lot of questions."

"You'll be sleeping under my roof. I have a right to ask questions, and to expect honest answers."

"Is that so?" He fiddled with a loose drawer pull. "All right, then. I'm from Oklahoma. Elk City, to save you the trouble of asking."

"Do you have family there?"

His jaw tightened. "Not anymore."

"Why do you say that? Did they move away? Did something happen to—"

"That's enough," he snapped, cutting off her words. "No more questions, Ruby. And no more answers. I'll pay my rent on time and treat you like the lady you are. But nobody has the right to pry into my past."

Stung by his vehemence, Ruby checked the impulse to back away. Summoning her courage, she took a step toward him and raised her eyes to meet his stony gaze. Her heart was pounding like a runaway locomotive. Could he hear it, echoing in the dark chamber of the cellar?

"It seems we have that much in common, at least," she said coldly. "Let's declare a truce. I'll respect your privacy if you'll respect mine. That should be suitable for both of us. Agreed?"

He stood glowering at her, tall and strong and over-poweringly masculine. He could break her bones with his bare hands if he chose to, Ruby thought. But the emotion that poured through her body wasn't fear.

Heaven help her, she wanted to feel his hands on her again. She hungered for a second helping of the sensual pleasure he'd ignited when he caught her in his arms and lowered her to the floor.

Leave before it's too late! a voice of caution inside her urged. But Ruby's feet would not obey. She stood rooted to the floor, straining toward him like a grass stem reaching for the sun.

The darkness pressed around them, intimate in its silence. She could hear the low rush of his breathing and smell the clean, musky-sweet aroma of his sweat. A warm, liquid ache rose from the depths of her body.

"Maybe we should just stop talking altogether." His voice had gone thick and husky. Heat sizzled over her skin as he bent closer. Her lips parted, anticipating his kiss.

What if she couldn't do this?

What if she froze in panic, as she'd done almost every time Hollis had touched her?

This was a mistake. She wasn't ready. Maybe she never would be.

A whimper escaped her throat. She stumbled backward, shattering the tension between them. Ethan watched in silence as she battled for composure. His dark eyes held a world of unspoken questions.

Questions she wasn't ready to answer.

She drew herself up and faced him again. "Perhaps we'd both be better off if you stayed at the hotel," she said.

His gaze hardened. "Ruby, if you're afraid that I'd—"

"Of course not!" Her cheeks blazed with heat. "It's just that—"

From the house above them, a muffled rapping interrupted her words. Someone was knocking on the front door.

Ethan froze, instantly alert. Wheeling away from him, Ruby raced up the cellar steps and into the blinding sunlight.

The kitchen door stood open, as she'd left it. From the front of the house, the rapping came again, more insistently this time. Ruby raced through the kitchen and dining room, into the parlor. Maybe Jace and Clara had brought the girls into town. Or maybe Marshal Sam Farley was coming by to check on her, as he'd promised Jace he would. Whoever it was, they'd be welcome. Being alone with Ethan was wearing down her all-too-fragile defenses.

Ruby wanted to make a good impression on the townsfolk, and that included being a proper hostess. If only she'd had the foresight to buy some cookies or cake from the bakery up the street and brew a pot of tea! It was too late for that now, and of course the house was an impossible mess. Why hadn't she been better prepared?

Hastily pinning up her hair and tugging her blouse closed, she hurried across the parlor and flung the door open.

Two men, both strangers, stood on the front porch.

The older, shorter of the pair was well into middle age, his heavy features punctuated by a Roman nose. The younger man, who looked to be in his late twenties, had mousy brown hair and a receding chin. Both of them were dressed in mail-order brown suits and matching fedoras. Despite the lack of resemblance, Ruby surmised they were father and son. Only the father was smiling.

"Thaddeus Wilton," he said, extending his hand. "I just heard today that someone had bought this old house. As mayor of Dutchman's Creek, it's my pleasure to welcome you to our town."

Ruby accepted the proffered handshake. The mayor's palm was baby smooth, his prolonged clasp uncomfortably warm.

"Ruby Denby Rumford. I'm happy to meet you." Ruby extricated her fingers and took a step backward. "Won't you come in? Please excuse the condition of the place. I've barely had time to start on the cleaning."

"Perfectly understandable, my dear." The mayor stepped across the threshold, removing his hat to reveal a polished mat of ebony hair. "Allow me to present my son, Harper."

"Ma'am." Harper Wilton gave her the barest inclination of his head. His neutral expression appeared to have been chiseled on his face. Only his basalt-colored eyes moved, glinting like a reptile's.

"Mind the broken glass. I had a slight mishap this morning." Ruby scurried ahead of the pair to place two chairs near the window. "Please forgive me for not having refreshments to offer you. I'll need to scrub the cupboards before I can unpack my kitchen things."

The mayor lowered himself onto the nearest chair. A ray of sunlight revealed the edge of his slick black toupee. "Quite all right, my dear," he said. "In fact, since you're still getting settled here, we'd be honored if you'd join us for dinner at the hotel this evening. I own the place, so I can guarantee you a good meal."

The offer caught Ruby off guard. "Oh, really, you needn't go so far as—"

"Please say yes, my dear," the mayor interrupted. "Since you'll be part of our community, we'd like to get to know you better. And we can tell you a great deal about this house. It used to belong to my late wife's aunt. In fact, Harper was born here, weren't you, Harper?"

"Can't say as I remember." Harper hadn't taken a seat. He stood just inside the door, leaning against the frame. His gaze flickered as if scanning every detail in the room. His behavior was beginning to make Ruby nervous.

She glanced toward the kitchen. Evidently, Ethan had decided not to show himself—strange behavior for a man who claimed to be writing a book about Colorado. One would think the mayor would be the first person he'd want to meet.

Maybe he was just being mindful of her reputation. But she wouldn't bet money on it. Ethan Beaudry, she sensed, had his own secret agenda. And her only chance of dealing with him lay in discovering what it was.

Ethan pressed against the wall behind the kitchen door. The narrow space along the frame allowed him a limited view of the parlor. From what he could see, Ruby's visitors looked harmless enough, but appearances could be deceiving. In any case, the mayor's reason for stopping by with his hatchet-faced son clearly went beyond sociability. Every time the strutting peacock called Ruby *my dear,* Ethan felt his teeth clench. Was it a simple case of a man playing up to a beautiful woman? Or did Mayor Thaddeus Wilton have some darker purpose in mind?

He took a moment to weigh the possibilities. If the mayor and his son were involved in the moonshine trade, it made sense that they'd stop by to make contact with the house's new owner. They'd spoken to Ruby as if meeting her for the first time. But that didn't mean it was true. She could easily have given them a signal, warning them that someone might be listening.

Weighing the facts, Ethan speculated that all three of them could be up to their necks in illegal activity.

Or it could be that the scene in the parlor was as innocent as a damn Sunday-school picnic!

Easing along the wall toward the open back door, he returned to the yard and went back down the cellar stairs. It wouldn't do for Ruby and her new friends to catch him eavesdropping. In any case, he should be able to hear what went on from under the floor. He'd spotted a battered study desk beneath a six-foot roll of moth-eaten carpet. Extricating it would give him reason enough to be down here. Meanwhile, he could keep his ears open.

"I insist that you be our guest, my dear!" The mayor's booming voice filtered through the floorboards overhead. "Some of the town's most important citizens dine at the hotel. We can introduce you to the right people, get you off to a good start."

The silence that followed suggested hesitation. Dared

he hope Ruby didn't like the oily pair? But what difference did it make? She was only a woman, after all—prettier than most, but with no less than her share of faults. He could take what she had to offer and walk away tomorrow, Ethan told himself. And maybe he would.

He'd come close to kissing her—close enough to know that the attraction was there for both of them. Given what he knew about her past, he shouldn't have been surprised when she'd backed away. But her retreat had left him with a powerful itch. He wanted her, pure and simple.

He had a job to do, Ethan reminded himself. But getting the beautiful widow in bed could be the most pleasant way to discover what she was up to. Call it workman's compensation.

The mayor's voice boomed into his thoughts. "No excuses, my dear. You'll be needing a good meal, and the Dutchman's Creek Hotel has the best food in the county. We won't take no for an answer, will we, Harper?"

The mayor's son muttered something Ethan couldn't make out. Again, a beat of silence passed before Ruby answered. "You're right, of course. And I do need to start meeting people. Very well, it would be a pleasure to accept your invitation. What time shall I meet you there?"

The reply was muffled. Evidently the mayor had risen and moved to a less audible part of the room. But Ethan had heard enough to conclude that further eavesdropping would be a waste of time. Whatever the mayor wanted, he would most likely save it for that evening.

With a vaguely muttered curse, Ethan turned back to the task at hand. The rolled carpet was thick and heavy, its woolen nap permeated with dust. He was dragging it out of the way when he happened to glance at the wall behind it. Where the furniture had blocked his view, a length of corrugated tin roofing stood against the rear wall. Behind it, a section of the wall was open.

Pulse galloping, Ethan held his breath to listen. From the direction of the parlor came the creak of a floorboard and the muted sound of voices. A quick look—that was all he dared risk. But it would likely be enough.

Lifting aside the tin, he peered into the opening. Musty odors of dampness and decay rushed into his nostrils. The place had likely been a root cellar for storing apples and winter vegetables. Maybe that was all it had ever been. But Ethan had his doubts. When he shifted to one side, allowing more light to shine in, he could see that the earth had been dug out farther under the house to make a chamber nearly a third the size of the original cellar. In its dark recesses, the dim light glinted on a motley assortment of glass jugs—scores of them, crowding the floor and stacked high on crude wooden shelves.

He knew at once what he'd found. Bootleg whiskey, brewed in an uncounted number of secret backwoods stills, had been brought here to be picked up and paid for by big-city crime syndicates. Ethan estimated the worth of the stash in the thousands of dollars.

Moving with quiet haste, he replaced the tin, the carpet roll and the other furniture that had concealed the opening. By the time he'd finished, he was sweating, more from nerves than from effort.

He'd found the evidence he was looking for. But pinning the crime on the responsible parties would take time and luck. Thaddeus Wilton's interest in the house made him a likely suspect. But even if the mayor was guilty, he probably wasn't acting alone. His son could have a hand in the dirty business, as well. So could any number of people in this close-knit little town.

And what about Ruby?

Had she known about the stash? Had she been prepared to take action if he found it? Ethan remembered how she'd sat with her hands folded, watching him like a cat as he lifted the furniture away from the wall. Only the arrival of visitors upstairs had kept her from being here when he found the whiskey.

Was she involved, or had she simply stumbled into a bad situation? Ethan had no proof either way. He was certain of only one thing.

He'd be a fool to let the woman out of his sight.

Chapter Three

Closing the door behind her guests, Ruby sank onto a chair with a sigh of relief. It wasn't that the mayor and his son had behaved improperly. In fact, they'd been perfect gentlemen. But she wasn't used to dealing with unexpected company. Back in Springfield, the family butler would have answered the door, taken the visitor's card and checked to make sure Mrs. Rumford was receiving callers that day. If she wasn't up to socializing—more often than not because she was nursing bruises—she would have the luxury of being "indisposed," and no one would think the worse of her for it.

Those days were gone forever, Ruby reminded herself. Dutchman's Creek was a small town, and she was no longer the socially prominent Mrs. Hollis Rumford. She was a struggling widow, newly arrived and in need of friends. The sooner she got used to that reality the better.

And the sooner she got this wreck of a house in shape, the sooner she could start renting out rooms and bringing in some income.

Rising, she seized a broom and began sweeping up the glass from her earlier mishap. First she would get the parlor looking presentable. Then she'd take the time to scrub down her own room, put clean linens on the bed, unpack her clothes and set out her personal toiletries. That would allow her to change and freshen up before having dinner at the hotel, and to fall exhausted into bed when she returned.

Would Ethan be spending the night here? The thought of him lying upstairs, alone in the darkness, sent a freshet of heat through her body. She remembered the velvety roughness of his voice, the sensual parting of his lips as he'd leaned toward her. She could almost imagine…

But she was fantasizing like a schoolgirl. Ethan was a stranger and she was a lady, whatever that was supposed to mean. Nothing would happen between them, not even if she wanted it to. Ruby knew herself all too well. Let a man get too close and she would turn to ice in his arms. It had happened last year with a charming Dutch businessman she'd met in Europe. He'd soon lost patience with her and gone his way. Professor Ethan Beaudry would be no different.

As if summoned by her thoughts, Ethan strode in through the kitchen, carrying a battered table with one crooked leg. His face, arms and clothes were smudged with dust. Ruby willed herself to ignore the quickening of her pulse. "Is that the best table you could find?" she asked.

He shrugged. "It'll do if I brace the leg. Did you see anything else you wanted from down there?"

Ruby realized she'd paid scant attention to the furniture in the cellar. "Nothing that can't wait. No use bringing anything else upstairs until the rooms are clean."

He glanced around the parlor. "Your visitors didn't stay long," he commented. "Did you drive them off with that broom?"

A twitch of his eyebrow confirmed that he was teasing her. Ruby couldn't be sure whether she liked it or not. "It wasn't supposed to be a long visit," she said curtly. "The mayor and his son just stopped by to welcome me to town and invite me to dinner this evening."

"Oh? Do they do that for every newcomer, or just for the pretty ones? No one here has invited *me* to dinner."

"Maybe they would have if you'd come upstairs and introduced yourself instead of hiding in the cellar like a grumpy old troll!"

His rough laugh startled her. "Ruby, I'm your tenant," he said. "That doesn't give me the right to come barging in when you have company. I'll introduce myself to the mayor another time, on my own terms."

"You strike me as a man who does most things on his own terms."

"Should I take that as a compliment?" He had lowered the table and appeared to be studying her, taking her measure with those fathomless gold-flecked eyes. What was he seeing? Pride? Vulnerability? Shame and fear? All those things were there, locked deep inside her. The past eleven years had taught Ruby to keep her emotions hidden. But no part of her seemed safe from his penetrating, curiously gentle gaze.

She felt as if he was probing into her soul—and the only response she knew was to fling up barriers.

"You can take it any way you like." She turned away from him and resumed sweeping the floor, plying the broom like a weapon.

"Careful," he teased. "The way you're handling that poor old broom, you could break it."

She stopped sweeping and glared at him. "Don't you have anything better to do?"

"Now that you mention it…" Ethan picked up the table again, turned toward the stairs, then paused.

"If there's nothing else you need, I'll start on my own room," he said. "The mattress could use a good whaling."

"Fine." Ruby resumed her sweeping. "When you're finished I'll find you some clean sheets and a quilt for your bed."

"No hurry. I'll be staying at the hotel tonight."

Surprised, she glanced up at him. Only then did she remember what she'd said to him in the cellar. Had he taken her at her word? Heaven save her, had she *wanted* him to sleep here tonight?

"My hotel room is already paid for," he said. "Might as well not waste the money. There'll be plenty of time to move in here tomorrow—that is, if you haven't thrown me out by then."

"Don't tempt me." Ruby scooped the broken glass into a dustpan. In truth, she'd been a bit nervous about spending her first night alone in the old house. But surely her fears were groundless. What could possibly happen to her in a quiet place like Dutchman's Creek?

"Will you be all right here alone?" Ethan asked. "If you're worried, I'd be glad to offer you my hotel room—gratis, of course. I can always bunk here."

"I wouldn't think of putting you out! Don't concern yourself. I'll be fine."

He shifted the table higher against his shoulder. "You're sure? I'm not one to argue with a lady."

"Quite sure, thank you." Ruby emptied the dustpan and started on the rest of the bare wooden floor. Clara's family had offered her the loan of some lightly used carpets, an overstuffed set, a dining-room table and other odds and ends from their storage shed. Jace would be bringing it into town when he delivered the girls at the end of the week. Meanwhile, she would have to make do with a few rickety wooden chairs for parlor seating.

She stole a glance at Ethan as he climbed the stairs to the landing and disappeared. Maybe she should have taken him up on his offer of the hotel room. The thought of a safe, clean, comfortable night was as tempting as a siren's song.

But since she couldn't pay for the room, and wouldn't accept charity from the man, that wasn't going to happen. She would spend the night here, in the saggy double bed that had come with her run-down, spider-infested house. And she would try to be proud of herself for getting this far on her own. Months, or maybe years from now, she would look back on this period as a time of growth, a time when she'd found the strength and courage to meet new challenges.

But right now, just getting through today seemed challenge enough.

Ethan had dragged the mattress into the backyard and propped it on end against a sturdy clothesline pole. Using an abandoned baseball bat he'd found in the grass, he delivered blow after blow against the faded, cotton-stuffed ticking. He'd half expected a veritable Noah's ark of small vermin to come rushing out through the seams, but so far the vigorous beating had only raised clouds of dust.

And that was just as well, since his mind was scarcely on task. Most of his thoughts had been about Ruby, who was slowly driving him to distraction.

Why would a woman turn down a comfortable hotel room to stay alone in a place that wasn't fit for habitation? Maybe she was too proud to accept his offer. But he couldn't rule out the possibility that something was going down tonight—something that involved that stash of moonshine in the cellar.

Either way, there were things about the woman he couldn't explain. If she was planning something, why had she shown him the furniture in the cellar and left him free to look through the stack? And why had she offered him sheets and a blanket for his bed, as if she'd assumed he would be staying the night?

Her actions pointed to innocence. But something about the beautiful widow didn't fit the picture. She was as out of place in this house, and this town, as a swan in a chicken coop.

Perhaps we'd both be better off if you stayed at the hotel.

When Ruby had spoken those words he'd been on the verge of crushing her in his arms and kissing her until she whimpered for mercy. Every instinct had told him she'd wanted that kiss. But at the last second, she'd pulled back, almost as if she'd been afraid. Then, before anything could be resolved, the mayor and his slit-mouthed son had come knocking at the damn door, and now it seemed that Ruby was going to dinner with them.

Ethan laid into the mattress with the power of frustration, landing blows that stung all the way up his arms. He was a seasoned professional lawman who'd achieved his rank through the coolheaded performance of his duty. He prided himself on his detachment, avoiding any personal involvement in his cases. So far the practice had served him well.

But Ruby Rumford was driving him crazy.

He'd known more than a few women in the four rootless years since the loss of his family. Pretty women. Charming women. Ruthless women. Ruby was not like any of them. She was a bundle of contradictions—strength and fragility, passion and aloofness, fire and ice. Every word she'd spoken rang true. But he sensed a hidden darkness lurking behind that innocent gaze. That air of mystery only made her more intriguing.

He wanted her, damn it.

And he needed a way to uncover her secrets—even if it meant she'd end up hating him for it.

In any case, he didn't really plan to spend the night at the hotel. Let her think he was safely out of sight. He would be close by, watching the back of the house. If any business was going on with that stash of illegal booze in the cellar—and if Ruby was involved—he would soon know.

When the mattress was beaten to his satisfaction, he picked it up and lugged it into the house. Ruby was gone from the parlor, but he could hear the faint thud of shifting furniture from one of the back bedrooms. Leaning the mattress against the stair railing, Ethan strode in the direction of the sound. It appeared that the lady could use some help, and he'd be remiss not to offer his two strong arms.

He found her in the larger of the two downstairs bedrooms, struggling to move an iron-framed double bed away from the wall. She was straining backward, her hands gripping a corner post. Perspiration had plastered her linen blouse to the back of her shoulders.

She paused, turning as he stepped into the room. Her blue eyes were wide and startled. Her tousled hair, caught by a shaft of light from the high window, blazed like an Arizona sunset. Lord, but she was beautiful, he thought. A man could lose his mind just looking at her.

"You could have called me," he said. "I was just out back."

"No need. I can manage this fine." She returned to tugging on the bedpost, dragging the heavy frame away from the wall by inches. A drop of sweat glistened on her temple.

"You hired me to work for you, remember?" Stepping behind her, he clasped her shoulders to guide her away from the bed. Her body tensed beneath his palms, but she made no effort to resist. "Let me help you, Ruby," he said. "That's why I'm here."

She stood with her back toward him, her seductive fragrance wafting into his nostrils. Ethan knew that he should let her go, but his hands wanted more of her. He imagined his fingers sliding down her shoulders to cradle the lush, warm weight of her breasts, his arms pulling her back against him, molding her ample rump to his body until he could feel...

Hellfire, what was he thinking? She'd probably slap him silly.

Willing himself to let go, he released her and stepped away. She turned to face him, her lips moist, her breathing quick and shallow. When she spoke, her voice was a husky little rasp.

"This mattress could probably use a good beating, as well. While you have it outside, I can dust the springs and clean the floor under the bed. With the mattress gone, it should be easy enough to move the frame...." The words poured out of her in a nervous torrent. Ethan fought the temptation to stop her mouth with his.

"Stand back," he said. "I'll have it out of here in a minute."

Ethan bent over the mattress. It was heavier than he'd expected, and years of wear had made it as floppy as a big pancake. He wrestled with the cursed thing, tackling it from the side, from the middle and from the end, without being able to pick it up. From somewhere behind him came a delightful sound. It took him a moment to realize it was Ruby giggling. Her laughter was as sweet as a girl's.

He collapsed facedown across the mattress, letting the sound wash over him. Memories stirred inside him, blurred by pain and years—memories of love and happy warmth he had no wish to ever feel again.

Ethan forced the memories from his mind. They faded slowly, like tears on sun-parched earth.

How long had it been since she'd allowed herself to laugh? Ruby gazed down at Ethan's prone body, savoring the giddiness that had swept over her. It was oddly comforting to know that this big, strong man had his limitations.

"This strikes me as a job for two people," she said.

"So what does the lady have in mind?" He had risen onto one elbow. The look in his lazily sardonic eyes suggested he was in no hurry to get up. He was teasing her again, stopping just short of impropriety. Ruby struggled to ignore the thread of heat uncoiling in the depths of her body.

"If you take one end of the mattress and let me steady the other, we should be able to carry it outside together," she said. "Shall we try it?"

A beat of silence passed. "Sounds like a good idea," he said, rising and shifting to the foot of the bed. "We'll tip the mattress onto its edge and slide it out the door. I'll take this end. You take the other. Ready?"

"Ready." Ruby clasped the mattress where it lay against the headboard. With no place to grip, holding on was awkward at best.

"Now." He seized the foot of the mattress, tilting it until it slid off the spring and onto the floor. Ruby braced to keep her end upright. A rigid mattress would have been easy to support. But this one was as limp as a noodle. Wherever it wasn't being held, it sagged.

"Here we go." Ethan backed out of the room, sliding the mattress along on one side. Ruby followed, swaying with effort. Perspiration drizzled down her throat to pool in the damp hollow between her breasts. The narrow space of the hallway lent some stability. But getting the thing through the parlor and dining room, into the kitchen and out the back door would be exhausting.

Ethan backed out of the hallway and into the parlor, giving the mattress full play. Holding it was harder than ever now. Ruby's legs were beginning to quiver. "We could lay it down and drag it across the room," she suggested.

"We'd just have to stand it up again to get it through the doors," Ethan grunted. "We might as well—" His words ended in a curse as something clattered under his boot. Only then did Ruby remember the dustpan she'd left on the floor.

Swearing out loud, Ethan lost his footing and went down, taking the mattress with him. The momentum yanked Ruby off her feet. She spun, staggered sideways and collapsed facedown with her legs sprawled across his.

For a moment she lay stunned and gasping. A slow,

sensual heat rose from the point of contact. She felt it tingle upward from her legs into her thighs, pool between her hips and flow upward to tighten her nipples into aching nubs.

"Well, this is a fine how-do-you-do." Ethan's voice was a growl next to her ear. Turning her head, Ruby met his smoldering eyes. His face was no more than a handbreadth from her own, his mouth so near that the slightest forward movement would bring her lips into contact with his. Yearning rose inside her like a silent cry. She ached with the need to be kissed, to be cradled in tenderness and love by a man who respected and cared for her.

Could Ethan Beaudry be that man?

Did such a man even exist?

She strained toward him, ever so slightly. Sensing her response, he brushed her mouth with his own, once, then again. His lips were weather chapped and clean to the taste, claiming hers with a sureness that spoke of an experienced lover. As he deepened the kiss, Ruby's heart broke into a gallop. The heat between her thighs pulsed and liquefied. Bolts of sensation rippled through her body, awakening a hunger for more.

With a low mutter he caught her waist and rolled her onto her back. Now he lay partly above her, his mouth plundering hers, his knee resting lightly between her legs. She felt the hardening pressure against the side of her hip. Instinctively she pressed against him, heightening the waves of shimmering need flowing between them. He groaned and shifted his weight, moving until his chest and pelvis settled into place, fitting her like the missing piece of a jigsaw puzzle. "Tell me what you want," he growled, his weight pressing down on her. "Tell me, Ruby."

Panic exploded in Ruby's brain, shooting darts of ice through her body. She couldn't move, couldn't breathe. She was trapped and at his mercy. Her pulse slammed with irrational fear. She began to struggle.

"Please…" she gasped. "Let me up. Let me go…"

He rolled off her at once, his expression as dark as a thundercloud. "Lord, Ruby, what is it? Do you think I'm going to hurt you like your husband did? Don't you know me better than that?"

"Actually I don't know you at all." She sat up and began rearranging her blouse, fussing needlessly with the collar. "I'm aware that we agreed not to pry into each other's pasts, but under the circumstances, you can hardly expect me to—"

"Save your breath, lady. You don't have to draw me a picture." Ethan exhaled raggedly as he sat up. "Come on, let's get this damn mattress out the door. For what it's worth, I promise not to lay an ungentlemanly hand on you."

"Fine. And if I gave you the wrong impression, I'm sorry." Ruby stood, turning away from him to hide her burning face. Ethan was one of the most compellingly attractive men she'd ever met. His kisses, and the casual contact of their bodies, had filled her with a pleasure so sweet she could have wept with it. But when he'd pressed her for more, she'd been unable to hold back the gut-clenching panic, the fear of being hurt again.

Hollis was dead. She had fired the three shots that

killed him and been acquitted of his murder. But it seemed that the memory of her late husband, who had so relished causing her pain, would never leave her in peace.

Ethan had heaved the mattress back onto its edge. He and Ruby were scrambling to get it headed in the right direction when the knock came—this time as a discreet tap on the front door.

"Oh!" Ruby dropped her end of the mattress and flew across the parlor. Letting the mattress sag to the floor, Ethan moved back into the hallway. Maybe the mayor and his son were making a return call. Whoever it was, he'd be smart to stay out of sight until he knew what was going on.

From where he stood, he could see that Ruby had reached the front door. She hesitated a moment, smoothing her clothes and tucking in strands of hair that had come loose during their tussle on the mattress.

It had been a delicious tussle, Ethan mused. Or, at least it might have been. Kissing her had been as sweetly intoxicating as sipping hot buttered rum. She'd responded with a hunger that seemed to match his own. Then, suddenly, it was as if he'd become her enemy. What was going on here? Had he done something to spook her or was the woman playing games with him?

To say the least, Ruby Rumford was a challenge.

But then, he'd enjoyed challenges before.

The click of the latch jerked his attention back to the present. Ruby opened the door a few cautious inches, then swung it wide to reveal a rangy, slightly stooped man with a thatch of silver-white hair.

"Hello, darling girl!" His voice was an old man's, pleasantly gruff.

"Sam!" She flung herself into his arms for a welcoming hug. Only as he released her to step away did Ethan see the silver star pinned to his worn tweed vest.

Ethan's memory clicked back to the briefing he'd been given for this assignment. The man would be Sam Farley, who'd been the marshal in Dutchman's Creek for more than thirty years.

Farley had a trustworthy reputation. But experience had taught Ethan to be cautious. In Kansas, he'd brought down a bootlegging operation that had involved the mayor, the sheriff and the bank president. Until he had evidence to the contrary, everyone was a suspect.

He'd seen the story played out before—a public servant who'd received scant reward for a lifetime of honest work and felt he deserved better. Sam Farley would be nearing retirement. He could probably use some extra cash to see him through a comfortable old age. Who could blame the marshal for turning a blind eye to the sale of illegal booze for a share of the profits? Especially if the extra money was needed to catch the attention of a beautiful woman?

That possibility, and the fact that Ruby had greeted him like a long-lost uncle, didn't exactly put a shine on Farley's reputation. Or on Ruby's.

Ethan pressed against the wall to better hear what was being said. Whatever he learned, it was bound to be interesting.

* * *

Ruby had met Sam Farley a year ago, when she'd come to Dutchman's Creek to get her brother out of Sam's jail.

During the awful months Jace had been on the run, charged with Hollis's murder, she'd developed a contempt for lawmen that bordered on hatred. Most of them had been in the pay of Hollis's wealthy friends, and they'd gone out of their way to make her life miserable. Only fear for the safety of her daughters had kept her from blurting out the truth—that *she* was the one who'd killed her husband, and Jace had taken the blame to protect them.

When Clara had telephoned her with the news of Jace's arrest, Ruby had commandeered her lawyer and caught the next train west. Fearing the worst, she'd been astonished to find her brother in the custody of a gentle, silver-haired man who was the soul of fairness. By the time Jace had been cleared of all charges, Ruby and the aging marshal had become fast friends. They'd remained so to this day.

"Son of a gun, girl!" Sam's gaze roamed the drab parlor, coming to rest on the mattress. "Don't tell me you're trying to fix up this place by yourself. Where's your brother?"

"Jace offered to come. But with Clara's time getting so close, I didn't want to keep him in town."

"Couldn't you have borrowed a couple of the ranch hands?"

Ruby shook her head. "I couldn't afford to pay them, and I won't impose on Jace or on Clara's family. They've done so much for me already. Besides, I did manage to find some help. A man who'll be living here is doing some work in exchange for his first week's room and board."

"A man, you say?" The marshal's face creased into a suspicious scowl. "You mean you hired some stranger who just happened by? And you're going to be here alone with him? Lordy, girl, where's your common sense?"

Ruby bristled slightly. Sam Farley might be old enough to be her father, but that didn't give him the right to treat her like a fifteen-year-old. "He offered to help and his price was right. As for my being alone with him…" She paused. "You, of all people, should know that I can take care of myself."

The marshal's scowl deepened. "Well, you let him know that I'll be checking on you—and on him." His gaze swept from the kitchen to the stairs. "I don't see much work getting done. Where is the lazy so-and-so, anyway?"

"Right here." Ethan stepped out of the hallway. His expression was guarded, but he extended his hand. "Professor Ethan Beaudry. It's a pleasure to meet you, Marshal. You're just in time to help me haul this mattress outside for a beating. The lady and I managed to get this far before you knocked on the door."

"Sam Farley. And it looks like I got here at the right time."

As the two men shook hands, Ruby glanced away to hide the flash of color to her face. Moving the mattress wasn't the only thing they'd managed before the marshal showed up.

Sam's long arms and added strength eased the work of hauling the mattress out to the backyard. Ruby stepped aside to let the men pass. Lugging the mattress outside, they laid it against the raised entrance to the cellar.

Ruby closed the screen door behind them. She had plenty of work to do in the house. But on second thought, leaving the two men alone might not be a good idea. On her first visit to Dutchman's Creek, she'd made it clear to Sam that the scandal of her husband's death was to be kept private. Sam had promised to respect her wishes. But the marshal did like to gossip a bit. If his tongue slipped, she wanted to be there to stop him from saying too much.

As for Ethan… Ruby struggled against the memory of his kisses. What she needed was some time away from him to regroup her emotions. But that would leave him alone with Sam, and a conversation between those two could lead anywhere.

There was only one thing to do. With a sigh, Ruby opened the door again. She came out onto the stoop just in time to hear Ethan saying, "So, Marshal, how is it you know Mrs. Rumford? Something tells me there's an interesting story here."

Chapter Four

Ethan had hoped to get the marshal talking. But now Ruby had come outside. It was she who answered his question.

"My brother lives near Dutchman's Creek. Sam and I became friends last year when I came for a visit."

A glance flickered between Ruby and the old man. Whatever she'd said, Ethan sensed that her words had fallen short of the real story.

"Ruby's brother, Jace, married into one of the finest families in the valley," the marshal said. "His father-in-law, Judd Seavers, owns the biggest ranch in these parts."

"My brother and his wife are expecting a baby," Ruby added. "I moved here from Missouri to be near them. But I wanted to live in town, on my own. That's why I bought the boardinghouse." She paused. A clever smile lit her face. "But enough about me, Professor. Why don't you tell us about the history book you're writing. I've never met a real author before."

Ethan picked up the baseball bat and gave the mattress several solid whacks. A too-innocent story followed by a deft evasion. The woman had outmaneuvered him and he wasn't happy about it. First thing tomorrow, he'd begin the process of checking out everything she and the marshal had to tell him. If there were any holes in their combined stories, he would find them.

Ruby's link to the prominent Seavers clan might put her in a more favorable light, but it didn't wash her clean. The best of families could have its black sheep, and she could be using the Seavers connection to win people's trust. Ethan had learned to suspect anyone who hadn't proven themselves innocent. That included politicians, elderly lawmen and beautiful, seductive women.

"We're waiting," Ruby's tone rang with challenge. Her folded arms pushed her ample breasts upward in a way that made Ethan's mouth go dry.

"I haven't started writing yet," he hedged. "There are plenty of books on the general history of Colorado, but I wanted something more personal—history as it affected the people of a typical small town. After some research I chose Dutchman's Creek."

"So you'll be going around talking to folks?" The marshal assessed Ethan with narrowed eyes. Plainly, the old man didn't trust him.

"Yes, I plan to. If they're willing to talk to me, of course."

"Have you got some identification, some kind of credentials you can show me?"

Ethan had been given the proper documents by the agency. "I have. But my papers are in my hotel room. I can bring them by your office tomorrow."

"Do that." Sam Farley spat a stream of tobacco into the grass. "I have a responsibility to folks in this town, and I take it seriously. You're not to bother any of these good people unless you can prove you're who you claim to be."

"Understood." Ethan lifted the bat and stepped back for another swing at the mattress. The marshal's next words paused him in midmotion.

"Then understand this, Professor. You lay so much as an ungentlemanly finger on this sweet lady here, and I'll have you behind bars before you can say Jack Robinson!"

"I hear you." Ethan smashed the bat against the ticking again and again, raising a cloud of cottony dust. What would Sam Farley say if he knew he was talking to a U.S. deputy marshal? Probably the same damn thing. The old man seemed very protective. If he knew what had happened on that mattress seconds before his knock, he'd likely be breaking out the handcuffs.

"The mayor and his son came by, Sam," Ruby broke the awkward silence. "They invited me to dinner at the hotel. Maybe you can give me some idea what to expect."

"The mayor?" Sam punctuated his words with a snort. "If I was a pretty woman, I'd be on my guard. Thaddeus has always had an eye for the ladies, and now that his wife's gone to her reward, he's like a hound off the leash. I'm guessing he sees you as a candidate for

Mrs. Wilton number two. Probably licking his chops at the prospect."

"Oh, dear. I certainly have no intention of—" Ruby shook her head. "He said he'd introduce me to some important people. And of course his son will be there. Nothing about that arrangement seems improper."

The marshal frowned. "I'm not saying you shouldn't go. Just warning you to be careful."

Ruby's head went up. Ethan caught a flicker of defiance in her blue eyes. "I'm not a child, Sam. If anything makes me feel uncomfortable, I'll just get up and leave."

"You do that." The marshal nodded. "You leave and come straight to me."

Ethan was a practiced observer of people. In Sam Farley's eyes and voice he detected the sadness of an old man hopelessly in love with a younger woman—a man who knew he could never have her in this life. The poor devil.

But right now that wasn't his problem, Ethan reminded himself. It had occurred to him that there might be hidden motives behind Mayor Wilton's invitation. With Ruby at dinner the house would be left empty, giving the bootleggers a chance to move in and smuggle out their liquid treasure.

At the end of the day, he'd planned to stop by the hotel, get a meal and keep an eye on Ruby. But he couldn't be in two places at once. The smarter choice would be to stay here and keep watch on that cellar door.

Stepping away, he let the bat slide into the grass.

Suspect Everyone—that motto had always served him well. But in this case it was giving him one humdinger of a headache.

At the entrance to the hotel Ruby paused to brush a speck of dust off her dove-gray jacket. Anxious to make a proper impression, she'd dressed in a plain traveling suit and high-collared white blouse. Hollis would have called her ensemble schoolmarmish, but his opinion no longer mattered. When Ruby had packed for the move to Colorado, she'd sold her expensive pieces of jewelry and left behind most of the silken gowns her husband had favored, along with the opera-length gloves, the satin slippers and the dyed ostrich plumes that had decorated her hair. She was a different person now— businesswoman, mother and citizen of a conservative town. She was determined to look the part.

Twilight was settling over the valley. Along Main Street, shopkeepers were closing up for the day. Buggies, wagons and Model T Fords rolled their way homeward, deepening the ruts on the narrow dirt roads. The dimly lit saloon was open for billiards and card games, but business had trailed off since the recent prohibition of liquor. Clandestine spots set up in barns and backwoods cabins, where illegal whiskey flowed freely, were stealing the serious clientele.

Squaring her chin, Ruby opened the door and strode into the brightly lit hotel lobby. She'd insisted on joining the two men here. This was a business meeting, not a date, and she had no wish to create the wrong impression.

The dining room was to the left of the lobby. Ruby stood in the entry, scanning the half-filled tables. The mayor had told her that he and his son would be here by six-fifteen, but there was no sign of them. Maybe people were less concerned about punctuality in small towns. But she did feel awkward, waiting here alone.

She glanced around hoping to see Ethan. After Sam's departure, he'd put in a hard afternoon cleaning out the upstairs rooms, making some needed repairs on the plumbing and reaming out the chimneys for the stove and fireplace. After that he'd excused himself to go back to the hotel. One would think the man would be hungry. But for whatever reason, he wasn't here. In his absence, Ruby felt strangely vulnerable.

Her knees weakened as the memory swept over her— Ethan's lips brushing hers, the clean, masculine aroma of his skin, the hardness of his arousal pressing her hip. The sweet terror of it…

"Mrs. Rumford?" The low voice startled her. She turned to see a pimply-faced waiter in a white shirt and black vest.

"Yes, I'm Mrs. Rumford," she said. "I was looking for Mayor Wilton."

"He's expecting you. Right this way."

The young man ushered her down a paneled hallway, past two closed doors. The third door stood ajar. After a discreet knock, the waiter spoke. "Here's the lady, Your Honor. We'll be bringing dinner now."

Ruby's senses prickled as she stepped across the threshold. The candlelit room was small and window-less. In a garish attempt at elegance, the walls had been covered in red satin brocade. A gold velvet chaise occupied one side of the room. A circular dining table with a white cloth took up the rest of the space. There were two place settings and two chairs. In one of the chairs sat His Honor Mayor Thaddeus Wilton.

"My dear Mrs. Rumford. How delightful to have your company this evening." He rose from his place, his manner so unctuous that Ruby feared he was going to bow and kiss her hand.

She glanced uneasily around the room. "I thought your son would be joining us," she said.

"Oh, Harper had some urgent business come up. He asked me to extend his apologies. Please have a seat. As the owner of this hotel, I took the liberty of ordering for you. The roast beef is excellent here."

He stood while the waiter pulled out Ruby's chair. Ruby remained on her feet. "I'd prefer to eat in the dining room," she said.

"I quite understand, my dear." His thumb stroked a link of his gold watch chain, its motion slow and sensuous. "But most of the tables have already been reserved. Besides, with so much chatter in there, you can barely hear yourself think, let alone carry on a proper conversation. Please sit down. As a respectable widower and trusted public official, I can promise your reputation will be quite safe."

Ruby hesitated, then lowered herself to the edge of the chair. What alternative did she have—walk out on an influential man who could help her make friends, insulting him in the process? That would hardly be wise. Besides, she hadn't eaten since breakfast. She was ravenously hungry, and while the aromas wafting down the hall from the kitchen didn't quite seem to live up to the mayor's extravagant praise, they still triggered a growl in her stomach.

What harm could come to her here? If the mayor made an improper move, all she had to do was get up and leave. Ruby forced a smile as she settled back into her chair. She could handle this, she told herself. Still, she couldn't shake the idea that this meeting was some kind of high-stakes game. And Thaddeus Wilton was holding the trump cards.

Ethan returned to the boardinghouse at dusk, taking the backstreets and cutting through a weeded lot. Moving aside two loose boards, he slipped through the fence and into the backyard.

Tonight he was armed with his .38 Smith & Wesson revolver, and his U.S. marshals badge was pinned to his vest. He didn't plan to arrest anyone if he could help it. It was too soon for that. But in case all hell broke loose, he wanted the authority of his office made plain.

Pausing next to the six-foot fence, he scanned the yard for a hiding place. He'd considered watching from the safety and relative comfort of an upstairs room. But Ruby could easily discover him there; and a view from above wouldn't allow him to see faces, hear what was being said or, if necessary, trail after suspects when they left. For that he would need to be as close as possible.

The moon was a thin silver edge above the peaks. Fully risen, it would flood the yard with light. Only the deepest shadow would be enough to hide him.

In the far corner of the yard stood a dilapidated garden shed. Its door had rotted away, leaving the front open beneath the sagging roof. But the narrow space between the fence and the rear of the structure would be buried in shadow. Overgrown with brambles, it wouldn't be a comfortable hiding place, but it would have to do.

The twilight was deepening into darkness. Knowing he might be there for hours, Ethan eased himself between the shed and the fence, kicked aside the prickly stems and settled in to wait.

"So, how was your dinner, my dear?"

"Fine, thank you," Ruby answered. In truth, the roast beef had been overdone, the mashed potatoes lumpy and the piecrust like sodden leather. But since she'd been so tense she could barely swallow, the quality of the food had made little difference.

For most of the meal the conversation had been light and trivial—happenings in the town, people, businesses and her own plans for the boardinghouse. But she'd sensed that Thaddeus Wilton was biding his time, waiting to spring some unknown trap when she least expected it. That subtle awareness had kept her on edge throughout the meal.

The mayor had told her a little about the history of the house and implied that if she wished to sell it, he might be willing to make her an offer. "It's a big responsibility for a woman alone, especially a gently reared lady like yourself," he'd said, patting the back of her hand.

"You misjudge me," she'd replied, stiffening at his

touch. "I'm quite capable of doing whatever I put my mind to."

"So I gather," he'd murmured, withdrawing his hand and reaching for another dinner roll. "You're a very remarkable woman, Ruby—I may call you Ruby, mayn't I?"

"Yes, of course." Ruby had forced herself to take another bite of roast beef. All she'd wanted was for this interminable evening to be over.

Now the meal was at an end. The waiter cleared away their plates and brought coffee. Ruby sipped delicately, aware that too much of it would keep her awake. The mayor leaned back in his chair, studying her over the rim of his cup. His bushy black eyebrows looked as if they'd been dyed to match his toupee.

"Yes," he murmured. "As I said earlier, you're a quite a remarkable woman, Ruby. I didn't know how remarkable until I telephoned some contacts of mine this afternoon." His eyes narrowed, sending a chill of apprehension through her body. "When you say you can do whatever you put your mind to, I believe you. A woman who can murder her rich husband and get away with it is capable of anything."

Ruby's shaking hand sloshed her coffee, scalding her fingers and staining the white tablecloth. Sooner or later, she knew, her secret was bound to come out. But to have it revealed now, and in such lurid fashion, would be disastrous. She needed time to build a good reputation. Her girls needed time to make friends. She couldn't allow this conniving weasel of a man to ruin their chances. Willing herself to be calm, she set the cup onto its saucer and met Wilton's leering eyes. "I shot my late husband in self-defense," she said in a cold voice. "The jury acquitted me of all charges."

"Of course they did. What jury could convict a woman who looks like you? But don't worry, my dear. Your little secret is safe with me."

Ruby battled the urge to fling the hot coffee in his face. "What is it you want?" she demanded, keeping her voice low.

"What do I want?" He feigned a hurt expression. "Why, nothing, except your trust and friendship, Ruby. I understand that you wouldn't want the story getting out—you know how gossip can spread in a small town. And people here can be *so* judgmental, especially the women. Why, they'd turn their backs on you, every last one of them! As for your children…"

"Stop it!" She rose, her body quivering. "I did what I had to. In the eyes of the law, I've been judged innocent."

"As you doubtless are." The mayor remained seated, blotting his mouth with his napkin. His eyes gleamed with victory. "As I told you, Ruby, as long as we understand each other, you've nothing to worry about. Now, why don't you sit down and finish your coffee. Then I'll walk you through the dining room and introduce you to some influential friends of mine."

Ruby clasped the back of her chair, her stomach roiling. "Please forgive me, I'm not feeling well," she murmured. "I think the best thing would be for me to just leave."

"Of course." The mayor rose. "Please allow me to walk you home, my dear."

She shook her head. "I'm not much for company when I'm feeling unwell. I'd prefer to walk home by myself."

"Alone? But will you be all right?"

"I'll be fine. It's only a few blocks." Ruby edged toward the door.

"And you'll allow me to call on you tomorrow?"

"Of course. Whenever you like." Anything to end this wretched evening and get away, she thought.

"Very well, if you insist. At least let me escort you outside." He came around the table and took her elbow. Ruby willed herself not to recoil as he guided her through the hallway and across the lobby. This vain, obsequious little man had the power to cast a shadow over her future and the future of her daughters. She had no doubt he planned to put that power to use.

On the porch outside the hotel, he clasped her hand. She cringed inwardly as he raised her fingers to his lips. "Until tomorrow, then, my dear Ruby," he murmured. "Something tells me this evening will be the beginning of a beautiful friendship."

Ethan watched the moon crest the ink-black sky. Hidden in the shadows, he couldn't make out the time on his watch, but he calculated the hour to be well past midnight.

Ruby had come home around eight-thirty. He'd seen the light flicker on in her bedroom and glimpsed her moving shadow on the shade before the window went dark once more. So much for his theory about the mayor wanting to get her clear of the house. But at least she was safely home.

Now, alone in the darkness, Ethan imagined her lying in bed, drugged with sleep, her long legs sprawled deliciously beneath the sheet. The image triggered a stream of whispered curses. He'd give a month's pay to be in that bed with her right now, molding her satiny warmth to his, burying his face between her breasts and drinking in that sweet, womanly scent. Damnation, what he'd like to do to her. Do with her. And do inside her.

Maybe if she was half asleep, he fantasized, she wouldn't pull away from the passion that sparked between them whenever they touched. Ruby had shown signs of being a warm, responsive woman. But someone, most likely the bastard she'd married, had scarred her with fear. She would need some gentle loving, maybe a great deal of it, before—

Hellfire, this had to stop. He was driving himself crazy with those thoughts, and right now he had a job to do.

The spring night had turned chilly. Ethan shivered as the breeze penetrated his light woolen jacket. He'd been out here for hours with nothing to show for it but muscle cramps, a growling belly and brambles in his britches. If he had any brains he'd go back to the hotel and get some rest. But experience had taught him to trust his instincts. Right now those instincts were telling him to wait.

Needing to stretch his legs, he eased out of his hiding place and walked into the yard. Dimmed by moonlight, the stars shone like pinpoints of ice against the dark sky. Wind rustled the untended grass.

Standing still, Ethan listened to the night. A faint sound reached his ears. Had he really heard it? The prickling sensation at the back of his neck was enough to answer the question.

Now he heard it again, the snort of a horse and the jingle of harness brass, approaching from a side street. A wagon wheel creaked. The murmur of voices, barely audible, blended with the wind. Someone was coming, getting closer.

It made sense that bootleggers would bring a wagon. A motorized truck would make too much noise. Judging from the wheel tracks Ethan had noticed earlier, they probably planned to pull in and park in the shadow alongside the house, then walk around to the cellar. But had they come to deliver more whiskey or haul away the stash that was there?

Did they know the place had been purchased, and that Ruby was inside? Would she be in danger, or was she expecting them?

Maybe the next few minutes would give him some answers.

As the wagon pulled up in front of the house, Ethan drew his pistol and slipped back into his hiding place.

"You lying bitch! I'm going to kill you!"

Hollis's great, hammy fist pounded the locked bedroom door, accompanied by the sound of splintering wood. A few more blows would rip the door from its frame.

Frantic, Ruby scanned the satin-draped bedroom, searching for some weapon to defend herself. Any other night she would have submitted to a beating and slunk off to nurse her bruises. But tonight was different. Tonight she had stood up to him. She'd confronted him with what the girls' nanny had told her and threatened to expose him for the monster he was.

Now there could be no going back. When Hollis said he was going to kill her, Ruby knew he meant it. And with her gone, there'd be no one to protect her daughters.

Did he have a weapon? Probably not. But a hulking brute like Hollis could easily strangle her with his bare hands or beat her senseless and throw her out an upstairs window. Whatever story he might concoct to cover her death would be vouched for by his corrupt friends in the legal system.

"Open this door, you lying whore! By the time I'm through, you'll be begging me to kill you!" He was roaring loudly enough to be heard all over the house. But Ruby knew that the servants, fearful of losing their jobs, wouldn't come to her aid. No one would dare stand up to Hollis except her brother, Jace—and he lived in town, fifteen minutes away. Even if she could reach Jace by telephone there was no way he could get here in time to save her.

Hollis smashed at the door again, this time with his boot. The impact tore the lower hinge loose from the frame. The next blow would surely bring him inside.

Wild with fear, Ruby seized a brass lamp from the nightstand next to the bed. The electrical cord snapped as she ripped it loose from the wall. Only then did she remember the gun—the loaded pistol Hollis kept in the nightstand drawer.

The lamp clattered to the floor as her shaking fingers yanked the drawer open and closed on the pistol grip.

"Get ready to die, you bitch!"

The gun was a cold weight in Ruby's hand. How did one fire such a weapon? Her frantic mind scrambled to remember what little she knew.

The hammer—she thumbed it back and heard the click. In the same instant, her husband's burly shoulder crashed into the door and broke through.

As he lunged toward her, Ruby's finger jerked the trigger. The shot echoed like the crack of a thunder bolt. Reeling for an instant, Hollis kept coming. His face was beet red with fury. A red flower of blood had burst into bloom on his white dinner shirt.

Ruby fired again, twice in rapid succession. The first shot struck the left side of his chest. The second hit him higher. He staggered forward and collapsed at her feet.

From beneath him, a crimson lake of blood spread outward, soaking the Persian carpet and seeping into the toes of her pink satin mules....

Ruby woke up screaming.

Three men had climbed off the wagon and were moving stealthily around to the side of the house. They didn't appear to be armed, but Ethan, acting on reflex, thumbed back the hammer of his pistol. As they came closer, he could see that they were shabbily dressed, one in overalls, the other two in mud-stained work clothes. Probably backwoods yokels hired to lug the whiskey out of the cellar and load it on the wagon—unless they were crazy enough to be stealing it. Either way, he was here to watch and learn, not to interfere.

Too bad he wouldn't be able to follow them. He'd arrived a few days ago by train and had yet to rent a horse from the livery stable. Likewise, arresting the three small-timers would only blow his cover, allowing their bosses to get away. His best hope would be to see their faces or catch a name or two from their conversation. He could follow up on those clues later.

They were approaching the cellar door when, from the house, a crescendo of terrified screams shattered the darkness.

Ruby!

Ethan's pulse slammed. Whatever was happening, he had to get to her. Heedless of the men in the yard, he lurched forward. But the brambles behind the shed had worked into his jacket and trousers. Their hooked barbs held him fast.

The three men wheeled and bolted for the wagon. By the time Ethan yanked himself free and plunged from his hiding place, they were gone. Judging from their frantic departure, they wouldn't be back tonight.

Ruby's screams had stopped. Ethan pounded across the moonlit yard, ripped open the screen door and crashed his way into the kitchen. "Ruby!" he shouted. "Ruby, can you hear me?"

Fearing the worst, he raced through the parlor and into the darkness of the hallway. There he saw her. She was standing outside her bedroom door, phantom pale in her long white nightgown. Her hair was wild around her face, her eyes huge with fright.

Pausing to holster the pistol, Ethan strode down the hallway and gathered her close. Trembling, she huddled in his arms like a terrified child. Her skin was chilled beneath the light muslin gown. Ethan struggled to restrain his hands from wandering over her body.

"Don't worry," he whispered against her hair. "I'm here, and they're gone."

"They?" She strained backward to gaze up at him. "What are you talking about?"

"The men in the yard. Your screams scared them off. Didn't you hear them?"

She shook her head.

"Then what frightened you, Ruby? Was someone in the house?"

"In the house? No…I don't think so." She strained closer to him, her lush curves triggering a response that strained Ethan's trousers. The pressure was so urgent that he bit back a groan. If the woman pulled away again, he was going to need a long, cold dunk in a mountain stream.

"It was a dream," she said. "An awful dream. I've had it before, but this time it was so real…"

She was shaking again. Ethan's arms tightened around her. "Don't be afraid, Ruby," he muttered. "I'm here."

His lips found hers in the darkness, nuzzling her, nibbling her. She tasted of sleepiness and sex. So damn sweet he could hardly stand it. Unbidden, his hands slid down her back, cupping the full moons of her rump and pressing her in against his erection. She moved against him, her arms sliding around his neck.

"Don't leave me, Ethan," she whispered.

Chapter Five

Lifting her in his arms, Ethan carried her into the bedroom. Ruby clung to him, her heart thundering. She wanted him with a hunger that burned through every nerve and vessel in her body. And she needed the release he could give her, needed it desperately if she was ever to be free from her ugly past.

But what if she lost her courage? She'd been a virgin when she married Hollis. Despite his behavior, she'd remained a faithful wife. No other man had ever made love to her—if her husband's brutish lustful attacks could be called lovemaking. Whatever it was, it was all she'd ever known, and she'd grown to dread it.

"Give me a minute," Ethan whispered, lowering her to the bed. "I'll be right with you."

He vanished into the shadows. She heard the sounds of his boots coming off and the clink of metal, which she assumed to be his belt buckle, striking the floor. Ruby lay still, growing less confident by the minute. Maybe this was a mistake. Maybe she should send him away.

Then, as if by magic, he was next to her in the bed, gathering her close, cradling her in the darkness. He'd left his cotton drawers in place for now, but his upper body was bare to her touch. She closed her eyes, savoring his masculine warmth. His torso was smooth and hard with a dusting of crisp hair that spread over his broad chest and tapered to a dark trail down his belly. He smelled of hotel soap and good, clean sweat. She inhaled greedily, drinking him into her senses.

"You're shaking," he whispered, brushing his lips down the side of her face. "Is it the dream? Do you want to tell me about it?"

"Not now. It has nothing to do with…this." Finding the hollow of his throat, she tasted his salty skin with the tip of her tongue. His breath caught, then eased out in a groan. His arms tightened around her.

"You were made to be loved, Ruby," he murmured against her hair. "Let me show you how loving's meant to be. Let me give you the pleasure you deserve."

Ruby's throat tightened. She struggled to reply but no words would come.

"What is it? Are you afraid of me?"

She shook her head, finding her voice. "It's not you I'm afraid of. It's me. All those years of steeling myself against the things he did, the nights of lying there, wondering how he was going to use me next…" She exhaled raggedly. "What if I'm broken, Ethan? What if I can't—"

His kiss lasted just long enough to block her words. "Hush," he growled. "I always did enjoy a challenge."

The next kiss was warm and deep and intimate. When his tongue invaded her mouth, Ruby felt the contact as a spark that shimmered all the way to her toes. She whimpered as he feathered his way over the delicate surfaces, thrusting and withdrawing, taking time to arouse her with a gentle parody of what was to come. Her pulse skittered to a gallop. Sensations she'd never dreamed of, let alone experienced, trickled along her nerves. But the fear was still there, like a dam resisting a warm spring flood.

His hands found her breasts, shaping her softness to his palms through the thin muslin. She sighed, closing her eyes as he eased the nightgown off her shoulders, baring her body to the waist. Maybe it would be all right. He was so tender, so patient, so… "Oh!"

His mouth captured her nipple. She moaned out loud as his tongue laved the sensitive flesh, shrinking it to a tingling nub. Arching her back, she strained against him, heightening the wonderful sensation.

All too abruptly, he stopped. Her eyes shot open.

"Oh, so you like that, do you?" His rough velvet voice teased her. "Do you want more?"

Ruby couldn't answer. She felt as if she would do anything for more of that sweet madness; but no one had ever asked her such a question. She pressed toward him, shamelessly offering her breast to his mouth.

"Is that a yes or a no?" The wretched man was enjoying himself.

"Yes," she breathed, the need throbbing inside her.

"Yes, what?" Oh, he was insufferable!

"Yes…more!" she gasped.

"More what? Tell me, Ruby."

Blast him! Ruby's frustration mounted, building until the words exploded out of her. *"Suck my tit!"*

She lay there in shock. Never in her life had she uttered such an unladylike phrase.

Ethan chuckled as he bent over her. "That's my girl. You're making progress." His mouth closed over her nipple again and began its gentle tugging. This time it was as if a barrier had dissolved. The rush was so intense that it brought tears to her eyes. Her hands moved, fingers tangling in his hair, cradling his head against her. If they could just stay like this all night it would be enough, she thought.

But clearly it wasn't enough for Ethan. His hands had found their way under her nightgown, their touch like raw silk on her skin. His skilled fingers moved along her spine, pressing the tightness out of her muscles. She sighed deeply. "If I were a cat I'd be purring," she muttered.

"Good. That's the idea." His voice was a rumble in her ear. He kissed her mouth again with a teasing flick of his tongue, then, shifting, nibbled his way along her throat, between her breasts and down her belly. His hands caressed her body, tracing the curve of her waist, cupping her buttocks. Ruby drifted in a fog of pleasure.

As his touch became more intimate, more urgent, his breathing roughened. His erection pressed stone hard against the side of her leg. Ethan had been patient and tender with her, but she knew he couldn't hold out much longer. Soon his male urges would take over and his body would demand a pounding release. That would be her moment of truth.

As his hand slid between her thighs, her muscles instinctively clenched. Ethan sensed the change at once. "It's all right, girl," he murmured. "I'll make it all right. Lie still."

Ever so gently, his hand brushed over her nest of curls, then settled into place, resting there. The contact sent shimmers of heat spiraling through her. Beneath his hand she felt a tremor, like the first tentative beat of a butterfly's wing.

"Ethan…"

"Hmm?" She couldn't see his face, but something told her he was smiling.

"Nothing. It's just that I've never…" Her voice trailed off. She seemed to be teetering on the edge of the sky. If she found the courage to fling herself into space, would she soar or crash to earth?

"What if I told you it gets better?" Without waiting for an answer, he began opening her with his fingers, separating her labia like the petals of a rose. "You're wet," he muttered. "You're so wet I could float my way inside you." As if to prove what he was saying, he began stroking her, his fingertips gliding over the moisture-slicked folds.

"Oh…!" Ruby responded with a moan as he found the exquisitely sensitive nub at her center. Her legs parted wide, hips arching against his masterful hand as he stroked back and forth, each time easing his index finger a little way inside her. The feeling was unimaginable. After ten years as Hollis's wife, she'd thought she'd experienced everything a man could do to a woman. But not this. Nothing like this.

A delicious throbbing pulsed outward from his fingertip. The feel of it was driving her wild. Her hips moved, thrusting, demanding more. "Don't…" she whispered.

"Don't?"

"Don't…stop…" Her breath came in gulps as she felt the explosion building. Then everything seemed to burst. She shuddered against his hand, then lay back with a sigh. Her eyes were wide with wonder.

"Are you all right?" His voice was a breath in her ear.

She struggled for words. "It was so… Good heavens, I had no idea…"

He brushed a kiss across her mouth. "There's more where that came from. But you can always say no."

Fear awakened and stirred. Ruby willed it away. She needed to do this. She wanted to. She shook her head.

"Is that a no, don't go ahead, or a no, don't stop?" Ethan's tone was teasing, but Ruby sensed that her answer mattered to him. Strange, she'd never been given such a choice before.

She pulled his head down for a lingering kiss. "It's a no, don't stop."

"Then you'll have to excuse me for a few seconds." He eased to the edge of the bed and stood. Outlined by the moonlight that filtered through the shade, he stripped out of his drawers. He reached for his discarded pants and withdrew something small from a pocket. Turning away, he manipulated it discreetly. He was taking time to protect her, Ruby realized.

Back in bed, he pushed the covers aside and gathered her close once more, kissing and stroking her. Ruby willed herself not to be nervous. She'd always dreaded what was to come—being imprisoned under the crushing weight of a man caught up in his own pleasure, a man who didn't care how much he hurt her.

This was Ethan, she reminded herself. So far, he'd shown her nothing but tenderness. But as he shifted his weight, she struggled against a thread of panic. Her muscles tightened, bracing for the assault.

Then he did a surprising thing. Instead of moving over her, he rolled onto his back and lay with his sex thrusting straight up. His grin flashed at her in the darkness. "Mount up, lady," he said. "You're about to get a riding lesson."

Trembling, Ruby straddled him and poised herself above his jutting shaft. This was something new. Maybe something good. But the thought of the next step filled her with trepidation.

"It'll be all right, girl." He guided himself to her moist entrance and eased her hips downward a little. Her muscles clenched around him. She took a deep breath, willed herself to relax and pushed with her full weight.

"Oh…" she breathed as he slid inside her. "Oh, Ethan, it's…"

"Good?" He was smiling up at her. His length filled her completely and perfectly, leaving her free to move.

She laughed softly. "It feels glorious."

"Then I'm all yours." His hands reached up to cradle her breasts, fingertips teasing her nipples, triggering freshets of warmth. Instinct compelled Ruby to move. Leaning forward, she began cautiously, stroking against him, feeling the sensual heat flow upward through her body. Craving more, she pushed harder, faster, her senses erupting in waves of sensation. Suddenly, it was as if she'd sprouted wings and was flying. She spiraled skyward, shattered into starbursts and fell, only to rise again as his hands and body urged her on. And now Ethan was flying with her, his breath rasping, his hips pumping, deepening the thrust. A cry escaped her throat as they burst together in a shuddering climax. As they drifted back to earth, she heard Ethan chuckle. "Come down here, girl. Let me hold you."

As she slumped exhausted into his arms, Ruby felt the sting of tears.

She awoke, restless, a little before dawn. Ethan sprawled beside her, deep in slumber. For a time she lay wrapped in contentment, listening to the small sleep sounds he made. Last night had banished her fears and set her free. And she owed it all to Ethan Beaudry, a man she barely knew.

Did she love him? It was too soon for that, Ruby told herself. But she *could* love a man like Ethan. Believing she could love any man was a step forward.

Of course, she knew better than to think Ethan could love her in return. He'd enjoyed giving her pleasure and taking his own. But that didn't mean he would stay. She needed to prepare herself for the day when he moved on. That day would come, Ruby knew. Ethan Beaudry was a moving-on kind of man. But that didn't mean she couldn't make the most of their time together.

Stirring in his sleep, he snorted, turned over and buried his face in the pillow. Ruby resisted the temptation to kiss him awake and take up where they'd left off earlier. The sky was already fading with dawn. Soon people would be on the streets. It wouldn't do to have someone drop by and catch her in bed with her new tenant.

She would let him be for now. But for her, staying in bed much longer was out of the question. Her bladder was demanding relief, and her mouth was as dry as cotton. The sooner she got up and made herself presentable for the day, the better.

Easing out of bed, she pattered barefoot and naked across the floor, found her flannel wrapper and slipped it on. For her, the day couldn't go fast enough. She was already looking forward to tonight, the warm bed and Ethan's loving.

The windowless hallway was dark, but Ruby didn't bother to turn on the light. She could find her way to the bathroom easily enough, and she didn't want to wake Ethan. Moving with care, she stepped into the narrow space. Her feet inched along the floor.

Suddenly her toe stubbed something hard—something that hadn't been there yesterday. Ruby stifled a cry of pain. Whatever was there had been solid enough to hurt. Bending down to feel, she recognized Ethan's clothes, left where he'd taken them off last night. There were his boots, his trousers… But what was this? Her heart plummeted as her fingers closed around the cold shape of a holstered pistol.

She felt the blood drain from her face. *Who was this man? What had he been doing with a gun last night?*

Gathering everything up in her arms, she carried the burden into the kitchen, where dingy gray light was filtering through the east window. Dumping Ethan's clothes and pistol on the counter, she began a careful examination of what she'd found.

The .38 revolver was fully loaded, its holster attached to a well-worn cartridge belt. Recoiling as if she'd touched a snake, she laid it back on the counter and shoved it away. She detested guns and all they stood for.

Next she picked up his trousers, feeling the slight bulge of his wallet in the hip pocket. Its contents might provide important clues to Ethan's real identity. But she'd need more light to examine them. Putting the trousers aside for now, Ruby turned her attention to the jacket, shirt and vest.

The chambray shirt was worn to softness and smelled of Ethan's body. Aside from that it told her nothing. Nor did the jacket, which was of good quality wool serge, lined in silk. A clean handkerchief was folded neatly into the chest pocket. When Ruby picked up the leather vest, the first thing she noticed was a slight extra weight that caused the front to sag. Her fingers fumbled in the dim light. As they touched cold metal, her breath caught. Even without seeing it, she knew what she'd found. Pinned to the vest was an open circle with a five-point star at its center—the badge of a U.S. marshal.

The man in her bed was a lawman. And a liar.

* * *

Ethan woke to the solid thump of a boot striking his chest. His eyes shot open in time to see the rest of his clothes hurtling toward him like mortar shells. He flung up his arm to protect his face from the impact of the heavy cartridge belt. Lowering it, he saw Ruby standing in the doorway. Clad in her robe, with her hair flying loose around her face, she looked as majestic as a Valkyrie and as angry as a wounded bobcat.

Her right hand gripped his pistol, aiming the muzzle straight at his chest. Ethan cursed himself as he realized what had happened. He'd had one thing on his mind last night. Clearly it had been the wrong thing.

"You have two minutes to get your clothes on and get out of this house!" she hissed. "After that, I never want to see your sorry, lying face again."

Ethan scrambled for his wits. "Now, put that pistol down, Ruby," he soothed. "You wouldn't want me bleeding all over your nice linens, would you? And how would you explain having shot a naked man in your bed?"

Her eyes narrowed. "Never mind that, Marshal. If I'd known you were a lawman, I'd have sent you packing right away. You lied to me, and you took full advantage of my trust. Now, get dressed and get out of here before I decide to pull this trigger."

By now, Ethan was sitting up. "I can explain," he said. "But first I'd like to know what you've got against lawmen. You're friendly enough with old Sam Farley."

"That's none of your concern," she snapped. "I'm the one with the gun, and I'm asking the questions. You said you could explain. Fine. I'll listen while you're getting dressed."

"Only if you put that weapon down, Ruby. We both know you're not capable of using it."

Something flickered in her eyes. She hesitated, then sighed as she laid the pistol on the bed. Ethan picked it up and checked the cylinder. As he'd suspected, the bullets were missing.

Ruby folded her arms across her ample breasts. "I'm waiting," she said. "What are you doing here and why did you lie to me?"

The room was almost as chilly as her voice. Ethan slipped on his shirt, then swung his legs to the floor and reached for his drawers. If he lied to Ruby again, any chance of winning back her trust would be shot to hell. He had little choice except to tell the truth.

"I was sent here to break up a bootlegging ring and arrest the leaders," he said. "It started out as an undercover job, but now that you've found me out, I don't know how long I can keep it that way."

She sniffed disdainfully. "Why bother? I never did believe you were a college professor. Why should anyone else?"

Swearing silently, Ethan yanked on his socks and trousers. He'd known from the beginning that his assigned cover had been a lousy idea. His mistake had been accepting it without an argument.

"In any case, you've nothing to fear from me," Ruby continued. "Once you're out of here, I'm going to do my best to forget I ever met you. And the sooner you walk out that door, the sooner I can start. I never want to see you again, Ethan Beaudry, or whatever your name is!" Her voice choked on the last words. She was fighting tears and losing the battle. Either the woman was a superb actress, or she was completely innocent and he deserved to be horsewhipped for doubting her. Ethan was inclined to believe the latter. But he needed to be sure.

Feeling lower than a snake, he pulled on his boots, rose and walked toward her. His hands reached out for her shoulders. She wrenched herself loose and turned away.

"Listen to me," he said. "I know I've hurt you, but I can't leave now. Whether you like it or not, I'm staying."

"You're *staying?*" She wheeled to face him. "But this is my home. I just ordered you to leave."

He shook his head. "A crime's been committed in this house, Ruby. You could be in danger here. It might be wise for you to stay with your brother until I finish my job."

Ruby reeled as if he'd slapped her. "What on earth are you talking about?" she demanded. "You've got some explaining to do."

He exhaled slowly. His hair was tousled, his eyes bloodshot from too few hours of sleep. "Do you remember my saying something about men in the yard last night?"

"Now that you mention it..." She'd only been half awake at the time, Ruby recalled. But the memory was there, barely.

"There were three of them," he said. "I was behind

the garden shed, watching. They were headed for the cellar when your screams scared them off."

"The cellar? But there's nothing down there except dusty old furniture. You saw it for yourself."

"And I saw more. Sit down, Ruby, you look ready to keel over."

"I'm fine." She glared at him. "Just go on. Tell me everything."

He nodded, lips pressing together in thought. Those lips had thrilled her with caresses. They had also lied to her, Ruby reminded herself. They could be lying to her now.

"While you were visiting with the mayor and his son, I moved the rest of the furniture away from the wall," he said. "I found a covered hole there with a hidden room behind it. It was stocked with jugs of illegal whiskey, hundreds, maybe thousands of dollars' worth. I waited in the backyard because I figured somebody would be coming to get it. That's why I was close by when you started screaming."

"But why didn't you tell me about the whiskey right away?" she demanded.

His silence answered, and suddenly she knew. Her legs weakened, threatening to give way beneath her. "You thought I might be involved, didn't you? Maybe that's what you still think. Is that why you made love to me, Ethan?" She was shaking with rage now. "Did you think you might learn something that way, you scheming, contemptible—" She bit back the other, more colorful names she wanted to call him.

His expression could have been chiseled in granite.

"Forgive me, but it's my job to ask. *Are* you involved, Ruby?"

"No!" She flung the word at him with a blast of fury. "How could you even think it? And how can I let you stay here after this?"

"Because you have no choice, and because I told you, you aren't safe here alone. Those men, or others like them, are bound to show up again. My best advice would be to go and stay with your brother until this mess is straightened out."

Ruby met his challenge with a thrust of her chin. "This is my home, and I'm not leaving. If I have to, I'll go down in that cellar, take a hatchet and break every one of those whiskey jugs myself!"

He shook his head. "You'd only be making yourself a target. Besides, I can use that stash of whiskey for bait. It's my best chance of catching the rats who're breaking the law and lining their pockets. That's why I need to stay here." His eyes drilled into hers. "And if you're not involved, maybe you can prove it by helping me."

"Prove it by helping you?" She stared at him in shock. "Of all the arrogant, high-handed—"

"Think about it, Ruby." His voice was a lawman's voice, stripped of emotion. "The sooner we can arrest these people, the better it will be for both of us. You'll have a safe place to live. And as for me…" His words trailed off. He didn't have to say the rest. When this job was done he'd be leaving. He'd be out of her life for good. For Ruby, that couldn't happen soon enough.

And Ethan was right about the rest, as well. There was no way she could bring her little girls to this house while criminals were using the cellar to store illegal whiskey. And there was no way she could invite paying tenants to move in, either.

Ruby's shoulders sagged as the fight went out of her. Ethan had lied to her. He had used her shamelessly, and she despised him for it. But if she wanted to move on with her life, she had no choice except to do as he'd asked.

"It seems you have me at a disadvantage, Marshal," she said. "Fine, I'll work with you for as long as it takes to get rid of the bootleggers. But only on one condition."

"What condition is that?" His manner was as distant as a stranger's. How could she have let this man into her bed? How could she have imagined being in love with him? His charm, his teasing manner, it had all been an act.

"Just this," she said. "You're to take your things and get out of my bedroom. You can stay upstairs or at the hotel. I don't care which. And you can come and go here as you like. But don't you come near me, Ethan Beaudry. Don't you ever touch me again."

Chapter Six

Rumpled and unshaven, Ethan took a backstreet route to the hotel. By now the sun was coming up. Already there were people on the streets. He had no wish to be seen coming from the boardinghouse at this hour, especially given that he looked like something dragged out of hell.

He felt even lower than he looked. Ruby's tongue-lashing had gotten to him. He couldn't blame her for being furious. He'd behaved like a cad, telling her lies, making love to her, then acting as if their night together had meant nothing. But he was a professional lawman. Even if it meant hurting a vulnerable woman, his job had to come first.

Hurting Ruby now meant less chance of hurting her later, he told himself. But he was rationalizing now. The truth was, Ruby Rumford had class. The trust she'd given him last night had been precious and genuine.

And he'd ground it under his heel. For what he'd done to her, he deserved to be dragged buck naked through an acre of prickly-pear cactus. But some things couldn't be changed. And the truth was that no woman deserved to be shackled to what he'd become—a hollow shell of a man, incapable of deep emotion. The man he'd once been was buried back in Oklahoma with his wife and their two little girls. Now he lived for his work, and his only real satisfaction came from seeing justice done.

An hour later, clean-shaven, freshly changed and minus his gun and badge, he strode up Main Street to the low brick building that served as the railroad station. The telephone there was in a booth, and he needed to make a private call.

Entering the wooden booth, he lifted the receiver, deposited a coin and gave the operator the number of the U.S. Marshals' regional office in Denver. The switchboard transferred him to the Investigative Division. The voice that answered was one he recognized.

"Forrest, Ethan here."

"Hey, Ethan. How's the case going?"

"Don't even ask. More dead ends than a damn prairie-dog maze. But I need some background checks on a few people, pronto."

"I'm your man. Let me grab a pencil." Forrest White was a master of long-distance investigation with a network of contacts in every state. If anybody could help Ethan open up this case, it was Forrest.

"Ready." Static crackled on the line as Forrest shifted the phone.

"Here we go. First on the list is the mayor, Thaddeus Wilton."

"The mayor?" Forrest whistled softly. "This sounds interesting."

"It may or may not be," Ethan said. "Next you can add his son, Harper Wilton, to your list. Then the town marshal, Sam Farley."

"Got it. Anybody else?"

"Yes." Ethan cleared his throat, which had suddenly gone tight. "A woman—a widow named Ruby Rumford. She's new here in town, but you might want to talk to someone in Springfield, Missouri. She has a brother named Jace, but I didn't catch the last name. Find out what you can."

"Sounds like I'll have my work cut out for me." Forrest chuckled. "That widow, now—is she pretty?"

"That's neither here nor there," Ethan growled.

The chuckled deepened. "She's a pretty one, I'll wager. And it sounds like she's managed to get under that alligator-tough hide of yours."

Ethan ignored the gibe. "How soon do you think you'll have something for me?"

"No promises. The boys upstairs have me pretty well sandbagged today, but I'll make some calls as soon as I get a break. You can check back this afternoon if you want."

"Not sooner?"

"A bit anxious, are we? Sorry, but that's the best I can do."

"Fine, then, I'll call you back. And thanks." Ethan hung up the phone and stepped out of the booth.

Impatience gnawed at him, but there was little he could do. Forrest's time was in high demand, and this bootlegging caper wasn't at the top of his list.

Ethan's belly was growling with hunger. Maybe his disposition would improve if he got some something to eat. Adjacent to the train depot was a small café that bore the hand-lettered sign Mabel's. The food wouldn't likely be up to what he'd get at the hotel, but at least it should be faster and cheaper. After breakfast he could arrange for a horse, deliver his paperwork to Sam Farley and, providing he could work up the nerve, go back to the boardinghouse. He had some serious fence-mending to do with a certain redheaded landlady.

There was just one thing wrong with that plan. He'd hoped to learn more about Ruby and the elderly marshal before dealing with them again. For now, he might be better off taking the horse to explore the countryside, then returning after midday to put in another call to Forrest. Either way, there was no hurry. He could think about what to do over breakfast.

After buying a newspaper on the platform, he entered the café, sat down at an oilcloth-covered table and ordered a plate of bacon, eggs and beans with black coffee. He was reading the paper and sipping coffee while he waited for his food, when a familiar voice startled him.

"Fancy running into you here, Professor. Thought you might be eating at the boardinghouse this morning."

Startled, Ethan glanced up to meet the pale blue eyes of Marshal Sam Farley. So much for plans. Now he'd have to play it by ear.

"Mind if I join you?" Without waiting for an answer, Sam slid out a chair and sat down. "The usual, Mabel," he said, casting a smile toward the attractively plump, middle-aged woman behind the counter.

"Coming right up, honey." Mabel returned the smile and added a wink. He had a lot to learn about the people in this town, Ethan reflected—the friendships, the feuds, the secret jealousies and, last but not least, the most welcoming place to get a meal.

"So how's Ruby doing after her first night in that place?" Sam asked pleasantly. "Is she settling in all right?"

"I believe so." Ethan folded the newspaper and set it aside. "But she's not set up for meals yet, so here I am. Oh, you asked for my credentials yesterday." He drew a sheaf of folded papers out of his inner pocket. "I was going to bring these by your office later on. But as long as we're here…"

"I see." The marshal unfolded the letter of introduction from the president of Oberlin College, which was actually genuine, written as a favor to an old friend in the agency. "And if I telephone this fellow, he'll vouch for you?"

"Absolutely, providing he's in today."

Sam looked startled for a moment, as if he'd forgotten what he was doing. His fingers shuffled the papers Ethan had given him. "I see your diploma's here, even your driver's license."

"Good enough for you?" Ethan took a sip of his coffee while the old man made a show of inspecting the papers. "You're welcome to take them for a few hours."

"No, they look fine." Sam's coffee had arrived, along with a small pitcher of cream and a bowl of sugar. Returning the papers to Ethan, he sweetened the coffee liberally before he took a sip. "First-rate as always, Mabel," he said. "Thanks."

The woman beamed. "Your breakfast will be ready in a minute, honey. Yours, too, sir."

Ethan leaned back in his chair, studying the marshal over his coffee cup. The hand that lifted the sugar spoon had been unsteady enough to spill a few grains into the bowl. And he'd given Ethan's papers only a cursory glance, as if he might not be able to read the small print. Law enforcement was a job that demanded razor-sharp senses and lightning reflexes. Was Sam Farley still up to facing a dangerous situation? Ethan couldn't be sure. But after thirty years in office, Sam would certainly know every inch of his town and a great deal about its people. How would a man use that knowledge? Ethan wondered.

"It impressed me that you asked for my credentials, Marshal," he said. "You're very protective of your people, aren't you?"

"Damn right I am. The safety of this town is my responsibility. I don't take it lightly."

"That strikes me as a big job for one man. Surely you must have a deputy or two."

The old man snorted. "Might have, if I could find one worth his salt. My last deputy up and got married last month. His bride was worried about him gettin' shot, so he quit. Don't suppose you're interested in the job, are you?"

Ethan chuckled, shook his head and changed the subject. "I noticed how concerned you were about Ruby. You must know her pretty well."

The marshal scowled. "Ruby's one fine woman. But she's been through more hell than you or I can even imagine. The last thing she needs is some man giving her more of the same. You get my drift?"

Ethan nodded, wincing inwardly. He assumed Sam was referring to Ruby's marriage. Could there be more to the story than what he'd already guessed? "What do you mean, she's been through hell?" he asked cautiously.

Sam shot him a stern look. "That's her private business. If Ruby wants you to know about it, she can tell you herself."

"I see." The awkward silence that followed was broken by the arrival of breakfast. Served on spotless white plates, the food was fresh, well prepared and surprisingly good.

"Thaddeus Wilton at the hotel's been trying to buy Mabel out or hire her away for years," Sam said between mouthfuls of fluffy scrambled egg. "She competes with his business and she's the best cook in town. But she owns this little place, and she likes being her own boss, don't you, sweetheart?"

"That I do," Mabel replied with a grin. "And it looks like I'm about to get busy."

As if on cue, the early-morning train rolled up to the platform and stopped in a hissing cloud of steam. Travelers spilled out of the passenger cars, a rough dozen of them heading straight for the café. Jostling for tables and calling out orders, they filled the small space with their clamor.

Ethan had planned to bring up the subject of bootlegging to get the marshal's reaction. But with so much chatter around them, any attempt at private conversation would be wasted. There was nothing to do but finish his breakfast and be on his way.

Taking his leave of the marshal, he stepped outside. The sunlit air was brisk, the distant peaks sparkling with snow. It was a perfect morning for a ride, Ethan mused. As for Ruby, they could both use a few hours of cooling-off time. He would see her after he'd spoken with Forrest. Decision made, he strode back downtown and took a side street to the livery stable.

By now the shops were open and the streets were busy. Coming toward Ethan was a pretty young blonde woman flanked by two little pigtailed girls. Dressed in matching pinafores, they clasped their mother's hands, swinging her arms as they skipped along the sidewalk. Watching them approach, Ethan felt the pain twisting like an icy blade inside him. He might have wheeled in his tracks and crossed the street, but it was too late. They were almost upon him. As they came closer, their faces broke into friendly smiles. One little girl's grin widened. "Hello, mister," she chirped in her childish voice.

Ethan couldn't help it. He had to turn away.

Ruby sat in the hotel dining room, finishing her breakfast of English tea and a buttered roll. Worried about money, she'd ordered the cheapest items on the menu. Now she wondered why she'd bothered to order anything at all. She was so tense that she could barely swallow.

How could her plans for a peaceful life have turned into such a nightmare? She'd hoped the boarding-house would provide income and a home for her and her daughters. Instead, here she was, the owner of a criminal habitat, suspected of being in league with the hoodlums, betrayed by the man to whom she'd given her trust and blackmailed by a powerful man who wanted her favors.

This morning she'd been so furious that, if Ethan hadn't left on his own, she'd have thrown him bodily out of the house. How could he insist on staying after the way he'd lied to her? And how dared he try to blackmail her into helping him? *Helping him,* for heaven's sake! She'd just as soon help a chicken-stealing weasel! But whether she liked it or not, she found herself coming around to his point of view.

Over the past hour her anger had been undermined by a rivulet of icy fear. As long as the stash of illegal whiskey remained under her house, her life would be at risk. Since Congress's passage of the Eighteenth Amendment, bootleg liquor had become big business. The men who trafficked in it were the worst sort, capable of murdering anyone who got in their way. And they warred with each other as well as with the law. Any night, a gun battle could erupt right in her cellar, with bullets crashing everywhere. While that danger existed, there was no way she could rent out rooms or bring her precious daughters to town.

As she saw it, she had two options. She could give up the house and slink off with her tail between her legs, or she could stay here and cooperate with Ethan. Being around the man would be a constant strain. But she was through backing down, as she had for so many years with Hollis. This time she would stay and fight for what was hers. But, by heaven, she intended do it on her own terms, not Ethan's.

Dropping a few coins onto the white tablecloth, she rose from her chair. Right now there was just one thing she needed. One thing that couldn't wait any longer.

In the hotel lobby was a pay telephone, mounted around the corner from the desk. Hurrying toward it, she shoved a coin into the pay slot and gave the operator the number of her brother's ranch.

It was Clara, Jace's pretty young wife, who answered the ring. "Ruby! We've been wondering about you. How are things going?"

"Just fine." Ruby had already made up her mind not to burden Jace and Clara with her problems. "What I'm wondering is, how are you?"

"I'm as big as a Holstein cow! And this little mischief is kicking up a storm!" Clara laughed, clearly delighted with her pregnancy. "The doctor says one more week, but I'm not sure I believe him."

"How's Jace holding up?"

"Not too bad so far. He's out with the calves today. You know, Ruby, Jace is more than willing to come into town and help you."

"No, everything's all right," Ruby lied. "I've hired a man, and he's working out well. But I may need to impose on you to keep the girls a few extra days. The house is taking more time than I'd hoped."

"That's no problem. Mandy and Caro are darlings. They've actually been a lot of help to me."

Ruby felt herself beaming, as she always did when someone praised her daughters. "Are they close by?" she asked. "I'd like to say hello."

"They're out on the porch, playing with Patch's new kittens. I warn you, they're going to want one. I told them it was up to you. Wait, I'll get them in here."

Ruby waited, clasping the phone as she listened for the slamming of the door and the sound of running feet. Her little girls were her joy, her anchor, her reason for living. Only now did she realize how much she missed them.

"Mama?" Ten-year-old Mandy, short for Amanda, sounded out of breath. Ruby could picture her blue eyes dancing, her taffy-colored curls tumbling over her forehead. "Mama, Patch has kittens! They just got their eyes open, and they're so cute! Aunt Clara said we could have one if you'll let us. Can we, please?"

Ruby sighed. "We'll see, dearest. The kittens will be needing their mother for a few more weeks. Let's wait till they're big enough. Then we can decide."

"But can't you promise? Then we could pick one out and give it a name."

"I said we'll see, Mandy. Are you helping Aunt Clara?"

"She says we're the best helpers she ever had. Can't we *please* have a kitten?"

Ruby had to laugh. Mandy's persistence could be

wearing, but it would serve her well in life. "I love you," she said. "Now, let me talk to your sister."

"Hello, Mama. I miss you." Caroline was dark like her father's family. At eight, she was an avid reader and wanted to be an archaeologist when she grew up.

"I miss you, too, sweetie." Ruby blinked back tears. "Are you having a good time?"

"Uh-huh. It's nice here. But I want us to be together. When can we come and live with you?"

Ruby felt the ache of longing. "Soon, I hope. But there's still a lot of work to be done on the house."

"We could help."

"That wouldn't be much fun for you, sweetheart. You're better off with Uncle Jace and Aunt Clara. But I'll try to come and see you soon. And don't worry, everything's going to be fine."

Ruby ended the conversation, wishing she could believe her own words. She had never been away from her girls, and the yearning to see and hold them was like physical pain. Somehow she had to resolve this mess with the house. She owed it to Mandy and Caro to provide a safe home, where they would never again have anything to fear. Whatever the cost, she would make that happen.

Half-blinded by tears, she headed across the lobby toward the front door. She stumbled outside just in time to collide with two men—men she recognized only as she wiped her eyes clear.

She stifled a groan. The day, which had begun badly enough, was about to get even worse.

"Ruby, my dear, what's wrong?" Mayor Thaddeus

Wilton laid a proprietary hand on her shoulder. Ruby stiffened at his touch.

"Nothing that I can't fix by myself," she said icily. "Now, if you'll excuse me—"

"Excuse you? Why, we'll do nothing of the kind!" The mayor's sweaty clasp tightened. "Harper and I were about to have breakfast. We insist on your joining us, my dear. Don't we, Harper?"

"Whatever you say, Pop." Harper mouthed the words with no change of expression on his long, horsey face.

Ruby turned, freeing herself from his grip. "That's very kind of you," she said in a formal voice. "But I just finished breakfast and couldn't eat another bite. It's time I was getting back. I promised myself I'd get the kitchen cleaned and set up today."

"In that case, I hope you'll allow us to escort you home." Wilton's manner oozed friendship and goodwill. But Ruby sensed an undertone of menace in his oily voice. He had discovered her secret, and he was intent on showing her how he could use it to control her. For now, he'd taken the liberty of touching her and insisted on walking her home. Soon he'd be asking small favors, then demanding large ones. If she defied him, he had the power to make her pay, along with her innocent daughters.

As she began to walk toward home, he fell into step beside her and slipped his hand under her elbow. After a sharp exchange of glances, Harper turned away and strode back toward the hotel.

"Our meeting is fortuitous, my dear," he said. "I'd planned to call on you after breakfast to extend an invitation, which I hope you'll accept. I'm hosting a little dinner party at my home tomorrow evening. I'll be entertaining some important people and I'd like to see you there, dressed in your prettiest gown."

Ruby took time to weigh his words. She had no desire to attend, especially given the odds that she might find herself alone with him. But if she hedged, he would bring the threat of revealing her secret into play—a threat he could carry out only once, she suddenly realized.

Thaddeus Wilton wouldn't play his ace over an issue as trivial as a dinner party. It was far more likely he'd hold out for higher stakes. Ruby didn't want to think about what those stakes might be. But for now there was no need to bow to his every whim.

"I hope you won't be foolish enough to refuse, dear girl," the mayor said. "I have a lot of influence in this town. My backing, or lack thereof, can make or break your prospects here."

"You say there'll be important people at your party." She spoke slowly, daring to let the bastard dangle. "And who might those people be?"

"Well, as I said, it's just a small party."

"Who?" she insisted. "I'd like to know before I make up my mind."

His eyes narrowed beneath the straight black slash of his eyebrows. Until now, he'd evidently believed he had her in the palm of his hand. She could be playing a dangerous game.

He cleared his throat. "Very well, I've invited some business owners, the president of the ladies' auxiliary and a few members of the city council."

"Does that include Marshal Farley?"

He scowled, thrusting his lips into a pout. "Sam's a good soul, but he's a plain-living man. He'd feel out of place at an elegant party like mine."

"So you haven't asked him?"

The mayor shook his head. "Sam's getting on in years—he's outlived his usefulness. If he doesn't retire on his own, we have plans to vote him out and put in someone young enough to do a proper job."

"Oh?" A dark prickle crept down Ruby's spine. "And who might that be?"

Wilton laughed. "So you've guessed, have you? I think my boy, Harper, would do a first-rate job as marshal of this town."

"I see." The boardinghouse was less than a block away now. Ruby resisted the urge to tear herself loose and break into a run. Thaddeus Wilton repulsed and frightened her. But she knew better than to show it. A bully required a victim. She would not give him what he wanted.

"So, what's it to be? I'll be sending my car to pick you up at six-fifteen."

She paused, deliberately taking her time. "I'm not used to accepting invitations on such short notice," she demurred. "I hope you won't mind if I check my schedule and let you know. I can leave you a note at the hotel desk."

Wilton glared at her. "Your schedule!" he sputtered. "I've had my eye on you since you arrived here, and I know for a fact your social calendar isn't exactly full. I'm doing you a favor, woman! Just say yes!"

They had reached her front gate. Turning, she gave him the full impact of her gaze. "I'm sorry, but back in Springfield, where I came from, invitations were issued at least a week ahead, usually in writing."

He went rigid, and Ruby knew her barb had hit home. The implication that she viewed him as a social bumpkin was the last thing the mayor wanted to hear.

Taking her hand, he gave her a slight bow. "As you wish, my dear. Think about it and let me know. But if you want to succeed in this town, you'll need good connections. This party will be your best chance to make them."

"I'll keep that in mind." Ruby turned away and opened the low picket gate. Closing it behind her she watched the mayor stalk back up the street toward the hotel. Maybe she'd pushed him too far.

Thaddeus Wilton was in a position to do her some serious damage. Standing up to him, even in a small way, had been risky. But she'd needed to let him know that she wouldn't be pushed around. Judging from his expression, he'd gotten the message.

Drained by the encounter, she mounted the steps, unlocked the front door and went inside. The house was silent, giving no sign that Ethan had returned. In his absence, she felt strangely vulnerable.

Knees quivering, she sank onto a chair. The tick of the mantel clock she'd set that morning echoed in the stillness. She clasped her hands on her knees, fingers working creases into her skirt as she pondered her dilemma.

She'd vowed to be independent in every respect. But

trouble was rising around her like a river in flood, and she had nowhere to turn for support. The mayor couldn't be trusted. And, much as she needed his protection, neither could Ethan Beaudry. Jace had already proven he'd do anything for her. But with Clara's time so near, she couldn't, and wouldn't, involve him in her problems again.

There was only one man in Dutchman's Creek she could count on—a man who knew her secret and remained a steadfast friend, a man whose advice would be wise and in her best interest.

She would force herself to spend the morning scrubbing the kitchen, Ruby resolved. Then, after giving herself time to think things out, she would walk up the street and pay a call on Marshal Sam Farley.

By the time Ethan returned, it was past midday. Using back roads and trails, he'd ridden a broad circle around the outskirts of town. The ride had given him a mental map of Dutchman's Creek and the surrounding countryside, with its patchwork of fields, farms and ranch land.

Along the wooded foothills, he'd spotted a number of likely stills in run-down shacks and cabins. Taking quiet note of their locations, he'd kept his distance and ridden on. He was after bigger fish. Once the organization was broken, teams of deputies could come in, smash the stills and arrest anybody stupid enough to be hanging around. For now, it made sense to keep things quiet.

Leaving the horse at the livery stable, he walked back toward Main Street. By now he was getting hungry. He would take the time to order a sandwich at Mabel's. While she was making it, he could go next door to the railroad station and telephone Forrest White. He was anxious to hear what, if anything, the investigator had learned.

Mabel gave him a welcoming smile and took his order for a ham and cheese on rye. Ethan could understand why Thaddeus Wilton would want to shut her down. The food and the friendly service at this little place had the hotel beat six ways to Sunday.

"I'll be back in the time it takes you to put that sandwich together," Ethan told her. "Just need to make a telephone call."

"Don't be too long, honey." Mabel was already slicing the meat. Ethan grinned as he strode out the door. That morning she'd called him "sir." Evidently, he'd been promoted.

Stepping outside, he glanced both ways, an old habit that served him well. To his left, the station platform paralleled the tracks. It was empty now, except for a spotted dog sniffing at a sandwich wrapper. To his right, Main Street stretched four blocks to the boardinghouse at the far end. After the morning bustle, this was a quiet time of day, with only a horse-drawn wagon and a couple of Model Ts on the road. A few people strolled the boarded sidewalks, none of them rushing.

Ethan was about to turn away when something far down the street caught his eye—a flash of flame-gold hair, an elegant head on a statuesque, blue-clad figure. Even at this distance there was no mistaking Ruby.

And she was just coming out of the marshal's office.

Ethan cursed out loud. He should have known Ruby would go right to Sam Farley with what he'd told her. The illegal whiskey in the cellar, his own true identity, everything. And if Sam was trafficking with the bootleggers, the whole damn case would be blown out of the water.

Even if Sam was innocent, his knowing would create more complications than a loose bull at a county fair. The old man liked to talk; and one word to the wrong person could ruin everything. Worse, he might want to involve himself in the case. If Ethan was right about the man's eyesight and unsteadiness, Sam could be putting himself and anyone he was protecting in serious danger.

Damn! Damn! Damn!

Now what? Ethan watched Ruby until she disappeared into the dry-goods store. He had some decisions to make. But first he needed to know exactly who, and what, he was dealing with.

He strode back toward the railroad station, one hand fumbling in his pocket for change. He could only hope Forrest had something to tell him. Otherwise, he might as well be flying blind.

Chapter Seven

On his third attempt to call, Ethan heard the familiar voice on the line. His pulse skipped. "Got anything for me, Forrest?" he asked.

A chuckle punctuated the answer. "This must be your lucky day. Some time opened up and I was able to make a few calls. Highly entertaining, I must say. But I'll save the juiciest part for last."

"I'm listening." Ethan was grinding with impatience, but he knew better than to show it.

"I'll start with Sam Farley. According to what I was told, the old man's practically a legend. In his younger days, he put away enough bad guys to make your head spin. His reputation is above reproach. All I can say is, if you suspect he's crossed over, you'd better have solid proof before you act."

"Understood. What about the mayor?"

"Not much on him, I'm afraid. Certainly no criminal

record. But that boy of his—Harper, right? He was charged a couple of times in Wyoming, once for rape and once for assault. The charges were dropped later. I got the impression his old man paid off the victims."

"Thanks, that helps." Ethan filed the information away. The mayor and his poker-faced son would definitely bear watching. But Forrest had promised to save the most interesting tidbit for last. That meant it involved Ruby, and it was bound to be bad news. "Let's hear the rest," he said, bracing himself.

"About that widow of yours…" Forrest paused for dramatic effect. "It's quite a story. Wait till you hear it."

Minutes later Ethan exited the station house, too numb to feel the ground beneath his feet. Lunch forgotten for the moment, he walked slowly down Main Street. His bags were packed and waiting at the hotel. He'd planned to move everything to the boardinghouse this afternoon. But he needed to calm down and think things over before he confronted Ruby. That might take some time.

For now, he'd return to Mabel's and force himself to eat the sandwich she'd made him. After that he'd take some time to explore the town while he sorted out his thoughts. Turning around, he walked back toward the station. With every step his thoughts churned and roiled like clouds before a thunderstorm.

Ruby… Lord, what happened, girl? I know the bastard hurt you, but what could drive you to kill a man—a woman like you, so gentle and such a lady? Why in heaven's name didn't you just leave him? How could you pull that trigger?

Ruby's kitchen was spotless. The cabinets had been wiped clean, the linoleum floor scrubbed and waxed. The large black cookstove was polished and stoked with the coal the hardware store had delivered that morning. A pot of pinto beans simmered over the back burner.

Ruby was standing on a chair, stacking her precious Limoges china on the highest shelf when she heard the front door open. By now she'd spent enough time with Ethan to recognize the sober cadence of his footsteps. That, and the abrupt click of the closing door, told her he wasn't in a happy mood.

She brushed a stray curl out of her eyes. She was tired and sweaty and not feeling very amiable herself. Whatever happened next was bound to be unpleasant. But there was no use putting it off.

"In here," she said, her voice carrying into the parlor. "Mind the linoleum. It's been waxed."

She heard him set his bags down. Seconds later he appeared in the kitchen doorway. Weariness was written in every line of his face. Weariness and something else. Ruby recognized the look at once. As a U.S. marshal, Ethan would have access to the records of the entire American legal system. Checking her past would have been as easy as making a couple of telephone calls.

She looked down, meeting his gaze. "You know, don't you." It wasn't a question.

He exhaled slowly. "Yes, I know you killed your

husband, Ruby. Would you care to tell me how it happened?"

Ruby hesitated. Last night she might have trusted him with the whole, very personal story. But Ethan had betrayed her once. No doubt he was capable of doing it again. "A jury acquitted me on grounds of self-defense," she said. "That's a matter of record, and it's all you're entitled to know."

"I see." Something flickered in his eyes, but he remained where he was, feet planted in the doorway as if defying her to make him leave.

She stiffened with apprehension. "What is it? Something else?"

He scowled at her. "I saw you earlier, coming out of the marshal's office."

"So?" She feigned nonchalance. "Sam is a friend."

"What did you tell him, Ruby—about the whiskey and about me?"

She climbed down from the chair to stand facing him. "Except for what happened last night, I told him everything."

Ethan growled a curse under his breath. "Now, why did you have to go and do that? I told you this was an undercover case."

"Why not? Sam Farley is the marshal of this town. He's a good man, and he deserves to know what's going on right under his nose. I can't imagine why you'd keep this from him."

"Maybe I did it for his own protection. The marshal's getting old, and these are dangerous people we're dealing with. If he gets in the way, he could end up hurt, even dead."

Ruby studied the man who'd made love to her last night—the man who'd calmed her fears and awakened her to a thrilling new world of sensual pleasure. Everything he'd done, and everything he'd told her, had been a lie. Why should she believe him now?

"You aren't telling me the whole truth, are you?" she said. "You suspected me of being involved with the bootleggers. You probably suspected Sam, as well. Maybe you still do. Go ahead, deny it. What's one more lie to a man like you, Ethan Beaudry?"

His eyes had gone stony. She'd hit the mark this time. "Well?" she demanded.

"A man in my line of work learns to suspect everybody, Ruby," he said. "If I were a trusting sort, I'd be lying six feet under by now."

"I can understand that. But Sam Farley? He doesn't have a dishonest bone in his body! Ask the people who live here, the ones who've known him for years. They'll all tell you the same thing."

"And I'd be inclined to believe them," Ethan said. "I checked Sam's record with headquarters in Denver. They confirmed everything you're saying about him."

The ugly weight in her chest sank deeper. "You checked on Sam—and of course, you'd check on me, too. That's how you found out about my husband."

"Just routine." His voice was cold and flat. Ruby battled the urge to fly at him and pummel his impassive face with her fists.

"I shot Hollis Rumford to save my own life. The

servants heard him bellowing that he was going to kill me. It was their testimony, along with the evidence of the broken bedroom door, that saved me from hanging." Her voice broke under the strain. "Did the records tell you that?"

His silence answered her question. Ruby turned away to gaze out the window above the kitchen sink. Outside, the panes were overgrown with blooming honeysuckle vine. If she raised the sash, the sweet fragrance would flood into the room. Groping for some diversion, she leaned over the sink and tugged at the wooden framework. Nothing moved. The window was painted shut.

A tear welled and spilled over. Ruby swiped it away with the back of her wrist. The last thing she wanted was for this wretched man to see her cry.

The floor creaked under his boot as he moved. His hands settled lightly on her shoulders. She went rigid, torn between pride and need. She'd told him not to touch her again. But the urge to lean back into his arms was a burning hunger.

"Don't," she whispered.

His hands dropped away. "I'm sorry, Ruby."

She wheeled to face him. "How could you do it? How could you make love to me and feel…*nothing?* Was that just routine, too?"

His face had assumed its impassive lawman's mask. "I never said that I felt nothing. And it certainly wasn't routine. But when this case is wrapped up, I'll be leaving Dutchman's Creek. And it's not likely I'll ever be back. A man in my line of work can't afford to form attachments. You need to know how it is."

She glared at him. "I'm not a child, Marshal. I've learned enough from life to know when I'm dealing with a cold-hearted bastard."

Did he flinch? It would be satisfying to know she'd hurt him, even a little. But she didn't want to spend the rest of the afternoon trading insults. They had more pressing things to discuss.

"Well, now that we know where we stand, we might as well get on with our business," she said. "Did you check on anyone else?"

"The mayor and his fair-haired boy. Thaddeus is clean, but Harper's had some nasty brushes with the law. He could hurt you, Ruby. Stay away from him."

"Thanks for the warning, but it's not Harper I'm worried about. It's his father." Turning back to the sink, she resumed tugging at the stubborn window sash. "The mayor found out about my husband. He's threatened to make a scandal of it unless I cooperate with him."

"Cooperate how?"

"That remains to be seen. It's a threat he can only carry out once, so I'm guessing he'll save it for something big—something I might not otherwise be inclined to do. For now, he's invited me to a dinner party at his house tomorrow night."

"Here, let me do that." Ethan had his pocketknife out. Nudging Ruby aside, he began working the blade around the edge of the window sash, cutting through layers of dried, flaking paint. "So, will you be going?"

"I said I'd let him know. But I'd rather not suffer through it. I can't imagine he'd ruin my reputation over something as trivial as a dinner party."

"You're probably right. But then, it may not be all that trivial." He strained to lift the stubborn window sash. When it held, he tried the blade again, prying at the tight spaces between the sash and the frame. "I'd like you to attend, Ruby."

She stared at him. "Since when are you giving me orders?"

"I'm not. But the sooner we catch those bootleggers, the sooner you can open this place up for business. If the mayor's involved, you might be able to learn something from him. So it's in your best interest to help me. Agreed?"

"That depends." Ruby had mulled this part over while she was scrubbing the kitchen. She'd even rehearsed the words in her head. "This is my property, and I have my rights. I'm giving you a week, Ethan. If this mess isn't cleared up by next Saturday, I'm going down into that cellar with an ax and smash every last one of those whiskey jugs myself. You and your blasted bootleggers can take your fight someplace else!"

He shot her a stern glance. "That wouldn't be very smart, Ruby. You'd be putting yourself in danger."

"Then do the job yourself! One way or another, I want that whiskey gone! And unless you give me your promise that it will be, Ethan Beaudry, don't expect any favors!"

Laying the knife on the counter, he straightened. His gaze swept over her, taking in her tousled hair, her coal-smudged face and her faded calico apron. "Woman, you can be right mule-headed when you make up your mind to be," he grumbled.

"Those are my conditions. Take them or leave them."

"Will you go to the mayor's party?"

"I'll do whatever's reasonable to help you, but only for a week. If nothing's happened by then, I'm taking matters into my own hands."

He loomed over her like a thundercloud, his eyes drilling into hers. Had she pushed him too far? Ruby forced herself to stand her ground, her chin thrust outward, her gaze firm and challenging. Inside, she was jelly. Worse, inexplicably, she found herself aching to be kissed by him. Her heels rose off the floor as her body strained upward. What was the matter with her? This was all wrong!

He leaned over her. She heard the sharp intake of his breath. Then, abruptly, he jerked away and swung toward the window. His hands gripped the sash and wrenched it upward. With a squeal of sliding wood the window opened. The breeze-borne aroma of honeysuckle rushed into the room, so sweet that it made Ruby's head swim.

When Ethan turned back toward her his jaw was set, his expression steely. "I'll accept your terms, Ruby," he said. "But I won't have you putting yourself in danger. If the whiskey is still in your cellar by next Saturday I'll destroy the stash myself and seal up the opening. You'll never have to worry about it again. That much I can promise. Do we have a bargain?" He extended his hand.

Ruby accepted the handshake. His clasp was brief, the sort of gesture one man might make to another. Maybe it meant he would keep his word. But she knew better than to trust him. Ethan Beaudry was a lawman, and the law was his only code of honor. For the sake of that code, he would lie, betray and destroy anyone who stood between him and his idea of justice.

"Now that we've settled that matter, I know there's still work to be done," he said. "Is there something you'd like me to start on?"

There was nothing settled about the way Ruby was feeling. But she matched his casual manner. "Now that you've managed to open one window, why don't we open them all and air out the house. And with the windows open, we're going to need screens put up. I believe I saw a stack of them out back in the garden shed. And there's a ladder lying alongside the fence."

"That should be enough to keep me out of trouble for the rest of the day." He strode toward the back door, opened it and stepped out onto the porch.

"Oh, Ethan—"

He turned back toward her.

"Dinner should be ready in a couple of hours. I bought bread from the bakery, and I'm cooking some beans. I'll call you when it's time."

"Sounds good. As I mentioned when we met, I'm right partial to home cooking." The door closed behind him.

Ruby's legs sagged beneath her. Leaning against the counter, she closed her eyes and let the honeysuckle breeze cool her damp face. Why did dealing with Ethan always leave her drained? He was only a man, after all. A man with melting brown eyes and the physique of a Rodin statue. A man with a cold, prideful and thoroughly exasperating nature.

A man who would never love her.

But when had the idea of love entered the picture? She'd made a grievous mistake with Hollis. Ethan Beaudry would surely be another. Even if he came to her on his knees, something he would never do, she'd be a fool to accept him.

Besides, she wasn't exactly prime courtship material herself. What man in his right mind would pursue a widow who'd taken a .38 and blown her husband to kingdom come?

But why was she wasting time with such useless thoughts? She was struggling to make a place for herself and her daughters. Nothing else could be allowed to matter.

Pushing the whole idea aside, she lifted the lid of the big enameled pot to check on the beans boiling inside. She'd set them on the stove more than an hour ago, but they were still as hard as pebbles. Never mind, they'd surely be done by suppertime. And the bread she'd bought would be good, even without butter. When she got settled in, she would start making her own bread. She had a recipe somewhere, one of several she'd salvaged from the kitchen back in Springfield. A little flour, a little salt and yeast—how hard could it be? She imagined lifting the plump, golden loaves out of the oven. She could almost smell their fragrance, mingled with the sweetness of honeysuckle.

A sparrow chirped beneath the eave of the house. From the backyard came the scrape and thud of Ethan dragging the window screens out of the shed. A fleeting sense of contentment stole over her. Could happiness be as simple as this—supper on the stove, a man working in the yard and a woman waiting to welcome him inside?

The feeling vanished, leaving Ruby more troubled than ever. She'd come to Dutchman's Creek to find peace and start a new life. Instead, she'd stumbled into a morass of uncertainty and danger, led on by the most compelling man she'd ever known.

A week or two, surely no more, and Ethan would be gone. Until then she would keep her distance and guard her heart. She'd let one man destroy her life. It could never be allowed to happen again.

Ethan laid the screens flat on the grass and used a hose to wash away the dust and cobwebs. It felt good to be doing physical work. Anything was better than pacing the ground and stewing over what he'd learned.

Ruby's version of her story, what little he'd heard, rang true. No doubt she'd believed herself in mortal danger, and her acquittal was a just verdict. But questions buzzed like hornets in his mind. What had triggered Hollis Rumford's homicidal rage? Could Ruby have driven him to it? Had she *wanted* an excuse to pull that trigger?

It was a fair question. But none of the answers made sense. If she'd wanted to end Rumford's abuse, she could have left him. And if she'd been after his money, why didn't she have it? Why was she struggling to open a run-down boardinghouse in a backwater like Dutchman's Creek?

His lawman's nature demanded answers. But he couldn't blame Ruby for holding back. He'd lied to her. He'd violated her trust in the most callous way, and she wasn't ready to forgive him. Maybe she never would be.

After finding the screen that fit Ruby's bedroom window, he put up the ladder and mounted a lower rung. Taking care, he ran the knife blade around the edge of the sash, loosening it from the outside. Then he wiped each pane of glass with a rag, polishing it clean. Through the white lawn curtain she'd hung, he could see her neatly made bed with its quilted coverlet. Was it just last night he'd slept in that bed, with Ruby's lush body cradled in his arms, her long silky legs tangled with his?

His blood warmed as he remembered making love to her, remembered her surprising innocence, her delight at every new sensual discovery. She'd been fearful at first, but her eventual response had held nothing back. She had given him her all.

Now, looking through the window at that pristinely made bed, he ached to be there again tonight, loving Ruby as she was made to be loved, plundering her sweet mouth, holding her close as he filled her with his heat, stroking and thrusting into that slick honey chamber.

But he knew better than to think it might happen. Ruby was a proud woman, and he'd behaved despicably toward her. The rest of his nights in this house would be spent chastely alone.

He tried raising the window sash, but it was latched on the inside, probably painted shut, as well. It would need to be opened from the bedroom. For now, he could put the screen up.

Things were bound to be a bit tense with Ruby. But it felt good to be here protecting her. Ruby was a fiercely independent woman, but she was no match for the dangers that lurked around this house. Tonight he would keep watch, sleeping with one eye open and a pistol under his pillow. But he didn't expect any trouble. By now, the bootleggers would know there was someone living in the house. If he was right to suspect that the mayor was involved then they'd be more likely to show up tomorrow, when Ruby was at the mayor's party.

And that brought Ethan's thoughts to the mayor. He'd had a bad feeling about Thaddeus Wilton from the first time he'd come to the house. Initially he'd chalked it up to the man's interest in Ruby. But after Forrest White's report, the picture made perfect sense. The mayor oversaw the bootleg operation and pocketed the cash, keeping his hands lily white. Harper did the dirty work, protected by his powerful father.

Ethan's instincts told him he was right. But without proof he was whistling in the dark.

Was Wilton's dinner invitation a scheme to get Ruby clear of the house, or just a man's desire to possess a beautiful woman? Ethan's jaw tightened as he pondered the mayor's scheme to blackmail Ruby. Would he use his threat to get her into his bed tomorrow night?

But that would be up to Ruby, Ethan reminded himself. It wasn't his job to tag along and protect her. He needed to be here at the house, waiting for the bootleggers to come after the whiskey.

He lifted the screen to the window and hammered the wooden frame into place, giving it extra blows for good measure. Ruby was a grown woman, capable of making her own decisions. But for him, every minute she was with that bastard would be a little bit of hell.

It was nearly dusk when Ruby called Ethan in for supper. She'd set the table with her second-best dishes and a fresh gingham cloth with matching napkins. The bread had been sliced, the beans ladled into a blue china tureen. A single red rose, snipped from a wild bush in the yard, bloomed in a miniature crystal vase. This humble meal would be the first in her new home. She wanted it to be nice. And she'd taken a little time for herself. Her hair was freshly brushed and pinned, her face washed, her apron consigned to the laundry basket.

Her pulse quickened as he came in through the kitchen door, his face and hair glistening with water from the hose. He looked rumpled, sun-weathered and impossibly handsome. "Smells good," he said, pulling out a chair. "I've worked up quite an appetite."

Feeling strangely shy, Ruby took her seat on the opposite side of the table. "Sorry there's no butter," she said. "I'll buy some tomorrow, and some milk, too. This was all I could manage today."

"It looks right fine. I appreciate it, Ruby." He laid a slice of bread on the side of his plate and scooped some beans into his bowl. "Mind if I dip?"

Ruby felt her lips curve into a smile. "Since there's

nothing else to put on the bread, that strikes me as a good idea."

He broke off a chunk of bread, sopped it in the beans and lifted it to his mouth. A subtle change came over his face as he chewed. Ruby read surprise in his expression. Her heart sank. "Does it taste all right?" she asked.

He swallowed with effort and took a sip of water. "Tell me, Ruby, what did you put in these beans?"

She stared at him. "Why…nothing. I just put them in the water and cooked them. Why, is something wrong?"

"Have you tasted them?"

Ruby dipped a spoonful from her bowl, blew on the beans and took a cautious taste. They didn't exactly taste bad. In fact, they had no flavor. None at all. "Oh, dear," she said.

"Do you always cook beans this way?" Ethan asked.

Ruby sighed. There could be no more hiding the truth. "I've never cooked beans before in my life," she said. "In fact, I've never cooked anything. There were always servants around to do that."

Ethan leaned back in his chair. A smile played around his lips as he studied her. "Ruby, Ruby." He shook his head. "You are just one surprise after another."

"What am I going to do, Ethan?" She was fighting tears now. "Here I am, trying to open a boardinghouse, and I don't even know how to cook!"

"I suppose you could hire some help."

"Later on, maybe. Right now I don't have the money."

"Then I'd suggest you learn some quick basics, like salting the beans before you boil them. I'm no great hand in the kitchen myself, but I've spent enough time on my own to learn a few tricks. As long as we're here, I'd be happy to pass them on to you."

"You'd teach me?" She felt as if she were drowning and he'd just thrown her a life preserver.

His brown eyes twinkled, reminding her that he'd already given her lessons of a very different sort. "I said I'd be happy to. But in return, it would be a nice gesture if you'd forgive me for lying to you yesterday."

He looked as appealing as a puppy. The man had charm enough to melt granite when he chose to use it, Ruby reminded herself. He could also be as impassive as a brick wall. She'd seen both sides of him, and she wasn't sure which side she trusted less.

"I'll forgive you," she said. "But only on condition that you never lie to me again. Agreed?"

He grinned. "Agreed. No more lying. And I take my promises seriously."

"We'll see about that, Marshal," Ruby said. "Now, when do you start teaching me to cook?"

"First thing tomorrow we'll sit down and make a shopping list," he said. "As soon as we have something to work with, we'll get started. Meanwhile, go and get your wrap, lady. Tonight we're going out to dinner."

Chapter Eight

The spring day had been warm, but the evening was cooled by a chilly breeze. Wrapped in her merino shawl, Ruby strolled up Main Street with Ethan at her side. Shops and businesses were closed for the night. Traffic was sparse, with a few autos and buggies rolling homeward ahead of darkness.

"Aren't we going to eat at the hotel?" she asked as they passed the two-story structure on the far side of the street.

"Do you want to?"

She shook her head. "Not if we can find anyplace else."

"There's a little café by the station. Do you know it?"

"I've seen it. But I've never been inside."

He laughed. "Then you're in for a treat. It's Dutchman's Creek's best-kept secret. I only hope the place is open at this hour."

They passed the darkened windows of the dry-goods store and the barbershop. The ugly redbrick town hall, with its whitewashed Romanesque facade, was cloaked in shadow, as well. A golden sliver of moon had risen behind the far peaks.

Ruby stole a glance at Ethan's chiseled profile. He had turned on his charm once more. But she couldn't allow herself to be distracted. Behind that easy smile, Ethan was all business. "Do you have any solid reason to believe the mayor's behind the bootlegging?" she asked.

He was silent, as if lost in thought.

"Ethan, if I'm to help you, I need to know everything you know."

"And I need to be able to do my job without putting you in danger."

"In other words, you still don't trust me." Ruby stopped walking and caught his sleeve, yanking him around to face her. "You promised not to lie, remember? Are you still afraid I'll go running to that pompous little weasel with everything you've told me? How can you think that? I can barely stand the sight of the man!"

His hands flashed up to grip her shoulders. His mouth came down on hers in a rough, grinding kiss that ended without giving her time to respond. "Ruby, you're driving me crazy," he muttered, turning away. "Let's just walk."

He strode along in silence, his expression veiled in deepening twilight. Ruby kept pace with his long steps, her own thoughts racing and plunging. What was she to make of that kiss? What did he expect of her? What should she expect of herself?

"The truth is, I don't have a damn thing on the mayor," he said at last. "Not an ounce of proof against him or that snake-eyed son of his. All I've got is my own gut feeling that they're behind this operation."

"And that's where I come in."

"The man obviously finds you attractive," Ethan replied. "You own the house where the booze is stashed, and he thinks he has some power over you. If he shows his hand to anybody it could be you."

"In other words, you want to use me," Ruby said coldly.

He groaned. "Not at the risk of your safety. I wouldn't stand for that. But if you hear something, see something—"

"I'm to report back to you like a good little spy. Ethan, I've always minded my own business. I never wanted to be involved in anything like this. All I want is to be free of this awful mess!"

He sighed. "Ruby, I've seen what they do, the bastards getting rich from this business. I've seen the greed, the corruption, the innocent people who died because they got in the way or saw too much. We can close our eyes to it, or we can do what we can to stop it, even if it's only in this one little valley. I'm not asking you to do this for me. I'm asking you to do it because it's right."

The passion in his voice stirred Ruby as much as his words. Her mind pictured Dutchman's Creek and the good people who'd accepted her brother as one of their own. She imagined her daughters living here, growing into womanhood. How far would she go to keep them safe? Her chest tightened, constricting her voice to a hoarse whisper. "I understand. Of course I'll do it."

Ethan's throat moved, but he didn't speak. Ruby sensed the welling of emotions in him—all the things he tried so hard to keep hidden—the compassion, the innate decency, the tenderness. She could learn to love such a man, she thought.

The railway depot lay a half block ahead of them, its empty platform lit by a single electric bulb mounted over the doorway of the station house. On the near side of it, Ruby could see the small café. Its windows glowed behind lowered blinds.

"Looks like the place might be open," Ethan said. "Let's hope there's something left for dinner."

"Wait." She touched his sleeve, halting him as the door swung open and a lanky figure in a suit strode out onto the platform, paused, then vanished into the darkness.

"Damn," Ethan muttered. "That looked like Harper."

"What would he be doing here? His father owns the hotel." Ruby pressed forward, but Ethan pulled her back into the shadows.

"We don't want him to see us. Give him time to get clear, then we'll go on in."

They waited in silence. When, after a couple of minutes, Harper didn't reappear, they walked up to the café. The door swung open at Ethan's touch.

A woman sat alone at one of the tables. Her face was buried in her hands, but she looked up, startled, as Ruby and Ethan stepped through the door. She appeared to be in her late forties, with pink cheeks and graying hair that curled around her face.

When she'd seen Harper leaving, Ruby had suspected some sort of romantic assignation. But now that didn't seem likely. Harper was in his twenties. This woman looked old enough to be his mother. The checkered oilcloth table covers were wiped clean. There was no sign that Harper or anyone else had just eaten a meal. But the aromas lingering in the air made Ruby's mouth water.

"Are you all right, Mabel?" Ethan asked gently.

She rose, rearranging her features into a smile. "Why, it's the professor! Fancy you coming back here a third time today! And you've brought a lovely lady friend. What can I do for you?"

"We were hoping to buy dinner," Ethan said. "But if you're closed for the night—"

"Why, bless you, honey, I was just about to lock up," Mabel said. "But if you'll settle for leftover chicken and dumplings, I've got plenty. I was just about to have some myself and call it a day."

"We don't want to impose," Ruby said.

"Horsefeathers! If you don't mind my joining you, I could use the company, with the two of you as my guests, of course." She cocked her head, studying Ruby with gray eyes that might have sparkled at a different time. Tonight those eyes had a careworn look. "Aren't you Jace Denby's sister? The woman who bought that old boardinghouse?"

"How did you—"

"It's a small town, honey. And Sam Farley is a

good friend of mine. He sure thinks the world of you." Mabel bustled around the counter to where the bowls and plates were stacked. How much had Sam told her? Ruby wondered.

"Please let me help you." She hurried after Mabel, but the woman motioned her back.

"Sit down, both of you. I do this for a living. It won't take a minute."

True to her word, Mabel whisked the dishes, cutlery and napkins to the table. Disappearing into the kitchen, she emerged with a steaming pot, a platter of sliced bread, a saucer of butter and a small pitcher of milk all balanced on a tray the size of a bicycle wheel. Ethan sprang out of his chair to take it from her hands and lower it to the table. With a murmur of thanks she sank onto the chair he'd pulled out for her.

"Even the good Lord needed rest, Mabel," he said. "Something tells me you work too hard."

"The work keeps me going. It's the worry that gets me down." She lifted the lid off the pot and ladled the chicken and dumplings into the bowls. The rich, steamy aroma was sublime. "You'll want to let it cool a bit," she said.

The butter was fresh and lightly salted, the bread as soft and crusty as the baguettes Ruby had loved in France. The bakery she'd visited a few hours ago had nothing like this. Mabel must have made the bread herself.

Ruby blew on a piece of dumpling and took a cautions taste. The dumpling seemed to melt in her mouth. And the flavor…sweet heaven, she could have fainted with pleasure. "My word, this is wonderful, Mabel," she said between bites.

"Thank you, dear. Some people sing. Some people paint or sew. I cook. It's all I ever wanted to do."

"With food like this, I'm surprised anybody eats at the hotel."

"I'm afraid that's the trouble." Mabel sighed. "I wouldn't mind a little fair competition. But Thaddeus Wilton plays dirty, and he wants this place closed."

"We saw Harper leaving," Ethan said. "I take it he wasn't here for chicken and dumplings."

Mabel shuddered. "The man actually threatened me. Said this was my last chance. I could sell out to Thaddeus and go to work for him at the hotel, or start packing my bags."

"Did he say what he'd do if you didn't?"

"No. But it wasn't an empty threat. Harper's the sort who enjoys being cruel, and he doesn't care who knows it." Her head came up. "I worked hard to build this business after my husband died. I know the place doesn't look like much, but it's all mine, and I like being my own boss. It wouldn't be the same working for somebody else, especially an oily rattlesnake like Thaddeus!"

She was trembling. Ruby reached out and laid a comforting hand on her shoulder. "There's safety in numbers, Mabel. If you ever feel you're in danger, come to the boardinghouse. I'll take you in day or night, for as long as you need."

"Thanks for the offer, honey, but I'm used to taking care of myself. And as long as Thaddeus wants me to cook for him, I can't imagine he'd let Harper hurt me. Right now I'm more annoyed than scared."

"But you have to take the threats seriously," Ethan said. "Greed and cruelty are a dangerous mix, and the Wiltons don't seem short on either. Have you told the marshal what's going on?"

Mabel shook her head. "Sam's a good friend, but at his age, he's no match for those two skunks. I don't want him getting hurt."

Ruby glanced at Ethan. Now, she thought, would be a good time for him to tell the poor woman he was a U.S. marshal. But he kept his silence as he sopped a bit of bread in the sauce at the bottom of his bowl. Maybe he was weighing Mabel's needs against the demands of his job. If so, she had little sympathy for him. She turned to Mabel.

"Promise me, at least, that if there's any sign of trouble, you'll let me know," she said. "I have connections to people who might be able to help you. Don't I, Ethan?"

He looked up, his eyes narrowing. "Yes, I suppose you do. That's good advice she's giving you, Mabel. I hope you'll take it to heart."

And that, Ruby thought, was the best she was going to get from this duty-bound lawman.

When supper was done, she helped Mabel clear away the dishes and carry them into the kitchen. "I'd be happy to wash them for you," she offered.

"Thanks, dear, but I can do the job faster by myself." Ruby laid the dishes in the sink, added some soap shavings and poured hot water over them from the kettle on the big black stove. Adding a little cold water from the tap, she began washing. Her small, plump hands were a blur of efficiency. Without being asked, Ruby picked up a clean towel, lifted each dish out of the rinse pan and wiped it dry, but she was slower than Mabel. The dishes piled up in the clear water.

In the other room she could hear the light creak of the floorboards as Ethan waited for her. He was anxious to get back to the boardinghouse, she knew. With the fall of darkness, every passing minute increased the odds that someone might come after that accursed stash of whiskey.

Mabel had finished washing the dishes. She drained the soapy water and shook the drip off her hands. "I can finish here," she said. "You go on, dear. I can tell your gentleman friend is getting anxious to leave."

"He's not—" Ruby bit back the rest of the words. Explaining her relationship with Ethan was beyond her tonight.

"Thank you for everything." She handed Mabel the dish towel. "You've been so very kind, and the meal was delicious."

Ruby turned to go, but Mabel caught her arm. "Sam told me what happened back in Missouri," she said. "I admire your courage, Ruby, and I'd be honored to be called your friend."

Her words all but undid Ruby. She blinked back tears. "Thank you," she murmured, squeezing Mabel's hand. "Something tells me I'll be needing a good friend in the weeks ahead."

"Ready?" Ethan thrust his head around the door frame.

"Go!" Mabel shooed Ruby out of the kitchen. "Don't keep the gentleman waiting!"

Catching her shawl from the back of a chair, Ruby allowed Ethan to escort her outside. By now it was dark. The risen moon lay like a gold coin tossed against a spill of glittering stars. The breeze carried the scent of blooming honeysuckle.

Wrapped in her shawl, Ruby walked in pensive silence. She could feel Ethan's eyes on her, and she knew that soon the questions would start. His was a lawman's curiosity. It drove him to pry and probe beyond the point of annoyance. She understood that. But wasn't she entitled to her own questions? Ethan's personal life was a locked door. He might kiss her, even make love to her, but his privacy was sacrosanct. Could he have a sweetheart somewhere, or even a wife and family? What sort of game was he playing with her?

The answers to those questions could be painful. But Ruby knew she needed to hear them. She had to know the truth before she let him break her heart.

"Does Mabel know about me, Ruby? Is that what you were talking about in the kitchen?" Ethan glanced at Ruby and saw her flinch. "Sorry, but it's my business to ask."

"I'm well aware of that," she said. "And the answer is no. If I'd meant to tell her I'd have done it earlier, while we were eating." She took a deep breath. "Mabel does know about me, though—about my husband. It seems Sam's been talking."

"Does it matter?"

"It didn't to Mabel. But it might to other people. This is a small town." Her chuckle was laced with irony. "At this rate, Thaddeus's threat won't carry much weight, will it?"

"No, but it might be smart to play along with him. If he thinks he's holding that over you, he's more likely to talk."

"Of course." Her reply was crisp and cool. The breeze stirred her hair, wafting her fragrance to Ethan's nostrils. With it came the memory of holding her in the night, her glorious body naked and trembling against his own. He swore silently. For two cents he would sweep her up in his arms, carry her back to the house, fling her on the bed and forget this crazy mess for the rest of the night. He wanted to lose himself in the scent and taste and feel of her, to bury himself in her warm wetness and love her until the past washed away like an earthen wall in a spring torrent.

But that could never happen, not even with a woman like Ruby. Nothing on earth, in heaven or in hell, had the power to blot out the memory of who he was and what he'd done.

"Will you be keeping watch tonight?" Her tone was light, almost casual. Was it an invitation? Ethan's pulse quickened.

"We'll see," he said. "If the mayor's our man, I'm betting he'll send his boys in tomorrow night, while you're off at his party."

"I suppose that's another reason for me to be there." She touched his arm. "Be careful. This could get nasty."

"I know my job. I'll be fine."

"What if he's figured out you're staying here? Someone could easily have seen you working on the house."

"I thought of that. I'm still registered at the hotel, in case he checks. And I've gone in and out during the day, made sure the room looks lived in."

"You could go back there tonight," she said. "Put in an appearance, get some rest."

"I won't leave you alone in that house. Not while there's any chance of danger."

She clutched her shawl, gazing down at the sidewalk. "I didn't sign on for this mess, Ethan. I just want it over, so I can live my life in peace."

He dared to lay a hand on her shoulder. Her skin was warm through the light fabric of her blouse. "It'll be over as soon as we catch these people. And we will, Ruby. I promise you."

"I'll hold you to that promise." She moved ahead, breaking contact with his hand. The house lay ahead of them, dark and quiet. A cat, moonlight pale, fled across the yard as they came through the gate.

"Wait on the porch," Ethan said. "I'm going to check the back." He drew a small .22 pistol from the shoulder holster beneath his vest.

"No, I'm coming with you," she insisted.

"Then stay behind." He walked along the side of the house. Moonlight cast the ground into sharp relief.

There were no fresh tracks, no sign that anything had been disturbed.

"All quiet." He holstered the gun and checked the area for anyone who might be watching. "Go around front and let me in through the kitchen. I'm not expecting trouble tonight, but just in case, I'll be sleeping upstairs with one eye open. If you hear anything, just stay in your room and keep still." There, he'd defined the boundaries. She wouldn't need to worry about his expectations of sharing her bed.

Waiting in the shadow of the back porch, Ethan heard the opening and closing of the front door, followed by the light patter of her footsteps. The latch clicked and the door opened far enough to let him in. They stood in the dark kitchen, the sound of their breath filling the quiet space. If he were to take her in his arms he would be lost, Ethan thought.

She stirred, and cleared her throat. "I was planning to bathe before going to bed. Since the only tub is upstairs, you may want to finish with the bathroom ahead of me."

Ethan willed away the picture that flashed in his imagination. "I won't be a minute," he said. "I made sure the hot water was working yesterday. Let me know if it gives you any trouble."

"I will." She switched on the hall light and vanished in the direction of her bedroom. Ethan climbed the stairs and got ready for bed in the dark. No use advertising his presence in the house.

He was just stretching out between the sheets when he heard the sound of water running in the bathroom next door. The aroma of lavender bath salts crept through the paper-thin wall to tease at his senses. Forbidden images stole into Ethan's mind—scented bubbles sliding over satiny curves, water beading on rose-tinted nipples, fingers soaping places he had touched, places he had kissed…

Damn!

What if there were spiders in the bathroom? He knew for a fact that Ruby hated them. What if she were to see one on the edge of the tub and scream to be rescued…?

Damn! Damn! Damn!

He lay in torment, aching like a fool as the blissful sounds washed over him—the playful splash of water, the shift of her adorable bum against the slick porcelain surface of the tub. He fancied he could even hear her breathing. Then the gurgle of water down the drain drowned out everything else. The floor creaked softly as she stepped out and dried herself with a towel. Ethan heard the door latch click open, followed by the patter of her bare feet going back downstairs.

He was alone—and crazy with wanting her.

Ruby's slumber was plagued by fitful dreams. First she fancied that she was lying in Ethan's arms, blissfully contented. As he caressed her, she closed her eyes, trembling with anticipation. Their loving would be everything she'd ever wanted and needed.

At a chilling touch, she opened her eyes. She was staring up at Hollis. Heart slamming, she kicked and scratched with all her strength, but his massive hands pinned her down. "Bitch!" he snarled. "I'll teach you a lesson!" Even then she continued to fight him, doing little damage until her hands clawed his shirt open. There on his chest she saw three gaping, crimson bullet holes.

Sensing that this was a dream, she struggled like a drowning swimmer to bring herself out of it. Her thrashing legs tangled the sheets into a twisted mass. But it was no use. Sleep sucked her under again. And this time, the face leering above her belonged to Mayor Thaddeus Wilton.

His toupee was askew, his brows black and bristling. Beneath them, his eyes glittered with pure evil. "Double-cross me, will you?" he hissed as his fingers clenched around her throat. "You'll be sorry, my dear! I can hurt you in ways you never imagined!"

He was choking her. She fought for life, bucking against his iron grip, hands flailing, clutching at the sheet. In the instant before she abandoned hope, her fingers closed around something cold, hard and strangely familiar. It was a .38 revolver like the one she'd fired at Hollis. And this time she knew exactly how to use it. Thumbing back the hammer, she jammed the muzzle against Wilton's ribs and pulled the trigger.

The gunshot jolted her awake. For the space of a breath she feared it might have been real. But no, she lay alone and empty-handed in the dark, with no sign of any disturbance. She'd been dreaming again, that was all.

Turning onto her side, she huddled shivering in the twisted sheets. Her heart was racing. Her body felt cold and clammy. All she wanted was to be warm and to feel safe. And right now, her one source of warmth and safety lay in the room directly above her.

Still muzzy from sleep, she sat up, adjusted her night-gown and slid her bare feet to the floor. Ethan had made his boundaries clear. But he wouldn't have to make love to her—in fact, that wasn't what she had in mind at all. She only needed to be held and comforted until the fear went away. Surely he would understand that.

Pulse hammering, she mounted the stairs. In the quiet darkness, the small settling sounds of the house creaked around her. A cricket droned from a shadowed corner of the kitchen. The windblown honeysuckle made a brush-ing sound against the window screen.

She reached the landing and tiptoed down the hall. Ethan's door stood slightly ajar. From the dark space beyond came the low rasp of his breathing. Fully awake now, she hesitated.

Would she regret this later, running to him in the night like a frightened child? What would he think of her? What would she think of herself when morning came?

She'd set out from Springfield determined to be a strong and independent woman. She'd resolved to make a new life for herself and her girls, and to do it on her own terms. Those terms didn't include crawling into a man's bed just because she'd had a silly nightmare.

She turned away from the door, then hesitated again, remembering his muscular arms and the warm, manly aroma of his body. A tingling ache grew between her thighs, bittersweet and unbearable. Her hand reached for the door, then froze. If she walked into that room she would be lost. She could not—would not—let herself weaken.

Decision made, Ruby stole back to the landing and returned downstairs, to her own bed.

Chapter Nine

Ruby awoke to light streaming through the gauzy curtains. She sat bolt upright. Blast! What time was it? It had to be seven, at least. And she'd meant to get up before dawn to start her busy day.

From the kitchen came the clatter of someone shaking down the ashes in the stove. "Ethan?" she called. When there was no answer she rolled out of bed, swept her hair out of her eyes and tied on her flannel robe. This wouldn't do, she scolded herself. If she was going to run a boardinghouse, she would need to become an early riser.

Hurrying to the kitchen a moment later, she saw Ethan coming in through the back door with the empty ash receptacle. Freshly shaved, washed, combed and dressed in a clean plaid shirt, he looked annoyingly handsome.

He grinned at her. "Good morning, sleepyhead.

You're just in time for your first cooking lesson—bacon and eggs."

Ruby followed his gaze toward the counter. Three brown eggs and a thick slab of uncooked bacon rested on a tin pie plate. Beside the plate was a pint Mason jar filled with milk.

She blinked at the sight, wondering if she was fully awake. "It can't be time for the stores to open," she muttered. "Where did all this come from?"

"I paid an early visit to Mabel's. She was just opening for breakfast, and I talked her into selling me a few things. While I'm firing up the stove, you'll have time to get dressed. Then, as soon as you're presentable, we'll…"

Ethan's voice trailed off. His eyes roamed over her tousled hair, her sleepy face and the curves of her uncorseted body. His gaze deepening, he took a step toward her. Ruby's pulse skipped as he paused, then exhaled with a ragged breath. "Get a move on," he growled. "The sooner we start cooking, the sooner we can eat."

Ruby fled back to the bedroom, struggled into her underclothes, pulled on a clean cotton skirt and blouse and tied on an apron. In the bathroom she splashed her face, scrubbed her teeth and reached for her hairbrush. Her face was hot, her pulse still skittering. For an instant, Ethan had looked as if he wanted to eat her alive—and if he'd taken another step toward her she might have let him.

Stop that! Ruby gave herself a mental slap. She was a grown woman, not a boy-crazy schoolgirl. And life had taught her some hard lessons. One of them was that you mustn't throw caution to the wind with a man—any man. Especially a man as rootless and changeable as Ethan Beaudry.

As she twisted up her long hair and pinned it into place, her mind ticked over her agenda for the morning. After breakfast she would take the list of cooking essentials, which Ethan had surely drawn up, to the grocery store. Once the items were paid for, she would arrange to have them delivered to the boardinghouse. While she was out, she would stop by the hotel and leave a note at the desk, accepting Thaddeus Wilton's invitation.

She shuddered at the memory of last night's dream. The evil in Wilton's eyes had chilled her to the roots of her soul. Had the nightmare been some kind of warning? Her late mother had believed that dreams were sent for a reason and should be heeded. But Ruby had never held with such superstition. Besides, if the dream had told her Thaddeus Wilton was evil and she was destined to kill him, it had also hinted that Ethan could turn out to be like Hollis. The dream was best forgotten.

By the time she returned to the kitchen, a blaze was crackling in the big black stove. Ethan had put coffee on to boil and found a cast-iron skillet, along with a sharp butcher knife and a tin spatula. The bacon slab lay on the cutting board.

"First we cut the bacon, like this." He demonstrated with the knife. The marbled slice, as thin as fine shoe leather, fell neatly away from the edge of the blade. "Now you try it. Careful… Keep your fingers clear."

Ruby positioned the knife awkwardly and pressed

down. It was like cutting into a block of greased rubber. As she pushed harder, the blade slipped off the slab and clattered onto the cutting board. She breathed a mild curse. Ethan had made it look so easy.

"Try it this way." He moved behind her, reaching around to guide her hands. The press of his body ignited a warm tingle of awareness. His breath tickled her ear. Ruby willed herself to focus on the knife and the thick slab of bacon. "Hold it at a bit of an angle, starting at the corner. Now slide it along." His fingers were cool and firm. "That's it. See?"

The slice was too thick in some spots and too thin in others, but at least she'd managed to cut it. "I feel like such a butterfingers," she murmured.

"You'll be fine. Now do it on your own." He stepped back, releasing her. "One more slice, then we'll wrap up the rest for the cool box."

Ruby angled the knife the way he'd shown her and began to cut. She was a competent woman, she told herself. And this was a simple task, so easy that any fool could perform it. She could feel Ethan's eyes on her. She wanted to show him—she *would* show him...

"Oh!" The blade slipped, slicing into the finger that held the bacon in place. "Oh, drat!" Instinctively she stuck the finger in her mouth, tasting blood. The cut didn't seem to be deep, but it hurt.

"Here." Ethan turned on the faucet and ran cold water over her finger for a few seconds. "Let's have a look." He cradled her hand in his left palm, dabbing at the cut with the clean handkerchief that had come out of his pocket. "Not too bad. We'll wrap it up for a few hours till the bleeding stops." His eyes narrowed. "Better sit down, you look a little pale."

Ruby sank onto a chair and allowed him to wrap the handkerchief tightly around her finger. He knotted the ends as adroitly as he did everything else. "Does that mean the cooking lesson is over for now?" she asked.

"No. It just means you'll have to learn by watching." He laid the bacon slices in the cold pan. "Warm it up slowly and the slices won't stick. You find the best temperature by moving the pan on the stove top. Right over the fire is too hot. You're liable to burn the bacon or worse, get a grease fire. Here in the center should be about right."

Ruby watched from the chair, feeling like a backward child. Whatever had possessed her to think she could open her boardinghouse and just start cooking? So far, she was a walking disaster in the kitchen.

But never mind, she would learn, she vowed. Somewhere in this town she would surely be able to buy a cookbook. Her mother had always maintained that anyone who could read a recipe should be able to cook. That had to be true. There had to be a less embarrassing way to learn than taking lessons from a handsome U.S. deputy marshal.

The bacon was beginning to sizzle, filling the kitchen with its mouthwatering aroma. Ethan turned each slice with a fork, his movements sure and easy.

Ruby stood, moving closer to watch. "So where did you learn to cook?" she asked him.

"I taught myself, after…" He paused, his jaw tightening. "After I lost my wife it was cook or starve. I'm a pretty good hand with the basics. No fancy stuff, mind you."

"What happened to your wife, Ethan?"

His expression froze. A wall slid into place behind his eyes. "I thought we agreed. No personal questions."

"I know what we said. It's just that by now you know a lot more about me, and so I thought—"

"It's my business to know about you, Ruby. It's part of my job. Now, let's get back to cooking breakfast, all right?"

"Fine." She squelched the urge to fling up her head and stalk out of the kitchen. His brusqueness had stung her like a slap, but letting him know that he'd hurt her would serve her nothing.

What was she to make of the man? Two nights ago he had made exquisitely tender love to her. Last night he'd seized her on the street and delivered a rough, passionate kiss. This morning he was treating her like a stranger, little more than a person of interest in his case.

Blast his case! For two cents she would grab an ax, storm down to the cellar and beat that stash of moonshine into a heap of dripping shards. Then she'd march U.S. Deputy Marshal Ethan Beaudry to the railway station and kick his all-too-attractive butt onto the next outbound train. Case closed.

"I believe it's time for the eggs." He spoke as if nothing had passed between them. "Want to try this? I can crack the shells, and you should be able to do the rest with one hand."

Ruby almost said yes. It would satisfy her soul to show him she could do something right. But what if she failed again? How could she face that superior male smirk on his handsome face?

She shook her head. "I'll watch you for now and practice later, on my own," she said. "I've had enough humiliation for one morning, thank you."

After breakfast, Ruby set out on her errands. To spare her injured finger, Ethan had insisted on cleaning up. Ruby had gladly let him. Maybe she wasn't cut out for domesticity. Or maybe she was just plain spoiled. But either way, her old, pampered life was behind her. There was nowhere to go but forward.

The eggs had turned out magnificently. Ethan had shown her three different ways to fry them in the bacon grease—sunny-side up, with the gleaming yolk on top; easy over, which involved some deft work with the spatula; and the way she'd always liked them, with hot grease spooned over the top to cook the white to a soft pearl finish. And he'd made it look so easy. What a pity she couldn't hire him as a permanent chef. The women in town would be falling over each other to rent rooms.

Ruby sighed as she studied the list Ethan had drawn up. Flour, sugar, salt, baking powder, spices, yeast, bacon, eggs, coffee, oatmeal, maple syrup, butter, potatoes… Where did it end? By the time she paid for all this, she'd be scraping the bottom of her financial barrel. If she didn't get some boarders soon, she'd be penniless.

The store was a maze of ordered clutter, with goods stacked on open shelves and on the floor. A brindled cat slipped among barrels of dried corn, pickles, pinto beans and sacks of oatmeal. Orange and yellow wheels of cheese rested in a case next to the counter. Glass canisters held peppermint sticks, lollipops and horehound drops. Ruby imagined the simple pleasure of bringing her daughters here to pick out a sweet. She ached for the sound of their girlish voices, their laughter, the contrasting hues of their hair as they leaned together to share a secret. She swallowed the lump in her throat.

"Can I help you, ma'am?" The store owner was a small man, spare and quick, with wire-framed spectacles perched on his nose. Ruby thrust the list toward him. "I need everything here. I'll also need to arrange delivery to the big house at the end of the street."

He studied her through thick lenses. "You'd be Mrs. Ruby Rumford, right?"

"Yes." Ruby's heart dropped. Had word of her scandalous past gotten out already? "Is there some problem?" she asked.

"Not at all." He smiled, showing a badly chipped tooth. "The mayor told me you'd be coming in. He wanted me to make sure you were set up for a credit account. If you'll come over to the counter, we can do the paperwork while Max, here, fills your order." He gave the list to a towheaded youth who disappeared to rummage among the shelves.

Mention of the mayor had put Ruby on her guard. "I'd planned on paying cash," she said.

"You're running a business, Mrs. Rumford. You're certainly welcome to pay cash. But with an account, you can get what you need when you need it and pay when the money comes in."

Ruby took a moment to weigh her options. Buying on credit would make everything easier, especially now, while she had a world of needs and no income. All she had to do was sign a paper. So easy. So tempting…

But would the store owner be offering her credit if Thaddeus Wilton hadn't asked him to?

"Isn't that risky for you?" she asked cautiously. "What if I were to run up my account and not be able to pay you?"

"No reason to worry." He leaned toward her, his voice dropping to a confidential whisper. "Mayor Wilton assured me that if you run into trouble, I can just send the bill to him, and he'll take care of it. Quite generous of him, I'd say. Now, if you'll just step over here—"

The decision fell into place like a block of concrete.

"No." Ruby lifted her chin, standing proud. "I won't be in anyone's debt, especially the mayor's. I'll be dealing in cash, thank you kindly. And if this order comes to more than I can pay, I'll just put a few items back on the shelves."

Once spoken, the words swept over her with a wash of relief. Having little money and no credit was a fearful prospect. But accepting favors from Thaddeus Wilton was tantamount to bargaining with the devil.

"But surely you'll want to open an account. That doesn't mean you have to use it."

"If I open it, I might be tempted." Ruby's gaze flickered toward the boy, who was piling her purchases onto a flat wooden cart. "But there is one more thing you can do for me. By any chance, do you have a cookbook for sale?"

Since Ruby would be dining at the mayor's, Ethan had improvised his own supper by adding bacon and fried onions to last night's flavorless beans. The result wasn't half-bad. But hungry as he should have been, he'd managed to lose his appetite.

The blinds were closed, the kitchen dimly lit from the hallway. Ethan had made sure no one could see him from outside the house. Sitting alone now, at the kitchen table, he could hear the sounds of Ruby getting ready to go out—drawers opening and closing, the water running in the downstairs bathroom and the click of her dainty high-heeled slippers on the hardwood floor. He even caught a whiff of that man-luring French perfume she wore, probably as she scented herself with the little atomizer he'd seen on her dresser. He could just imagine who'd be smelling it.

Ruby was going to the dinner party because he'd asked her to, Ethan reminded himself. She would be keeping her eyes and ears open for anything that might tie Thaddeus Wilton to the bootlegging racket. But did that mean she had to spend so much time getting prettied up? Hellfire, the woman would look fetching enough smeared in mud and dressed in a potato sack!

Ethan broke off a chunk of bread, dipped it into the beans and forced himself to chew it. Truth be told, he didn't mind Ruby taking the trouble to look her best. What galled him was, she wasn't doing it for him. Wilton would be showing her off like some pretty new trinket he'd bought and paid for. Ruby professed to despise the man, but like most beautiful women, she certainly wouldn't object to his admiration. Didn't she know that *he* admired her, and for much more than her striking physical charms?

He remembered how she'd come home earlier in the day clutching her brand-new Fannie Farmer cookbook. While he'd busied himself replacing the cracked panes in the downstairs windows, Ruby had sat at the table poring over the recipes, exclaiming over the sauces, tarts and soufflés, rhapsodizing over the meals she was going to cook for her tenants.

Lord, what an adorable woman!

It had been all he could do to keep from flinging down his tools and striding across the floor to sweep her into his arms.

There was no denying it—she was getting to him in a way no woman had in the four years he'd been alone. He'd found himself wondering what it would be like to kiss her awake each morning and to share their stories at the end of each day—to build a real home somewhere, a place that would call him back from wherever his work took him.

The fact that Ruby had shot her husband bothered him less than one might expect. The woman had been brutalized. She'd acted in self-defense. Now that the past was behind her she deserved to forget what had happened. She deserved a gentler life with a man who cherished and loved her.

Loved her? Was that what he was feeling?

Ethan had told himself that after losing Sarah he could never love again. But maybe his heart was healing. Maybe it was time to take a chance.

Not that he was in a hurry. He and Ruby needed a lot more time to become acquainted. Meanwhile…

The sound of her approaching footsteps broke into his thoughts. She emerged from the hallway, a fragrant vision in peach-colored silk that skimmed her corseted curves like flowing water. Her flame-gold hair was pinned up in soft waves, accented with a cluster pin of baroque pearls. More pearls gleamed at her throat and earlobes. A shawl of cream lace trailed from one hand. Ethan swore under his breath.

"Ready to go?" he asked.

"Almost." She gave him a wan smile. "I can't say I'm looking forward to this."

Then don't go.

He almost spoke the words aloud. If anything happened to Ruby he would never forgive himself. But the real danger should be right here. Ethan's instincts told him that Wilton had contrived to get Ruby out of the house so his thugs could haul away the whiskey. If his hunch was correct, and if she stayed home tonight, anything could happen. Or, more likely, nothing would happen. The standoff would continue, perhaps until the only option left was to destroy the stash. Sending her off tonight was the only plan that made sense.

"Be careful," he said. "Don't take any foolish chances."

"I'm a big girl. I know how to be discreet."

"I've got that little .22 pistol upstairs. Let me get it for you."

"Don't be silly, Ethan. Where would I hide it? It would bulge under my dress, and my evening bag is tiny. After all, I'm only going to a party. Stop worrying. I'll be fine. But you can do me one favor."

"What's that?"

She turned her back to him, revealing a row of open button loops and flashes of the creamy skin beneath. "I hope you don't mind giving me a hand. The last time I wore this dress, I had a maid to help me do it up."

"Happy to be your maid anytime." Wiping his hands clean, Ethan rose and stepped behind her. Her scent crept around him, stirring his senses as he pulled the first silk-covered button through the opposite loop.

"Does this mean I'll need to unbutton you when you get home?" he asked huskily.

"Naughty man. We'll see when the time comes." There was a note of seduction in her throaty voice. Ethan's knuckle brushed her skin. The contact sent a feather tickle of warmth up his hand, along his arm and down into his body. The heat rising in his groin was all too familiar.

"Almost done." His fingers fumbled with the tiny buttons. Moisture gleamed on her gardenia-petal skin. It was all he could do to keep from leaning forward to kiss the back of her neck. He imagined circling her waist, drawing her against him, his hands sliding up to cup her breasts through the light silk. If he held her in his arms now, Ethan knew he would never be able to let her go tonight.

"Finished," he said, stepping back. "You look beautiful, by the way."

"Thank you." Her voice had dropped to a breath.

"Stay as long as you can," he said. "But not so long that everyone else has left. Don't let yourself be alone with him. You can always ask one of the other guests to drive you home."

"I told you, I'm a big girl. I can take care of myself."

"I mean it, Ruby. Don't get into a situation where you'll have to fight your way out. His Honor the mayor won't fight fair. You're liable to lose."

She turned toward him, her gaze soft in the shadows of the room. "You be careful, too, Ethan. I want you here safe and sound when I come back."

He forced himself to grin. "Of course I'll be here. Who else is going to get you out of that dress?"

The tinny chug of a Model T broke the evening stillness, approaching down the street and stopping to idle outside the gate. Ethan slipped behind the kitchen door. The driver would likely be one of the mayor's hired goons, sent to pick Ruby up and drive her to the dinner party. Ethan wanted a look at him, in case the man showed up later on a different errand.

Ruby had switched off the lights in the bedroom and hallway and was hurrying toward the front door. "Turn on the parlor light," Ethan whispered. "Leave it on until you step outside."

Ruby didn't answer, but she did turn on the parlor light. Instead of going out on her own, she waited for the knock, which came a few seconds later. Without looking toward Ethan, she opened the door wide.

Flooded by a rectangle of light, Harper Wilton stood on the front porch. His tie was loosened, his brown fedora slightly askew. One hand was braced against the door frame, as if for support. Ethan stifled a groan. Not only was Ruby's driver someone he already knew, but the man appeared to be drunk. And Ruby was about to leave with him.

"Ma'am." Harper touched the brim of his hat. "I've come to fetch you."

"I'm ready." Ruby tossed the cream lace shawl around her shoulders. Ethan was tempted to step into sight and stop her right then, blowing the whole investigation, but she glanced back with a barely perceptible shake of her head. Whatever the risk, she was determined to go through with this madness.

Maybe he'd oversold his argument about doing the right thing. Ruby had bought it all.

As she stepped through the front door, her hand reached for the light switch. Plunged into darkness, Ethan heard the closing and locking of the door; then, seconds later, the chug of the Model T pulling away up the street. She'd be all right, he told himself. The mayor's house couldn't be more than a few minutes from here. And Harper had to know he'd catch hell if Ruby didn't arrive safely. Still, Ethan didn't like this. Not one damn bit.

Why in heaven's name hadn't he forced her to take that pistol?

Churning inside, he paced to the front window and peered past the blind at the empty street. Ruby, his beautiful, brave, impossibly stubborn Ruby, had walked into danger tonight. And the thought of all the things that could go wrong made him sick with worry. He wanted to burst out of the house, run down the car, drag her out and carry her back to his bed where she'd have nothing to fear but his passion.

Damn!

But he couldn't afford to spend time brooding. Not when all hell could be priming to break loose outside. Now that night had closed in and Ruby was gone, it was time to prepare for his vigil in the yard. He could only hope that this time the tedious wait would pay off.

Steeling his resolve, he turned away from the window, strode across the parlor and started up the dark stairs to get his gun and badge.

"How far is it to your father's house, Harper?" Ruby had shrunk against the passenger-side door. She'd always disliked the smell of liquor, and her driver reeked of it.

"Not too far. Lives out on the cemetery road. Got hisself a real highfalutin place, Pop does. 'Fore long, I'll get me one that'll make his look like a brick shithouse, with a Cadillac in the drive and a pretty woman in the bed. An' I won't have to be his errand boy no more."

Harper swerved back to the right side of the road, and Ruby thanked her lucky stars for the scarcity of traffic. When she'd met Harper before, he'd barely spoken two words to her. Evidently the liquor had loosened his tongue. Maybe she could use that to her advantage.

"Where did you get the whiskey?" she asked. "Is it hard to come by in these parts?"

He flashed a toothy grin. "Wouldn't you like to know? Truth be told, if you've got the cash, you can get anything you want. All you got to do is ask. Interested?"

"Maybe." Ruby smoothed the knotted fringe on her shawl, her heart pounding. "Unfortunately, I don't have any money with me tonight. Perhaps we could arrange something later."

He snorted, swerving the car to miss a weedy ditch bank. Ruby braced her feet to keep from being flung hard against his side. "Pretty lady like you don't need money. Mostly I like my gals young, but you're a looker. I reckon you'd do for a couple of pints."

Ruby didn't know whether to laugh or slap Harper's insolent, horsey face. She willed herself to do neither.

"You're saying you've got some whiskey with you now?"

"That's right. I keep a case back there in the rumble seat, under that blanket. Never know when somebody might want to do a little business." He gave her a lustful smirk. "I know a road that goes behind the cemetery. We can drive out there, do our trade and have you back in time for Pop's fancy dinner." His eyes narrowed. "Don't worry, I'm a gentleman. Put your legs up nice, and I won't even muss that pretty dress of yours."

Fear seeped into Ruby like an icicle dripping down her back. Harper Wilton was bigger and stronger than she was. Even if she rebuffed him, he could drive her to an isolated spot, disable her somehow, and…

But she couldn't think of that now or she'd be paralyzed with fear.

Down the road, perhaps a quarter mile off, Ruby

could see a tall, brightly lit house. Beyond it lay the darkness of the cemetery and the open country beyond. Maybe it would be all right, she thought. Maybe Harper would simply stop and let her go inside to his father's dinner party.

But what would she do if he didn't?

Chapter Ten

The Model T didn't slow down as it neared the house. Ruby was running out of time to extricate herself. Her fingers clutched the beaded evening bag that held little more than her keys. If only she'd had the sense to accept Ethan's pistol.

"Isn't that your father's home?" she asked.

"Yup. All lit up for the grand shindig."

"Would you mind escorting me inside? I get nervous walking into strange places alone."

"Sure, after we've finished our business."

"That business can wait until I have money," Ruby said.

"Well maybe *I* can't wait." Harper sped past the turn-off, swerved left, then corrected with a drunken right swing. Ruby's stomach lurched.

"Take me back to the house. Now. I mean it, Harper."

Harper snickered. "I mean it, too. Might not be around to drive you home, and I've got a hankerin' now. C'mon, it'll be good quick fun, you bein' a widow lady and all."

Ruby's heart slammed. She glanced at the door handle, wondering if she could survive flinging herself out onto the roadside. The Model T was going at least thirty miles an hour. Even if she wasn't badly hurt, she'd be dazed. Harper could easily catch her again. When he did, he'd likely rape her. He might even kill her if he was drunk enough to ignore the consequences. Her best chance of survival lay in getting him to talk.

She willed herself to speak calmly. "Does your father know about this little whiskey-selling business of yours, Harper?"

"Pop's got his own line of business. I do all the work, and he doles out my allowance like I was a kid. Makes me drive this piece of crap while he parades around in his new Packard. But this little enterprise is local, and it's all mine."

Ruby studied his jut-nosed profile as the car careened along the rutted road. It was clear that Harper feared and resented his father. But could that fear be used to talk him into letting her go? Briefly she weighed the risk. If her ploy didn't work, she'd have to be prepared to fight for her life.

"In that case," she said, "I've got a proposition for you. Pull over so we can talk, and I'll tell you what it is."

He hesitated, his foot easing off on the gas. Ruby's fingers crept to the door latch. She didn't want to jump, but she'd do it if she couldn't change his mind. Pressing the brake he eased the car to a stop at the side of the road. "This better be good," he said.

"It's the best offer you'll have all night." Ruby met his thick-lidded gaze. "Take me back to the party right now, and I won't tell Thaddeus what you're up to. In fact, I won't even tell him what you had in mind to do with his lady friend. How's that for a deal?"

His breath hissed out, filling the car with the reek of booze. "So you're Pop's woman now? Funny, he didn't tell me."

"Your father doesn't tell you everything," Ruby said, hating what the lie implied. "So, do we have a bargain?"

He glared at her. "You promise?"

"I promise." Ruby crossed her heart with her index finger. "Not a word. Now, turn this car around and take me back to the party."

Harper hesitated; then with a muttered curse, he swung the Model T in a gravel-spitting U-turn and roared back up the road. As they neared the house, Ruby saw the line of automobiles parked along the drive. Her thundering pulse eased a bit. She'd been half-fearful of walking into the house and finding herself alone with Thaddeus Wilton. But it appeared she'd come to a real dinner party with actual guests.

Harper parked at the foot of the steps and came around the car to escort her inside. The house was a graceless structure of red brick with a facade of white-washed Romanesque pillars—a residential version of the hideous town hall. Thaddeus Wilton had likely worked out a deal to profit both himself and the builder.

As if the thought could conjure him up, Wilton opened the door and came out onto the porch. The entry light gleamed like brilliantine on his pomaded wig. "There you are, my dear," he scolded. "I was beginning to think my boy had decided to keep you for himself. Come on inside. Everyone is so anxious to meet you."

Harper turned away and slunk back down the steps. Evidently he wouldn't be joining the party. Did that mean he had other business—business back at the boardinghouse—that would put Ethan in danger?

Wilton's hand came to rest on the small of her back. Surreptitious fingers slid downward to brush the curve of her hip. Ruby stiffened as if she'd been shot. Long strides carried her out of his reach. If only she could turn around and leave right now. But if being here could help rid her home of danger she would stay and endure.

As the front door closed behind them, dread congealed in the pit of Ruby's stomach. To paraphrase an old saying, she'd managed to escape the frying pan. But something told her she'd just tumbled into the fire.

The moon had waned past fullness. It hung above the peaks like a ripening plum, imperfect in shape but mystical in its beauty. Wispy clouds, blown by a high wind, raced across the sky. Crickets sang in the grassy undergrowth.

Ethan prowled the fringes of the yard, keeping to the shadows. Except for a few late-nighters hurrying homeward, the streets were empty. Before long the town would be asleep. Then, if things went as expected, the thugs would crawl out of their holes and close in on their booty like coyotes on a sheep carcass.

As before, he planned to watch from behind the shed, listening for clues and looking for faces that might prove familiar. This time he'd tethered a horse in a nearby vacant lot. If they took the whiskey, he'd follow at a safe distance in the hope of learning where the rendezvous point was and who was making the deal. When he had the information he needed, he could call in reinforcements from Denver to help make the arrests. Right now the last thing he wanted was to scare the bastards into hiding or force a gun battle that could harm innocent people. He was a professional, and he knew his job. Solo heroics only worked in the picture shows.

To raise the odds in his favor, he'd used his version of an old Indian trick—red artist's chalk ground to a fine powder. Sprinkled lightly on the ground outside, and on the dark earthen floor of the cellar, it would cling to the shoes of anyone who walked over it. If the heist took place, he could always follow up tomorrow by perusing the town and keeping an eye open for red-flecked shoes.

He was about as ready as he could possibly be. All that remained was to quiet his grinding nerves and wait—something he did far too much of in his line of work.

Pausing in the shadow of the honeysuckle vine, he gazed down the empty street. Wind soughed through the gaunt Lombardy poplars that grew in the neighboring lot. The night breathed a hush of dark expectation.

Ethan's instincts told him something was going down tonight. Something bad. And somewhere out there, beyond the reach of his protection, was Ruby.

Lord, he should never have let her go. If she came home safely, Ethan vowed, he would never risk her again. He would keep her close, cherish her, love her.

Love? Was he capable of such a demanding emotion again? Did he have anything left inside himself to give a woman?

Something moved beyond the front porch. Ethan froze at the snap of a twig. His hand moved reflexively to the pistol. His senses strained. But as the seconds passed he heard nothing, saw nothing. Maybe it had been an animal, or maybe he was just jumpy. He waited, motionless, for a full two minutes before he moved, easing back along the side of the house. It was time he got out of sight. Sitting still would be uncomfortable, but he couldn't let himself be caught in the open. At least he'd remembered to cut back the brambles that had plagued him last time.

The wind had picked up, darkening the sky and fluttering the poplar leaves like castanets. With his kind of luck, it would probably rain, Ethan groused. But never mind that, he was here for the duration. Slipping into the space between the fence and the shed, he arranged his long legs and settled in to wait.

"I hear you've bought that old Enlow place, Mrs. Rumford," the balding pharmacist commented. "Rumor has it you'll be turning it into a boardinghouse."

And what else are the rumors saying? Ruby was

tempted to ask. The mayor's guests were polite enough, but she felt as if she'd been under a magnifying glass all evening.

"That's right," she answered brightly. "There's a lot of work to be done, but I hope to have it open for business within the week."

"And who do you propose to rent to?" The pharmacist's wife was a little prune of a woman, dressed in a flowery summer frock with a lace collar. "This is a family town. We don't get much—" She broke off as if catching herself, but Ruby could tell from the shape of her mouth that she'd been about to say *riffraff.* "We don't get the sort of people who wouldn't settle in a regular home," she finished awkwardly.

Ruby took a sip of home-brewed muscatel, which was illegal in the strictest sense but ignored by the law as long as no one tried to sell it. She shaped her mouth into a smile. "My brother says the town is growing. There'll be workers building homes, more teachers at the school, more clerks in the shops. Surely some of them will need an affordable place to stay."

"Yes," the woman sniffed. "I've noticed the man working on your property. Is he one of your tenants?"

Ruby's heart thudded as the mayor shot her a questioning glance. Until now he might not have known about Ethan.

"He plans to be a tenant once the place is open." She was talking too fast, the words spilling out like a child's schoolroom recitation. She forced herself to take a deep breath and slow down. "For now, he's staying at the hotel while he does a little work in exchange for his first week's room and board."

"And does he have any other job," the pharmacist asked, "or is he just a drifter?"

"He's a perfectly respectable man, a history professor on leave to do some local research." The lie rolled off Ruby's tongue, leaving the flat taste of fear behind. What if no one believed her? What if the mayor became suspicious of Ethan?

"In any case," she added hastily, "I don't expect my business to have much impact on the town. I only plan on renting out four rooms."

"And if I have anything to say about it, the lady won't be in a position to rent out anything much longer." Thaddeus Wilton winked at his guests from the head of the table. Ruby choked on her muscatel. Her stomach clenched into a knot. Heaven save her, was the man saying that he planned to propose? Maybe she should just tell him she'd rather marry a Gila monster, and get it over with.

She slumped a little deeper into her high-backed dining chair. The roast beef and gravy on her plate, most likely delivered from the hotel kitchen, had cooled to a grease-glazed mass. Ruby had lost what little appetite she'd arrived with, but she focused on her plate, pretending to eat. Maybe if she looked disinterested enough, the conversation would shift away from her.

For the moment, the strategy seemed to work. As the talk flowed around her, she felt herself relaxing enough to study her surroundings.

The mayor's house appeared to have been decorated

by his late wife. No man would have chosen the cabbage-rose-patterned wallpaper or the mail-order Louis XIV-style furniture upholstered in pink-and-gold stripes. And no man would have put lace doilies over the back and arms of every chair and under every movable object. But then, who was she to judge? Ruby reminded herself. The poor woman couldn't have had an easy time, with a husband like Thaddeus Wilton and a son like Harper. If the fussy decor had given her pleasure, she'd surely earned the right to enjoy it.

In addition to the mayor and herself, there were four couples at the dinner table. The pharmacist and his wife sat on her left, the owners of the local dry-goods emporium toward the other end, with a city councilman and his wife across from them. The women, plain and polite-spoken for the most part, cast furtive glances at Ruby's finery, confirming her fear that she'd overdressed. The peach silk gown was better suited for the soirees she'd attended in Springfield than for small-town society. When she got home she would consign it to the back of the closet.

It was the fourth couple, sitting directly across from her, who drew Ruby's attention. Brandon and Harriet Calhoun—he in his seventies, she a few years younger—made a stunning pair. President and founder of the Dutchman's Creek Bank, Brandon Calhoun was tall and fit, with twinkling blue eyes and a vigorous thatch of silver hair. His dark-eyed wife had clearly been a beauty in her youth. Now, dressed in a modest gown of sky-blue crepe with silver-mounted opals at her ears, she radiated grace and elegance. But what struck Ruby about the Calhouns was the way they kept glancing at each other, their hands touching in unguarded moments. They were in love, Ruby realized with a stab of envy. She could see it in their eyes. What she wouldn't give to have a man look at her the way the elderly banker looked at his wife.

But not just any man. It would have to be a rangy man with unruly black hair and gold-flecked brown eyes, a man whose hands and voice made her heart race. One man. Ethan Beaudry.

Ruby bit back a moan of dismay. Had she really done it? Had she fallen in love with him? What a muddle-headed, romantic fool she was! Loving Ethan would be like loving a wild horse that would wheel and bolt at a touch. He was as footloose as a tumbleweed, as evasive as a fleeting shadow. To make matters worse, he was a lawman, married to his job. What had she done to herself?

"Mrs. Rumford?" Brandon Calhoun's rich baritone startled her out of her musings. Chagrined, Ruby realized she'd been staring at the couple.

"I'm sorry," she apologized, flustered. "It's just that you're such a lovely pair. It's a pleasure to look at you."

Harriet Calhoun's laugh was musical. "What a nice thing to say! At our age, we don't get many compliments."

"Actually, I've been wanting to meet you since you arrived in town," Brandon said. "Dutchman's Creek can always use fresh business. If there's any way we can help you at the bank, please stop by and ask for me. I'll be glad to set you up with whatever you need."

"Thank you. I suppose I should at least open a checking account." Ruby felt a prickle of apprehension. After her experience at the grocer's, she couldn't help wondering if Thaddeus Wilton was manipulating the banker, as well. But on second thought, that didn't seem likely. A man like Brandon Calhoun would no more take orders from Wilton than a lion would take orders from a jackal.

Harriet squeezed his arm. "I've tried to talk this old fogy into retiring from the bank, but he says the work keeps him from slowing down. He'll be there for you any weekday."

The clang of metal on glass broke into the buzz of conversation. The mayor had risen to his feet, striking his fork several times against the side of his wine goblet. "I'd like to propose a toast," he declared in a theatrical voice that suggested he'd studied elocution at some point. Harper's speech, nothing like his father's, was probably a closer reflection of their true background.

"Here's to our friendship," the mayor intoned, "and to the bright future of our town." He paused. A few glasses went up, then lowered tentatively as he continued. "And here's to our lovely Ruby, who's come to walk among us like a goddess tending her garden. It's my sincere wish that you take her into your hearts, as I've already taken her into mine." His gaze rested on Ruby. She forced herself to look back at him. What she glimpsed in the depths of his citron-hued eyes was dark and cold and evil. Thaddeus Wilton meant to control her, to possess her absolutely. And he would use any means at his disposal to do so.

"Hear! Hear!" The pharmacist raised his glass. His wife and the other couples did the same, except for the Calhouns, who'd clearly noticed Ruby's distress.

As the glasses clinked above the table, Ruby felt her stomach clench. Her mouth tasted bile, a sign that she was about to be sick. Muttering an excuse, she pushed away from the table and stumbled to her feet. "This way, down the hall," a voice whispered in her ear. Only as a guiding hand slipped beneath her arm did she realize it was Harriet Calhoun.

In the small guest bathroom she bent over the bowl, taking deep breaths to battle the nausea. The last thing she wanted was to disgrace herself in front of this elegant woman.

Harriet had wrung a cool washcloth in the basin and laid it on the back of Ruby's neck. As the seconds passed, Ruby began to feel better. "Thank you," she murmured, straightening. "I should be all right now."

"Do you have a way home? We'd be glad to drive you." Harriet laid the cloth on the edge of the basin. Her dark eyes reflected genuine concern.

"Harper drove me here. He's not around, so I'm assuming the mayor is planning to drive me back. But I don't want to be alone with him. He's—" Ruby shook her head. "I'm sorry, I know he's your friend."

"Thaddeus, our friend?" Harriet chuckled wryly. "Hardly. Truth be told, Brandon and I can't abide the man. He'd sell his own mother for a profit, and no woman is safe within an arm's length of him. We only accepted this invitation tonight because he told us you were going to be here."

Ruby stared at her in surprise.

"You come with good connections," Harriet said. "We've done business with your brother, Jace. He's a fine man. And of course we've known Clara's family all their lives. We'd like to be your friends, Ruby, and to invite you to our home as soon as you're settled in."

Ruby blinked back a rush of tears. First Mabel, now Harriet had offered her friendship. But Mabel already knew about her past, and as much as Ruby wanted Harriet's friendship, she couldn't build it on a lie.

She braced herself for the rebuff that was sure to come. "There's something you need to know about me first," she said. "Back in Missouri, where I came from, I shot my husband. I was tried and acquitted on grounds of self-defense, so I'm clear with the law. But nothing can change the fact that I killed the father of my children. People will be shocked when the story comes out, so if you want to take back your offer, I'll understand."

Harriet's expression softened. She laid a hand on Ruby's arm. "We already know about it, dear. Brandon subscribes to a number of papers, including the *St. Louis Post-Dispatch*. We followed the story of your trial. How terrible that must have been for you."

A tear left its salty trail down Ruby's cheek. There were good people in this town, and she was slowly finding them—or they were finding her.

"You're not the only ones who know what happened," she said. "Thaddeus found out. He's been holding it over me, threatening to tell the whole town if I don't do what he wants."

Harriet's delicate brows shot up. "Oh, he has, has he? Why doesn't that surprise me?" She studied Ruby's face. "Your color's improving. Do you want to leave now? I can drive you home myself and come back for Brandon."

Did she want to leave? Right now there was nothing she wanted more. The thought of Thaddeus Wilton's leering face and groping hands was enough to make her feel nauseous all over again. But Ethan was counting on her to stay. How could she turn tail and go home, knowing she'd let him down?

She gave Harriet a wan smile. "I'd be ashamed of myself if I took the easy way out," she said. "I'm feeling well enough. Let's go back to the party."

Harriet grinned. "That's my girl. I'll be right behind you. And don't let Thaddeus manipulate you. The man's a coward and a bully. He can only take as much control as you'll give him."

Wise words. Ruby willed herself to take them to heart. What if Thaddeus made good on his threat? She could just imagine the shocked look on the face of the pharmacist's wife and other likeminded people. But two strong women who knew her story had already offered their friendship. She had to believe that more people would do the same.

Ruby had hoped to keep back the scandal until her girls arrived and had the chance to make friends. But waiting might do more harm than good, especially if it was viewed as living a lie.

What would be best for Mandy and Caro? That was the only question that mattered. Unfortunately, there was no simple answer. She had a fearful decision to make—a decision that would shape her daughters' future and her own.

Ethan crouched in the darkness, resisting the urge to step out and stretch his cramped muscles. The night was eerily quiet. Moonlight glinted through scudding clouds, casting a moiré of light and shadow on the ground. Tension lay so thick in the air that he could almost taste it. Nothing moved in the yard or in the empty street beyond. But Ethan's instincts were screaming. Something was about to happen.

He heard the wagon before he saw it—the creak of a wheel, the nicker of a horse. Then there it was, turning stealthily out of a side street to head toward the house. Flashes of moonlight revealed a two-horse team, a driver and four other men on the flatbed hay wagon.

He slid the .38 from its holster, hoping to hell he wouldn't have to use it, tipping the men off to the lawman on their tail. The man in charge of this racket wouldn't be with the wagon tonight. If Ethan's suspicions were right, he'd be at home, entertaining a roomful of respected guests who'd give him the perfect alibi.

And Ruby would be with him.

He'd been thinking about her all night. But right now he needed to put his worries aside and do his job. Thumbing back the hammer on the pistol, he waited.

The hay wagon was too big to turn around in the backyard. But the driver knew how to handle a team of horses. With some help from his cohorts, he backed the wagon into the space alongside the house. From there, it would be easy to load from the rear and drive away.

Leaving the driver with the horses, the other men approached the cellar door. They'd taken the precaution of masking their faces with bandannas. But it didn't take a genius to recognize the lanky frame of Harper Wilton.

Taking charge, Harper strode to the cellar entrance, worked the hasp free and flung the door open. "Get to work, boys. The sooner we can load up and clear out, the better. When we're done, you'll have time to get the wagon away 'fore I finish the job." He laughed. "There'll be a hot time in the old town tonight!"

At first the words didn't penetrate. Then a lantern flared, casting Harper into full silhouette. Ethan went cold as the man's intention sunk in.

Harper was holding a metal gasoline can with a spout. Once the whiskey was loaded and the wagon removed, the bastard planned to torch the place.

Chapter Eleven

The dinner plates had been cleared away, the wine-glasses refilled, and the dessert—soggy mince pie drenched in raisin sauce—laid out before the guests. Ruby's gaze met Harriet's across the table, seeking and finding a flicker of support. It was time.

Clasping her goblet by its stem, Ruby rose to her feet. Her silk-clad knees shook beneath her. But she'd done harder things, she reminded herself. She could, and would, get through this.

And when it was finished, she'd be free to spit in Thaddeus Wilton's eye.

There was no need to tap her glass with the cutlery as Thaddeus had. All talk ceased at the sight of Ruby on her feet.

She cleared her throat. "I'd like to propose a toast," she began, "to those of you at this table and to everyone else who's made me feel so welcome in this town."

Her tongue moistened her dry lips. So far, so good. But there was more to come. "I'm especially grateful for your acceptance because of where I've come from—a place where I was tried and acquitted for shooting my husband in defense of my life."

The pharmacist's wife gave an audible gasp. The other guests stared at her in stunned silence, except for the Calhouns, who smiled and nodded their approval. The mayor glowered at her over his muscatel.

"I know the people in this town to be fair-minded," she continued. "Fair enough to acknowledge that in the eyes of the law I committed no crime. If I hadn't defended myself I wouldn't be standing here tonight, and I'd wager that most, if not all, of you would have done the same.

"But enough about my past. Tonight is about the future. Dutchman's Creek is growing, and I, with my humble little business, will be honored to grow with it. I look forward to working with all of you to this end." Ruby raised her glass. "To our friendship and to the prosperity of our town!"

There was a beat of silence. Ruby could feel the sweat beading under her clothes. "Hear! Hear!" Brandon Calhoun's glass came up, swiftly followed by Harriet's. The other guests sat thunderstruck. Tentatively at first, the councilman's wife lifted her glass, then the pharmacist, then, one by one, the others. Last to join the toast was Thaddeus Wilton. Ruby had defied his control and made an enemy—one who would not likely forget or forgive.

She glanced at him. Wilton's mouth wore a pasted

smile, but when their eyes met, the glint of malice was like a cold blade tracing a line along her throat.

While Harper's stooges hauled jugs and demijohns out of the cellar, Ethan purpled the air with half-mouthed curses. He should have known things wouldn't go as expected. He should have been ready with a plan. Now he had no choice except to play the cards he'd been dealt.

Harper stood next to the cellar door, hip cocked in a casual pose as he supervised the hirelings. From his point of view, and his father's, setting fire to the board-inghouse would make perfect sense. The blaze would burn up telltale evidence and create a distraction while the wagon got away. A source of competition with the hotel would be gone, and a devastated Ruby would be left vulnerable to Thaddeus Wilton's manipulation.

The plan made so much sense that Ethan should have figured it out ahead of time. Slipups like that tended to happen when a man had a beautiful woman on his mind. But this was no time to kick himself. He had more urgent things to deal with.

There was no way he'd allow Harper to set fire to Ruby's house. The issue was how and when to stop him. Ethan's plan to follow the loaded wagon to the rendez-vous had just gone up in smoke. That left him several options, none of them good. He could wait till the wagon was loaded or he could act now. He could fire a warning shot to scare the entire gang off or try to arrest Harper on the spot, in the hope of getting him to make a deal and implicate his father. The last solution made the most sense, but it wouldn't be easy.

The three workers, who'd stripped down to shirt-sleeves, appeared unarmed and would likely scatter at the first sign of trouble. The driver was more of a guess, but he'd probably just want to get away, with or without the wagon. That left Harper.

The bulge under the man's jacket told Ethan he was packing a gun. Given Harper's record, he probably wouldn't hesitate to use it. And the last thing Ethan wanted was to return fire and kill the man who could close his case.

The best chance of taking him alive would be to get the jump on him before he could draw his weapon. For Ethan, that meant waiting until Harper was distracted or until he moved closer to the shed.

Adjusting his crouch, Ethan eased forward to the edge of the shadows. He felt raw with strain and fatigue. His eyes burned. His nerves were strung taut, his patience worn as thin as frayed silk, but he willed himself to keep still and stay alert.

The lantern had been carried downstairs into the cellar. Through the open door, its flickering light reflected upward, dancing like fire on the back of the house.

Ethan's imagination saw a different house, flames roaring skyward, windowpanes exploding in showers of glass. Acrid black smoke scalded his nostrils. Heat blistered his hands as he smashed against the door, clutching at the searing doorknob in a frantic effort to get inside. In the next moment unseen arms were hauling him back, dragging him across the yard. Cold water shocked his senses as they doused his smoldering clothes with buckets from the watering trough. He listened for screams from the house, but the only cries he heard were his own....

An abrupt silence yanked him back to the present. Something was happening.

The men emptying the cellar had frozen where they stood. Harper drew his pistol as a tall, stoop-shouldered figure stepped into the lamplight, Colt .45 in hand. Ethan stifled a groan.

"Hold it right there, boys." The voice was all too familiar. "Shame on the lot of you. You ought to know better than to break the law in my town."

Ethan swore as his muscles tensed for action. He had to do something fast, or Sam Farley was liable to get himself killed.

Sam's pistol was drawn. But so was Harper's. If it came to a shoot-out, the old man would be lucky to survive. Rising to his feet, Ethan stepped into sight.

"U.S. marshal," he barked. "Throw down your weapon and put your hands up."

That was when all hell broke loose.

The wagon driver whacked the leathers down hard on the rumps of the big draft horses. Startled from a drowse, the massive beasts reared and bolted. Whiskey jugs crashed to the ground as the half-loaded wagon careened toward the street.

Seizing on the distraction, Harper slammed the elderly marshal to the ground and sprinted after the departing wagon. A rear wheel crunched into an irrigation ditch, giving him precious seconds to gain ground.

As the team pulled the wagon free, Harper tossed the gasoline can onto the back and vaulted up behind it. He lay flat, clinging like a tick as the wagon clattered up Main Street and swung around a corner. By the time it vanished, the men loading the whiskey had fled into the night.

Ethan considered giving chase on the horse he'd brought. But Sam was still sprawled facedown next to the porch. The old fellow could be hurt.

"Sam?" Worried, he crouched beside the aging marshal and shook his shoulder. "Sam, are you all right?"

Relief washed over Ethan as he felt movement and heard a moan. Moving by painful inches, Sam managed to sit up. "Knocked the wind out of me, that's all," he muttered. "I'll be fine. Go on. Get on after those dirty skunks."

"Not much use doing that," Ethan said. "First chance they get, I'm betting they'll leave that wagon behind and hightail it for cover."

Sam hitched himself onto the edge of the stoop, his bony knees jutting upward. "Damn, I saw the wagon pull in and thought I could catch those boys in the act. I really put my foot in it this time, didn't I?"

He had. But there was no use rubbing it in. "You were only trying to do your job," Ethan said. "And it's partly my fault. I should've told you what I was planning."

"Yes, you should've." Sam spat into the grass. "You know that was Harper Wilton, don't you?"

"I know."

"So which one of us is going to arrest him?"

"I'd say, whoever can make sure the charges stick. As

things stand, a decent lawyer could probably get Harper off for tonight."

"Lawyers!" Sam spat into the grass again. "So what makes you say that?"

"Neither of us saw Harper's face. I heard his voice, but I barely know the man. And you can't swear you heard him say a word."

Sam swore. "So neither one of us could testify under oath that we knew it was him."

"Right. The lawyer will argue that it could've been somebody else. As long as he can establish reasonable doubt, Harper walks and we've wasted our time."

"So what do we do?"

"We keep an eye on him, wait till he messes up again. And he will. But don't take him on by yourself, Sam. If you see or hear anything, let me know. We'll take him down together. All right?"

Sam nodded grumpily. The aging lawman was clearly more accustomed to giving orders than taking them.

"Why don't you go on home and get some rest," Ethan suggested. "I'll keep an eye on the place till Ruby gets back. Tomorrow, if you want, we can haul what's left of those whiskey jugs out of the cellar and bust them up."

"Sounds good. It'll take a load off Ruby's mind to have them gone." Sam rose a bit unsteadily. "I'll be getting along. Meet you back here tomorrow morning at nine with some busting tools."

"Fine." The two shook hands. Ethan watched as Sam mounted the gray gelding he'd left out front and headed up the street. He could only hope his argument had convinced the old man not to go after Harper on his own. Ethan knew he'd made an impact when he'd talked about lawyers and evidence. Hellfire, he could almost have bought the story himself. But he'd left out one detail. The red chalk powder he'd sprinkled on the ground would be on Harper's boot soles, and on the soles of every man who'd been there except the wagon driver. It was tenacious stuff, that powder, working its way into every little crease and furrow of a sole. When damp, the color would soak into the leather, leaving a permanent stain. Find the boots, and he'd have enough proof to haul Harper Wilton's sorry ass to jail. But not yet.

Harper wasn't the biggest fish in the puddle. So instead he could be used. If offered a deal to keep him out of prison, Ethan was betting the coward wouldn't hesitate to betray his own father.

A fresh wind had sprung up, scattering clouds across the sky. Sheet lightning flared above the mountains, setting off a murmur of approaching thunder. The hour was late, and there was no sign of Ruby.

He'd told her to stay as long as possible, Ethan reminded himself. But that didn't mean she was all right. Anything could have happened by now.

He remembered how she'd looked tonight in that peach silk dress that almost matched her skin. His senses recalled the scent of her, the feel of her skin as he'd helped her with the buttons, the little spot at the back of her neck that he'd ached to kiss. The hunger to hold that womanly body naked in his arms, to make love to her again and again, was like a knife in his gut.

Where in hell was she?

Letting himself back into the dark house, he stood at the parlor window, staring out into the empty street. Slowly at first, then in a rapid staccato, raindrops drummed against the windowpane, breaking to stream down the glass with the fury of tears.

What if something had gone wrong?

He should never have let her go.

Tension hung over the table after Ruby's dramatic toast. It lingered through dessert, thickening the air like clabbered milk. The pharmacist's wife had hustled her husband out the door early, pleading a headache. Except for the Calhouns, the other guests sat in awkward silence, picking at their pie and looking everywhere but directly at Ruby.

Thaddeus sat at the head of the table, nodding attentively as Harriet described the visit she'd made to her daughter's family in Boston. When he glanced toward Ruby, his smile was unctuous, his eyes as frigid as an eel's. His expression sent a shudder through her body. He knew something she didn't. She felt more certain of it every time he looked at her.

Had she done the right thing, making her secret public? Would she take it back if she could? No, Ruby resolved. The truth was the only weapon she had—and better that it come from her lips than someone else's. Her revelation had left her open to gossip and ostracism. But in the days ahead, she would learn who her true friends were. She could only hope her daughters would find true friends, as well.

Outside, a storm had blown in. Wind lashed the trees and set a loose shutter banging against the side of the house. Rain pelted the windowpanes and streamed off the eaves. Shivering, Ruby reached for her shawl. She was grateful beyond words that the Calhouns had offered to drive her home. But unless they'd brought slickers along, it was going to be a cold, wet ride.

The hour was getting late, the guests growing visibly restless. Soon the interminable evening would be over. Ruby's one regret was that apart from what Harper had told her earlier, she'd learned nothing worth passing on to Ethan.

What would she find when she returned home? Had anyone come for the whiskey, or had the weather kept things quiet? As long as Ethan was all right nothing else mattered. She just wanted to be with him, to feel safe and protected as she always did when he was there.

The hotel waiter was serving cups of sweetened coffee when the front door burst open. Seated on Thaddeus's right, with a view of the entry hall, Ruby saw Harper stumble across the threshold. His brown suit was torn and muddy, his hair plastered wetly to his head. His eyes were as wild as a half-crazed steer's.

Ruby's heart slammed.

Ethan.

What if he'd faced down Harper? What if the unthinkable had happened?

With a muttered oath, Thaddeus pushed away from the table and strode to where his son stood dripping in the entry. "In here," he growled, shoving Harper through the open doorway of what appeared to be a study. The door clicked shut behind them.

Ruby strained to hear the muffled voices behind the door. She couldn't make out words, but the crisis seemed to be escalating. Each exchange was louder than the last, rising in volume until Thaddeus ended it with a shout.

"You stupid fool, you've ruined us!"

There was a resounding slap, followed by dead silence.

Numb with shock, Ruby turned back to the Calhouns. "I need to go now," she whispered. "Could you please take me home?"

Nodding, Harriet rose calmly from her seat. "I think it's time we were all going. Brandon, could you be a dear and bring the auto up to the house for us?"

Waiting with Harriet under the porch eave, Ruby stared through the gray downpour. Could Ethan be out there somewhere, bleeding in the rain? Would she find him alive? Silently and fervently she prayed.

Veiled by sheeting rain, the boardinghouse was dark and silent. Ruby forgot to breathe as Brandon pulled his Hudson Phaeton up to the front gate. There was no flicker of light, no sign that Ethan was there.

"You're sure you don't want me to see you inside?" he asked.

She shook her head. "Thank you, but I've put you to enough trouble. I've got my key. I'll be fine— No, please don't get out, Brandon. There's no need, and you'll only get drenched again."

"At least take this." Harriet thrust an umbrella toward

her. "If you're worried about returning it, you can drop it off at the bank."

Thanking her new friends, Ruby opened the umbrella and scrambled out of the auto. The ground was a sea of dancing mud, but her ruined kidskin slippers and water-splotched dress were the last things on her mind as she opened the gate and raced for the shelter of the porch. Sick with dread, she paused under the eave to close the umbrella and fumbled in her evening bag for the key.

Where was Ethan?

What if she found him dead?

Brandon was still parked at the gate, waiting to make sure she was all right. Turning, she gave him a wave and a forced smile. The things that had happened here were private. Whatever lay beyond that door, she would face it alone.

As the auto pulled away, she thrust the key into the lock. The tumblers clicked. Ruby's chest contracted, squeezing back her breath as she pushed the door open.

The parlor was deep in shadow, the blinds tightly drawn. For the first few seconds the room appeared empty. Then, in a sudden flash of lightning, she saw him step out from behind the door.

"Ethan!" Thunder exploded behind her as she flung herself into his arms. Kicking the door shut, he crushed her against him, molding her damp body to his chest. Ethan. Solid, real, unhurt, alive.

His mouth found hers, rough, hot and hungry. Her response flamed like torched gunpowder. So many questions. So many answers. And right now, none of them mattered.

"I was so afraid for you," she whispered. "I thought you might be—"

His lips stopped her words. She strained upward, arms clasping, hands groping, knowing that tonight she wouldn't be satisfied with anything less than all of him.

Her damp silk gown clung to her skin. Through the thin fabric she could feel the long ridge of his erection bulging against the seams of his trousers. Wild with need, Ruby hiked up her skirt. Straddling his thighs with her stocking-clad legs she rocked against that stone-hard, pleasure-giving length, feeding the bonfire that blazed in the roots of her body. Her breath came in whimpering gasps. She couldn't get enough of him. All she wanted was more.

He groaned, his hands splaying over her hips, supporting her against him as she moved. Lightning flashed through the blinds, chased by a thunder crash that shook the house. With a muttered oath, Ethan swept her up in his arms and strode down the hall to the bedroom.

She clung to him, whimpering with need as he carried her through the door. There'd be no time to undo the intricate web of loops and buttons that fastened her gown. And there'd be no need for the tenderness he'd shown the last time he'd made love to her. She wanted him now—wanted his manly strength filling the hunger inside her, his body pumping like a piston in rhythm with her own. And Ethan's urgency told her he wanted the same thing.

Flinging back the coverlet, he lowered her to the bed. She lay waiting, her skirt and slip rucked up around her hips, as he stepped back to kick off his boots and drop his pants and underdrawers. Framed by the tails of his open shirt, his erection jutted like a marble flagpole. It was hard to believe that the full size of him would fit inside her. But she knew he would. He had.

Under his touch her lacy bloomers were as insubstantial as a cobweb. He stripped them down her legs, taking her shoes but leaving her silk stockings in place. "Damn it, Ruby," he muttered, lowering himself between her open thighs. "I've wanted this every minute. Wanted it so much I could—"

"Hush." She caught his hips and pulled him toward her moist entrance. His thrust did the rest, driving him deep into her aching center. She was all hunger, all raw need as her pelvis thrust upward to meet him. He rammed into her like a stallion, igniting every nerve ending in her sensitive passage, almost making her scream with pleasure. Her hands clawed his shoulders as sensations ripped through her body like wildfire, thrilling and unspeakably deep. Her lips formed his name again and again, but the only sound that emerged was a primitive keening from the depths of her throat. Never, ever had she dreamed such sensations could be so powerful.

He was breathing hard, his chest heaving with the impact of each thrust. Ruby wrapped her legs around his hard-driving hips, letting his momentum carry them both. She felt the pressure, the pounding approach of his climax. Then she exploded like a sky full of holiday fireworks, convulsing around his heat as he filled her. Tremors ripped through her body, subsiding slowly, like the echo of the storm outside. As he relaxed above her she cradled him in her arms, overcome by what they'd given each other.

In a few hours tomorrow would arrive, bringing whatever was to come. But for the moment he was hers—all hers to love and treasure.

The peach silk gown, with its matching slip, lay in a sodden heap next to the bed. Pooled beside Ethan's clothes were the mud-soaked kidskin slippers, the silk stockings, the corset and the twisted wisps of lace that had been Ruby's underwear.

As the morning sunlight stole through the curtains, Ethan opened his eyes. Moving slowly, so as not to wake Ruby, he propped himself on one elbow to gaze down at her sleeping face. Naked as the day she was born, she lay curled against his side, her amber-gold hair spilling over the pillow. Seized by tenderness, he brushed a stray curl with his fingertip. Lord, but she was beautiful. If he could have his way, he would never be away from her again.

The memory of last night crept over him, stirring his sex between his legs. He wanted her again, but he wouldn't wake her. It was early yet, and she needed the sleep.

His eyes traced the contours of her lovely mouth, remembering how he'd bruised those sweetly swollen lips with his kisses, and more… He'd taken her urgently, almost brutally, with no thought except to lose himself in the deep, warm honey of her body. Surprisingly, it had seemed to be what Ruby wanted, too. She'd responded to him like a wildcat in heat, bucking and clawing beneath him, driving him to a frenzy with her raw need. He hadn't even taken time to—

Oh, hellfire…

He'd always made it a rule to use protection with a woman, or at least to withdraw if nothing was at hand. But last night that had been the furthest thing from his mind. What if he'd gotten her in a family way?

But that didn't matter, he told himself. If Ruby would have him, he meant to haul her in front of the nearest preacher and make her his lawful wife, the sooner the better.

Ethan felt the familiar cold weight shift and resettle in his stomach. He loved Ruby. That much was beyond doubt. But was he ready to be a husband again, let alone a father? What if he was no longer capable of the closeness a marriage required? What would he do if he failed her?

Ruby stirred and opened her eyes. Awake, she was even more beautiful. Leaning toward her, he brushed a kiss on her nose. "Hello, sleepyhead," he murmured.

"Hello." She smiled, stretched and yawned. "Mmm, you were delicious last night."

He grinned. "I could be delicious again this morning, but I wouldn't want Sam to show up early and catch me here with you. The old man would barbecue my hide."

Last night, before sinking into sleep, they'd briefed each other on the evening's events, including what Ruby had learned about Harper's small-time bootlegging operation, and his intimation that his father had something bigger going on. Ethan had heard enough to convince him that Thaddeus Wilton was the man behind the bootlegging. Ruby could rest assured that, before the day was over, the remaining whiskey jugs in her cellar would be hauled off and smashed. And there would be no more masquerading. Ethan would appear before the town as the U.S. deputy marshal he was.

Ethan had yet to round up Harper Wilton and get the goods on His Honor the mayor. And Ruby would still need his protection. In keeping with procedure, he would get a search warrant for Harper's auto and the property where it was stored. He would also telephone headquarters for a check on Ruby's new friends, the Calhouns. But he didn't expect to learn anything out of the ordinary. All in all, Ethan reflected, the night could have gone worse.

Spooning Ruby against him, he kissed the back of her neck. "Ready to start the day?" he asked.

"In a minute." She wriggled closer, nesting her lovely bum against his crotch—a surefire strategy for delay. "I've been thinking, Ethan…"

"Never a good idea," he teased, feeling his cock rise against her.

"No, listen." She shifted onto her other side, breaking their intimate contact as she turned to face him. "I came clean at the party last night, and I still feel it was the right thing to do. Now I need to do the same with you."

"I already know you shot your husband, Ruby."

"Yes, but you don't know why. Until now I've refused

to tell you the whole story. If you're ready, I'd like you to hear it."

Ethan willed himself to ignore a sense of foreboding. "Why now?" he asked.

"Because I have feelings for you. And I don't know what lies ahead for us. Whatever happens, I need you to know this."

"Fine. I'm listening." He waited, watching the play of sunlight on her face, loving her for her honesty, yet, somehow, dreading what he was about to hear.

"You already know that Hollis abused me for years," she began. "You asked me why I didn't leave. I stayed because of my children—my two little girls."

Two little girls. Something tightened like a noose around Ethan's throat.

"I knew that if I left, Hollis would use his power to take them away from me," she continued. "Whatever the price, I couldn't let that happen. So I endured the beatings, the drunkenness, the other women…"

She closed her eyes for a moment, as if gathering her strength. Heartsick beyond words, Ethan gazed at her.

"One night the girls' nanny came to me, terribly upset. She'd walked into their bedroom earlier that evening and caught Hollis there. He was…touching our oldest daughter, Mandy, while she slept. Touching her in a way no father should. When he saw the nanny, he made an excuse and left."

Ruby shook her head. "I knew the woman was in danger, so I gave her some money and sent her away. Then that night, after our dinner guests had left, I confronted my husband. I told him that if he didn't let me leave with our daughters, I was going to expose him for the monster he was."

She was trembling. Her hand reached out, seeking Ethan's. He clasped her cold fingers, loving her for her courage, loathing himself for what he was feeling.

"You know the rest," she said. "My brother, Jace, tried to take the blame for me. But after his arrest, I owned up to what I'd done and faced trial. Thank heaven the jury saw things fairly."

Ethan willed himself to breathe. He felt as if he were staring up the barrel of his own .38 revolver, about to pull the trigger.

"Where are your daughters now, Ruby?" he asked gently.

"They're staying at my brother's ranch while I get this place ready," she said. "With the whiskey cleared out, I should be able to bring them here in the next day or two. They're darling girls—eight and ten years old. There's no way you won't fall in love with them, Ethan."

Ethan's stomach clenched. A bead of cold sweat trickled between his shoulder blades. Two little girls, eight and ten. Could this be God's punishment for what he'd allowed to happen?

Ruby had said he would fall in love with her daughters. But how could he love them when he couldn't bear the thought of seeing them, hearing them or touching them?

Heaven save him, what was he going to do?

Chapter Twelve

Ethan swung the sledgehammer overhead and brought it down, shattering the jug of bootleg whiskey into glassy shards. The morning was cool, the earth fresh and damp after last night's rain. The flawless blue sky and cheerful bird songs should have put him in a decent mood. But each jug he smashed was like pounding his own head. He hadn't felt this black in years.

Why hadn't it occurred to him that Ruby might have children? Not just children, but girls—two little girls the same ages Ellie and Missy would have been if their father hadn't been such a proud, stubborn fool.

Not that he blamed Ruby. It wasn't that she'd been keeping her daughters a secret. It was just that he'd never thought to ask her about children. The subject had never come up between them. He'd assumed she was childless. But he'd assumed wrong. Now what was he supposed to do?

He loved Ruby. Loved her so much he could hardly stand it. He wanted a life with her—no matter that she'd burned the bacon and eggs that morning and neglected to salt the oatmeal. He could live with her deplorable lack of cooking skills. But how could he endure being around those sweet little girls, seeing their warm, bright eyes and hearing their childish voices? A baby might have been all right. Or even boys. But two girls? Every time he looked at them, the memories would tear him apart.

And when he couldn't take it any longer, when the blackness became unbearable, he would leave, and what would that do to her?

"You all right?" Sam Farley paused to rest his pickax on his shoulder. Most of the jugs loaded on the wagon last night had fallen off and broken in the street or been carried away by the fleeing hired help. Earlier that morning, Sam and Ethan had loaded the rest onto a buckboard and hauled it to the open land on the far side of the cemetery. There they'd dug a trench, lined up the jugs along the edge and set to breaking them. When they were finished, the broken glass would be shoveled into the trench and buried.

"I'm fine." Ethan crashed the sledge into another jug, releasing the rank smell of moonshine.

"You don't act fine."

"I said I was fine," Ethan growled. "Just wishing last night had turned out better, that's all."

"Hell, it could've been worse. At least nobody died. And those galoots won't have any more reason to bother

Ruby. Half the town saw us hauling this moonshine out here. I'm surprised we don't have an audience."

"Maybe we do." Ethan glanced back toward town, where Thaddeus Wilton's redbrick mansion rose on the far side of the cemetery. "Anybody with a good pair of binoculars could see us from one of those upstairs windows."

"Well, let's hope they're enjoying the show." Sam waved his hat toward the house, spat into the trench and resumed his work.

"Where do you suppose Harper's gone to?" Ethan asked casually.

"Nowhere." Sam smashed another jug. "Saw the son of a gun this morning, on my way to pick up the buck-board. He was stepping out of the hotel with his daddy, the two of them looking like butter wouldn't melt in their mouths. They must've figured out we can't prove he was there."

"Looks that way." Ethan had already resolved not to mention the red chalk. He didn't want Sam risking his safety again. But he wanted to get a look at Harper's boots before anything else went wrong.

As the sun climbed the sky, Ethan struggled to keep his mind on his work. But his thoughts kept returning to Ruby. He loved her to the depths of his lonely, miserable soul.

But he knew better than to believe he could make things work with her and those little girls. He needed to make a clean break soon, before he hurt her any worse than he was bound to. It had to be done, damn it. But parting from her would be like ripping out his own heart.

Lord help him, how could he just walk away?

How was he going to live without her?

Ruby stepped back to admire her newly installed telephone, mounted on the wall at the foot of the stairs. It had cost her a pretty penny, but she would need it for the boarders, as well as for herself. And now that she had service, she knew exactly who she was going to call.

Giving the operator the number, she waited for the ring. After a few seconds' pause, her brother's voice answered.

"Jace, it's me," she said. "How are Clara and the girls?"

Jace chuckled. "All fine. No sign of the baby yet. Your girls are off fishing with Clara's sister Katy this morning. They've been having a grand time, but I can tell they miss their mother. Just last night Mandy asked me when you'd be ready to have them come live with you."

"That's why I'm calling," Ruby said. "The house isn't ready for boarders yet, but Mandy and Caro should be fine here. If you can spare someone to bring them into town, along with the furniture…"

"How's this afternoon? Clara's grandmother will be coming over for a few hours. While she's here with Clara, I could drive the wagon into town myself."

"I'd love to see you. But are you sure Clara will be all right?"

"She's feeling fine. And believe me, if something

does happen there's nobody I'd rather have with her than Mary Gustavson."

Ruby felt herself smiling. "All right, then. As long as Clara isn't in labor, I'll expect you and the girls this afternoon. If there's a change of plans you can call me."

After giving Jace her new telephone number, Ruby hung up the receiver and finished tidying the kitchen. Her first breakfast had been a disaster, but she was learning. Next time, she'd know better than to set the skillet on the hottest part of the stove. And she'd remember that anything she boiled had to be salted.

At least Ethan hadn't said anything about the charred bacon, caramelized eggs and tasteless oatmeal. He'd cleaned his plate without a word of complaint, thanked her brusquely and disappeared down the cellar stairs. By the time Sam arrived with the buckboard, he'd carried most of the remaining whiskey jugs outside and had them ready to load.

Come to think of it, Ethan had been unusually quiet over breakfast. She'd been hoping they could talk a little. Now that she'd opened up her past, wasn't it reasonable to expect the same of him? But no, that all-too-familiar wall had slid back into place. He was a stranger again, taciturn and guarded.

Ruby blinked back a tear of frustration. Maybe he was upset about last night's debacle with the whiskey. Or maybe his mind was focused on his work. But how could she even think of a future with a man who swung from hot to cold with no warning at all?

Then again, maybe the future wasn't what Ethan had in mind.

Don't worry about it, she told herself as she wiped the counter and rinsed out the dishrag. This afternoon her darling girls would be here, and the pieces of her life would fall into place once more. She would fill her days with the sight of them, the sound of their laughter, the silky feel of their hair between her fingers. She would wake them up in the morning and tuck them in at night, and everything would be as it should.

Being the mother of Mandy and Caro was more important than anything in the world, and that included a man. Any man.

By the time the girls arrived, she wanted to have their room ready. It had come furnished with a pair of metal frame beds with mattresses, a washstand and a wardrobe with two drawers in the bottom. But there was nothing homey or cheerful about the dingy space. In the slanting light it looked as dreary as a cell.

The quilted pink coverlets the girls had used in Springfield were tucked away in one of the trunks. They would brighten the space and make it look more like home, but what was she going to do about that grubby yellow wallpaper?

She examined the faded pattern. The pale blotches on the surface appeared to be lambs and cupids. Maybe if she wiped the walls down, the paper would at least look cleaner. But even new, the color would have been ugly. And with pink? Hideous. Why hadn't she done this room first, instead of getting the rental rooms ready?

But she knew the answer to that question. If she didn't get some boarders soon, she would run out of money.

Painting over the paper would show every line; and even if she had time to strip the paper off first, the paint smell would linger for days. But maybe she could put new wallpaper over the old.

The more Ruby thought about that idea, the better she liked it. Surely the hardware store would have wallpaper and paste. And the room was small. The job couldn't take more than a couple of hours. She'd have plenty of time, especially since Ethan had told her not to expect him for lunch.

Now, if only she could find a nice pattern…

Almost before she had time to think, Ruby had flung off her apron and was racing out the door with her pocketbook. Twenty-five minutes later she was back with several rolls of paper, a flat pan, a wide brush and a one-pound bag of powdered paste. The supplies had cost more than she'd hoped, but the clerk had assured her she could bring back any unused rolls for a refund.

And she'd found the perfect paper—tiny pink roses and ribbons on an ivory background. With the pink coverlets, it would look adorable. The girls would love it.

Opening the bedroom windows and pushing the furniture into the center of the room, Ruby scanned the label on the paste for mixing directions. She'd never hung wallpaper before. But how hard could it be? You just cut the paper to the right length and pasted it onto the wall. Any fool could do it.

Rummaging in her own drawers, she found a

measuring cup, a spoon, scissors and a dressmaker's tape measure. A chair would do to stand on.

As the clock chimed eleven, with everything assembled, she set to work.

After the jugs were broken and buried, Ethan treated Sam to lunch at Mabel's. The place was filled with passengers off the 12:15 train, but they managed to find a corner spot and catch Mabel's eye. Today Ethan wore his U.S. marshal's badge openly. It was a relief to be done with the pretense.

The wait for lunch gave him a chance to ask Sam about the Calhouns. "Just routine, you understand. In this business you don't take anybody for granted."

Sam blew his nose on a wrinkled bandanna. "Well, you can cross the Calhouns off your list. They're the closest thing to royalty this town's got. Brandon's been president of the bank for more than thirty years. Been asked to run for mayor more than once, but he's not much for politics, which is how we ended up with the likes of Thaddeus. Brandon's wife was a schoolmarm. A real lady, that one. Her kid brother, Will, married Brandon's daughter by his first wife. They own the feed-and-hardware store. Fine folks, all, and as honest as saints. They'd no more sell moonshine than I would. Any more questions?"

"Not now. I asked because Ruby met the Calhouns last night at the mayor's. They drove her home. Evidently they've befriended her."

"Best thing that could happen. With what she's got going against her, Ruby could use some powerful friends. No woman in town would stand up against Harriet Calhoun."

At that moment Mabel bustled up to bring their coffee and take their orders for ham sandwiches and apple pie. Despite her friendly greeting, she looked haggard, as if she'd passed a sleepless night. Ethan wanted to ask her if the Wiltons were making more threats, but her tables were crowded with customers. Unless he came back later, there'd be no time to talk.

Sam spooned sugar into his coffee. "Always did like it sweet," he said. "And speaking of sweet, now that her cellar's cleared out, I'm guessing Ruby will soon be open for business."

"I suppose so." Ethan took a sip from his cup. The presence of boarders in Ruby's house would end his time alone with her. Under the circumstances, that would be for the best. But he'd miss those nights in her bed.

"And she'll be bringing her little girls in from the ranch," Sam continued. "I know she's anxious to have them with her."

The coffee had turned acid in Ethan's mouth. He swallowed the hot brew, half choking. Sam was staring at him with a puzzled frown. "Are you all right?" he asked.

Ethan nodded, forcing his mouth to smile. "Ruby told me about her daughters," he said. "Have you met them?"

"Yes, indeed. I was with Ruby's brother when he picked the three of them up at the depot. Cutest little princesses you ever saw, and smart as whips. They'll win you over in no time."

Yes, Ethan thought, that was exactly what he feared—not that he would dislike Ruby's children, but that the little girls might work their way into the hollows of his heart, touching places no one had been allowed to touch in four long years.

Maybe it was time he moved back to the hotel. Ruby would be all right now, and he could keep an eye on her from a distance. As soon as this case was wrapped up he could be on the next train out of town.

"Do you have a family, Sam?" he asked, changing the subject as their food arrived.

A wistful look passed across Sam's rugged face. The old man would have cut a handsome figure in his younger days, Ethan thought.

"I had a wife," he said. "She's been gone fifteen years now. Died of influenza—she was a frail little thing, never could have children. But she was my sweetheart. We were happy for the time the good Lord gave us."

"Then you were luckier than most." Ethan focused on cutting his sandwich in half. Too late, he realized what was coming next.

"How about you?" Sam asked. "You got a wife and kids somewhere?"

"Not anymore. Sorry, but it's something I don't like to talk about."

"I see." Sam sounded slightly hurt, causing Ethan to give himself a mental kick. They finished the meal in silence and awkward small talk. When they were done, Ethan paid for the food and, leaving Sam to return the buckboard, walked slowly down Main Street toward the boardinghouse. Knowing what awaited him, he was in no hurry to arrive. But the sooner he cleared his things out, the less painful his departure would be. For everyone's good, he needed to be gone before Ruby's daughters arrived.

By now it was early afternoon. Main Street was bustling with shoppers and strollers out to enjoy the sunshine. Some of the faces had begun to look familiar to Ethan. But it was the shoes of the men he found himself watching. Would he see any traces of red chalk? True, most of the powder would have stuck to the bottoms of the shoes. But there could be flecks on the sides, as well.

Because he was focusing down, Ethan didn't notice the two men walking toward him until they were a scant twenty paces away. Only as he glanced up did he look into the faces of Mayor Wilton and Harper. Both of them were nattily dressed in mail-order suits and fedoras. Harper sported shiny black oxfords and a line of purplish bruises along the right side of his jaw. Ruby had mentioned hearing a slap behind the closed door. But if the two men had quarreled, it appeared they'd patched up their differences. Father and son looked as thick as thieves.

"Marshal." Pausing, Thaddeus Wilton tipped his hat. "I understand you're on the trail of some bootleggers. As mayor, I want to offer you my full cooperation. Dutchman's Creek is no refuge for the lawless."

Harper didn't speak. Only his shifting gaze and a twitch along his bruised jaw betrayed his unease. For the moment he had little to worry about. Last night he'd been wearing boots, not oxfords.

"Do you have any suspects?" The mayor's question was bold, his eyes unflinching. Ethan was practiced at reading people. Harper was a bully and a bungler. His father was cold, calculating and as dangerous as a shark.

"Right now we're in the process of gathering evidence," Ethan said. "We won't make an arrest until we're sure we have a solid case. But you can rest assured we always get our man—or men, as the case may be." Ethan's stern gaze fixed on the son, then the father. Harper's Adam's apple jerked above his collar. The mayor didn't so much as flick an eyelash.

"Well, however it goes, I expect you'll keep me informed," Wilton said. "It's my business to know what goes on in this town. Soon it'll be my son's, too. Harper here is going to run for marshal of Dutchman's Creek in the special election we're holding next month. We're on our way to the clerk's office now to file the paperwork."

"I thought Sam Farley was the law in this town," Ethan said.

"Not for long. Dutchman's Creek needs a younger man for the job. If Sam won't retire on his own, he'll have to be voted out of office."

"I see." Ethan could imagine how the mayor would see to that. True, Sam was getting frail. But electing Harper in his place would be like appointing the fox to guard the henhouse. Not that it would matter. Harper couldn't run for office if he was in jail, and that was where Ethan intended to put him. Even if Harper made a deal and gave up his father in exchange for immunity, there wasn't much chance responsible citizens would elect the son of a convicted bootlegger.

"Pleasure to meet you, Marshal." The mayor extended his hand. His flesh was cold, his grip too hearty. "A word of support from you could turn some voters in Harper's favor."

"Sorry, but meddling in local politics isn't part of my job," Ethan said. "Anyway, I should have this case wrapped up and be long gone by the election."

"Well, maybe Harper could help you with your case. He's a smart lad, knows the town and could use the experience. Maybe he'd even learn a few things from watching your methods."

Harper's expression had gone as blank as a plastered wall. Ethan gave the request a few seconds' consideration before he shrugged it off. There might be some advantages to having Harper around, like getting a look at his boot soles. But no, the offer had been too readily made. Odds were, Harper would waste time with false leads, warn off his cronies and report every development to his father.

And it was the father Ethan wanted.

"Thanks, but for now I'm fine," Ethan replied. "If I need help later on, I'll certainly know who to ask."

"Then we'll bid you good day, Marshal." The mayor touched his hat and moved on past. Harper trailed him like a beaten hound. There was more to that pair than met the eye, Ethan reflected. Once understood, their relationship could be the key to busting this case wide open.

Arriving at the boardinghouse, he opened the gate

and moved toward the porch like a man trudging to the gallows. The longer he waited to end things with Ruby, the more painful it would be. He would tell her now—tell her the whole story so she'd at least understand. Then he'd pack up and move back to the hotel.

With leaden feet, he mounted the porch. The door stood slightly ajar. Ethan gave it a light rap, then, hearing no answer, he stepped into the parlor. "Ruby?" he called.

"In here!" Ruby's voice, coming from one of the back rooms, was a rasp of exhaustion. Maybe this wasn't the best time.

"Ruby, are you all right?" Ethan made his way down the hall toward the back room, which she'd kept closed until now. Only as he stepped through the doorway did he see her.

She was standing on a chair in the far corner, struggling to mount a sagging length of paper on the wall. One end was stuck to her skirt, the other end curled away from the spot where she was holding it. More strips of paper were plastered to the wall at cockeyed angles. Drying paste spattered Ruby's face, her disheveled hair, her arms and her clothes.

What a sight! Caught by surprise, Ethan did the very worst thing he could have done.

He laughed.

Neck craning, Ruby swiveled her head. Her violet-blue eyes held a murderous expression. "Don't just stand there, you jackass!" she hissed. "Give me a hand!"

Ethan had never loved her more than he did at that moment.

Stripping off his vest, he tossed it into the hallway and rolled up his shirtsleeves. Now what? He'd never hung wallpaper before and clearly, neither had Ruby. But at least an extra pair of hands should make things easier. Striding through the mess, he nudged her off the chair and took her place. "I'll line up the top and you smooth out the bottom," he growled. "We'll follow the seams of the old paper. If we can get one piece hung straight, the rest should go up easier."

The paste was still damp. Peeling the strip free, Ethan managed to align it with the corner of the room. While he held it in place, Ruby stood below him and used her hands to rub out the air bubbles.

"What made you think you could do this job by yourself, Ruby?" he asked. "And why now?"

She glanced up at him, her expression so vulnerable that it almost broke his heart. "Jace is bringing my girls this afternoon. This will be their room. I wanted to make it pretty for them." She shook her head. "How was I to know what a miserable job this would be?"

Ethan battled a rising sense of urgency. He'd wanted to be gone by the time Ruby's daughters arrived. But how could he leave her with this disaster on her hands?

He'd climbed down from the chair and was helping Ruby measure another strip of paper when she suddenly leaped to her feet. "Listen! It's them! They're here!"

Through the open window, Ethan's ears caught the jingle of harness brass, the snort of a horse and the faint murmur of voices. By then Ruby was already gone, dashing through the parlor to fling open the front door.

Ethan lagged behind her, wishing he could be anyplace but here.

A wagon, piled high with furniture and drawn by a team of massive Percherons, was just pulling up to Ruby's gate. The man driving the horses was young and rangy, with an air of competence that Ethan could sense even at a distance. Flanking him on the wagon bench were two little girls clad in bright gingham dresses and straw bonnets.

A cold weight thickened in Ethan's chest. He would have no choice except to stay and face what he dreaded more than knives and bullets.

As Ruby hurried toward the gate, the driver reined in the team and vaulted to the ground. Reaching up, he boosted each of the girls off the wagon bench and swung them, giggling, over the picket fence. They raced up the walk to their mother, almost bowling her over with their exuberant hugs.

Ethan could already feel the ache, like lye eating into his gut.

"Ethan!" Disentangling herself, Ruby beckoned him out the door. "Come and meet my family!"

The wagon driver was checking the brake on the front wheel. He straightened as Ethan approached. Dressed in work clothes, he was tall and muscular, with dark blond hair and eyes the same deep blue as Ruby's. "Jace Denby," he said, extending a callused hand.

"Ruby's brother, I take it." Ethan introduced himself and accepted the firm handshake. "I've heard good things about you." And not all of them from Ruby, he recalled. Forrest White had passed on the story of Jace

Denby's taking blame for his brother-in-law's murder. Denby had resolved to hang rather than risk his sister's arrest. Cleared at last by Ruby's confession, he was a man whose presence commanded respect.

"I hope you won't mind helping me haul this furniture inside," Jace said. "I could use another strong back."

"That's what I'm here for," Ethan nodded as Jace singled out a hefty-looking sofa on the back of the wagon. The overstuffed pieces, in dark shades of brown, green and gold, were worn in spots but appeared comfortable and well made. They would do nicely for the boardinghouse.

Ethan got a grip on the far end of the sofa. Ruby's daughters stood next to the fence, watching. Painful as it was, he couldn't help stealing glances at them. They were pretty little things, the older one fair like her mother with a tumble of strawberry-blond curls, the younger one dark, with large, serious eyes. His own daughters had been as pale as angels, with hazel eyes and hair like corn silk… But if he went down that road, the memories would kill him.

Ruby held the door while Jace and Ethan lugged the heavy sofa inside and set it under the window. The girls followed, dancing around their mother, tugging at her hands.

"Where's our room, Mama? We want to see it!"

Ruby's stricken gaze met Ethan's. One hand peeled a blob of paste out of her hair.

Without taking time to think, he sprang to her rescue. "Your mother was working on your room when she found out you were coming," he said. "It's not ready yet, but maybe you can help her finish."

Until now the girls had scarcely noticed Ethan. Now two pairs of young eyes were turned on him, their look so soft and curious that it was all he could do to keep from bolting out of the house.

"Girls, this is Marshal Ethan Beaudry," Ruby said. "He'll be boarding with us for a little while. Marshal, I'd like to present my daughters, Amanda and Caroline, otherwise known as Mandy and Caro."

"Ladies." Feeling as if his heart were wrapped in barbed wire, Ethan forced himself to extend a hand. The girls shook hands in turn, eyes sparkling, smiles a bit shy. Their small fingers felt like the delicate petals of a flower.

Lord, how long could he stand this? He couldn't get out of here soon enough.

The moment was saved from awkwardness by the sudden jangling of the new telephone. Dashing to the foot of the stairs, Ruby lifted the receiver.

"Oh!" Her eyes went wide. "Oh, my goodness! Yes, he's right here!" She jabbed the receiver toward her brother. "It's for you!"

Jace was already reaching for the earpiece. His words were rapid-fire, ending with, "Thanks, Mary. I'll get home as fast as I can."

Ruby's girls were bobbing like little Mexican jumping beans. "Is Aunt Clara having her baby?" Taffy-haired Mandy tugged at her uncle's arm. "Can we go back with you and see?"

"It looks that way," Jace said. "But no, Mandy, you're

staying here. Your mother needs your help. Come on, let's get that wagon unloaded!"

"Leave it and take a horse if you want," Ethan offered. "I'll get the furniture inside and see to your team."

Jace shook his head. "This job won't take long with everybody helping. Clara's mother and grandmother are there, and the doctor's coming from town, so she should be fine. But let's get this done!"

He spoke calmly enough, but when he headed back to the wagon, it was at a dead run. Soon everyone was moving at a frantic pace. Jace and Ethan lugged the heavy furniture. Ruby managed the lighter pieces, and even the girls pitched in, dashing back and forth to bring in smaller items like lamps and cushions. In what seemed like no time at all, the wagon was empty and Jace was back on the bench with the reins in hand. "Call me!" Ruby shouted as the wagon rumbled down the side street, headed for the road out of town. Jace waved his hat as he disappeared around the corner.

"Will Aunt Clara and the baby be all right?" Dark-eyed Caro slipped a hand into her mother's.

"They should be, darling," Ruby answered. "Your aunt Clara's young and healthy, and her doctor said everything looked fine. Just think, you're about to get a new little cousin."

"We've never had a cousin before, have we?" The little girl's smile drove a dagger into Ethan's heart. He couldn't help it. He had to look away.

"We've got work to do," he growled. "Come on, all of you. Maybe we can get this place put together before nightfall."

He strode up the walk, into the house, his jaw clenched against the welling emotion. His instincts told him to march upstairs, pack his things and get out before he became any more entangled. But he couldn't leave Ruby and her little girls with so much work to be done. She was counting on him to stay and help, and he couldn't let her down.

For now, heaven help him, he was trapped.

Chapter Thirteen

Ruby surveyed the parlor and dining room, where the overstuffed set, coffee tables, rugs, bookshelves and curio cabinet had been arranged to her liking. In the dining room the sturdy, well-used pine table had been set up with its extra leaves inserted and enough chairs for her boarders, her family and any guests that happened by.

The place needed a few finishing touches, like curtains on the front window and pictures on the walls. But in the soft glow of the electric lamps that flanked the sofa, it had a cozy look. Already, it seemed more like home than the twenty-room mansion in Springfield where she'd spent so many miserable years.

Arranging the furniture had taken a couple of hours, with Ethan patiently shoving the heavy pieces where she pointed, and saying nothing when she changed her mind. The rest of the day and evening had been spent wallpapering the back bedroom. Mandy and Caro had pitched in, mixing the paste and helping brush it onto the paper while Ethan aligned the strips on the wall and Ruby rubbed them smooth. The girls had made a game of it, chattering and laughing the whole time. To Ruby, the sound of their voices was like music, the sweetest she'd ever heard.

At five-thirty, Ethan had rushed out to the hardware store for enough spare paper to replace what Ruby had wasted that morning. He'd come back with sandwiches and a jug of root beer from Mabel's, which they'd wolfed down before going back to work. By tomorrow the walls would be dry, the room ready to be set up.

The mantel clock chimed the three-quarter hour. It was nearly eleven, high time she was asleep. She had tucked the girls into her own bed at nine, planning to join them after a little quiet time. Ethan had cleaned up the wallpaper mess and retired to his upstairs room half an hour later. Only on finding herself alone had Ruby realized how tired she was.

Now, dressed in her white lawn nightgown and flannel wrapper, she curled on the sofa, leafing through the pages of an old *Good Housekeeping* magazine she'd found in one of the boxes. She was exhausted, but too strung out to sleep. Maybe if she stayed up long enough, she'd hear from Jace. There was every reason to believe Clara and the baby would be fine. But things could go wrong, and Ruby knew she wouldn't stop worrying until the call came.

Restless, she put the magazine down, rose and walked to the window. Moving the blind aside, she gazed out at the deserted Main Street, so quiet, so different from what she'd known in Springfield. She could only pray her daughters would be happy here.

"Ruby?"

Startled, she turned. Ethan was standing at the foot of the stairs. He'd pulled on his trousers, but his feet and torso were bare. The sight of him, half-naked and disheveled from sleep, awoke a stab of memory—his arms, his body...

"I woke up and saw that the lights were on. Are you all right?" he asked.

"I'm fine. Couldn't get to sleep, that's all." She gestured, encompassing the room with a sweep of her hand. "Thank you for all this. I couldn't have managed without you today."

"Don't mention it. Glad I could help. Here, as long as you're looking out..." Crossing the room, he switched off the lamps at either end of the sofa. Then he raised the blind. Light from the waning moon flooded the room.

They stood a little apart, gazing out into the night. Where would they go from here? Ruby wondered. She was warmly aware of his body in the darkness, even more aware of the desire that made her womb ache with need. But they wouldn't make love tonight. Not with Mandy and Caro in the house. The girls' coming had changed everything.

Moving behind her, he laid his hands on her shoulders. His strong fingers began massaging the tightness from her muscles. Ruby closed her eyes, arching against the contact. Her breath escaped in a low moan. Ethan's touch was pure heaven. But even as she savored it, Ruby sensed that something wasn't right. He'd been far too patient today. And now he was too quiet, too gentle.

"What is it?" she whispered. "Tell me."

His hands dropped away from her shoulders. He exhaled with a raw breath that scraped like broken glass across her nerves. "Ruby," he said, "I need to— Lord, what's that?"

A sudden flash lit the night at the far end of Main Street. Flames shot skyward, staining the dark with crimson. Smoke rose black against the stars. Cursing, Ethan yanked the front door open and plunged out onto the porch. Ruby rushed after him, feeling the chill through the soles of her bare feet. Sick with dread, she stared at the awful glow.

Still swearing, Ethan strode back inside and headed for the stairs to get his clothes. "Those bastards!" he muttered. "Those dirty, stinking bastards! I can't believe they'd do this, and to a woman! That's Mabel's place they've torched!"

By the time the volunteer fire brigade arrived, Mabel's café was a roaring inferno. All the firemen could do was hose down the railroad depot and other nearby buildings to keep the blaze from spreading.

At least Mabel was safe. She'd been asleep in her small house, a block away, when the fire started. Awakened by the noise and light, she'd flung on her clothes and rushed to the café. By then it was too late to save anything. Now she stood quietly weeping between Sam and Ethan as her livelihood crumbled into smoking ruin.

"It was Harper." Mabel's face was streaked with tears

and soot. "I know it as sure as I'm standing here. He came in tonight just before closing time and said I had one last chance to accept his family's offer or face the consequences. I told him where he could take his offer and ordered him to leave. The last thing he said was that I'd be sorry...." Her voice broke. "I know the man's a hoodlum. But I never imagined he'd do anything like this!"

Sam laid an arm around her shoulders. "He'll pay for this, darlin', I promise. Harper Wilton's gotten away with plenty." Sam's eyes flickered toward Ethan. "But this time he's gone too far. I'm going to haul that galoot to jail and make sure the judge keeps him locked up till his damn teeth fall out. You'll never have to worry about him again."

Ethan watched the dying flames. Beyond the place where he stood, the fire crew was hosing down the embers, preparing to shut down and leave. Onlookers who'd come running at the sound of the siren were already wandering home.

He knew what Sam was thinking. If they'd arrested Harper after the debacle at the boardinghouse, he wouldn't have been free to start the fire. But how could you hold a man, let alone convict him, without evidence? Even the fact that Harper had threatened Mabel was hearsay. Guilty as the man likely was, Thaddeus's lawyer would have him back on the street tomorrow. Case dismissed.

At first light, Ethan would be back here. He would bring his evidence kit and inspect every inch of ground, every speck of ash for proof that Harper had started the fire. He would use whatever he found to get a search warrant, giving him the legal right to go through Harper's Model T and the Wilton house. With luck, he would find enough solid evidence to nail Harper for the bootlegging as well as for the fire. And hopefully, under threat of a long prison term, Harper would deliver Thaddeus.

It wasn't how things were done in the old days, when Sam Farley was a hot young lawman. But it was the way things had to be done now. It was the law.

"There's nothing more we can do tonight, Sam," he said. "Why don't you walk Mabel home and meet me here first thing tomorrow. We can look for proof that the fire was set, and that Harper did it. Once we've found what we need, we can go after the bastard together."

The old man stiffened, his eyes blazing. When he spoke, his voice was as cold as the edge of a chisel. "Don't patronize me, Marshal. I'm not working for you, and I don't have to take your orders. You came here to catch bootleggers, and that's fine. But Dutchman's Creek is my town and this fire falls under my jurisdiction. I'll handle it any way I see fit."

His vehemence was like a punch to the jaw. Ethan knew he'd overstepped his bounds. Sam deserved an apology and would get one, but Sam also needed to understand the importance of doing this right. The last thing either of them wanted was to arrest Harper and have his case thrown out of court.

"Sam, I'm sorry—" he began, but Sam turned away.

"Come on, let's get you home, Mabel," he said, slipping an arm behind the woman's waist. "Then I'll see what I can do about rounding up the low-down skunk who did this!"

As she turned to go with him, Mabel cast an urgent glance back toward Ethan. He could see the worry in her eyes. She cared about Sam and she was afraid for him. Maybe he would listen to her on the way home. Maybe she could talk some sense into the old man. But Ethan couldn't depend on that.

"Sam," he called after the vanishing pair. "Don't do anything crazy. I'll wait right here for you. When you come back, we can talk."

Sam paused. His mouth worked in a way that suggested he was going to spit. Then, as if thinking better of it, he checked himself and looked back at Ethan. "I may be an old man, Marshal," he said, "but I'm a helluva lot smarter than you seem to think I am."

With that parting shot, he ushered Mabel down the dark street and disappeared into the night.

It was after 1:00 a.m. when the call from Jace finally came. The sound of the telephone startled Ruby from a fitful doze on the sofa. She flew across the dark parlor to answer the ring, stumbling over an ottoman in her haste.

"It's a boy!" Her brother's voice rasped with joyous exhaustion. "Husky little fellow, bright as a button. And Clara's fine. The doctor said the birth couldn't have gone better." His voice broke slightly. "Lord, Ruby, I'm just… overcome. I never understood the way you felt about your girls until now. I'm happy, I'm scared spitless…." He laughed. "Sorry, I know I sound like an idiot."

"You sound like a brand-new father," Ruby said. "The girls will be thrilled when I tell them in the morning. They'll probably want to rush right out and see the baby, but I'll give Clara a day or two to recover first. Kiss her and the baby for me."

"I will, when they wake up."

"You'd better get some sleep yourself. Believe me, you're going to need it later."

He laughed. "I'll take your advice, sis."

Ruby was smiling when she ended the call. Nobody deserved happiness more than Jace, who'd been prepared to make the ultimate sacrifice for her and her daughters.

But fate could be brutally unfair, she reminded herself. Mabel, a good woman who'd been first in town to offer Ruby her friendship, had suffered a terrible loss tonight. Ruby would have gone to support her friend if she hadn't been afraid of leaving her girls alone. She wouldn't know the extent of that loss until someone brought her more news. But she knew that life was fragile and precious, and that nothing in this world could be taken for granted.

On impulse, she pattered down the hall and cracked open the door to her room. In her bed, Mandy and Caro lay curled like sleeping kittens, the sound of their breathing sweet in the darkness. Her babies. Her darlings. They were the center of her world. There was nothing she wouldn't do to keep them safe and give them happy lives.

As she closed the door, she realized she hadn't heard Ethan come back. Had he returned while she was dozing and crept upstairs without waking her? That seemed odd. Surely he'd have known she was worried about the fire.

She climbed the stairs to the dark landing and opened the door to Ethan's room. His rumpled bed was empty, the covers thrown aside. His jacket, boots and the gun belt he'd taken were missing from the wardrobe.

He'd left the house more than two hours ago. Had he gone after Harper? She shuddered, remembering the cold, reptilian look in Harper's eyes. What if something had gone wrong?

Burdened by growing dread, she trudged back downstairs, opened the front door and stepped out onto the porch. The air smelled of smoke, but the street was deserted and the fire appeared to be out. There was no way she could learn more without leaving the girls alone. For now, at least, she had no choice except to wait.

Huddling on the sofa, she covered her legs with an afghan and tried to rest. But sleep was out of the question. Her nerves were jumping. Her mind kept picturing all the horrible things that could happen to Ethan. This was pure misery. How could she have been foolish enough to fall in love with a lawman?

And she *was* in love with Ethan Beaudry. She'd known it for certain today, seeing him with her daughters—a bit shy with them, perhaps, but at the same time so gentle, so tender. Working together to get the house arranged and the wallpaper hung, she had almost imagined them as a family.

It was too soon to let Ethan know how she felt.

But after last night's lovemaking, how could he not be aware of it?

Time crawled as she waited, growing more and more worried. Outside, a wind had sprung up, moaning in the trees. The honeysuckle vine scratched against the kitchen window. The clock ticked away the seconds, each one like slow torture.

It was nearly 2:00 a.m. when the front door opened and Ethan walked in. Ruby was on the verge of running to him. But the sight of his face stopped her. He looked like a man who'd been wandering through a nightmare.

"What is it?" she asked. "Is Mabel all right? Tell me."

He sank onto the sofa with a sigh of exhaustion. "Mabel's safe at home. Her café's a total loss, but even that's not the worst of it. I've lost Sam, and I'm afraid something's happened to him."

The story came out in broken pieces—how they'd quarreled at the scene of the fire, how Sam had left with Mabel, promising he'd bring Harper in. "I knew I couldn't let him face Harper alone," Ethan said. "So I waited outside Mabel's, planning to tail him when he left. Only I never saw him leave. At first I thought he might be staying the night there. But I finally figured out the old fox had sneaked out the back way. By the time I got to his place, his horse and saddle were gone. I picked up another mount from the livery stable, and I've been looking for him ever since."

Ethan raked his hands through his hair. His damp clothes reeked of smoke. "I don't have a good feeling about this, Ruby. Sam's a proud old man. I tried to tell him how to do his job, and he lost his temper. If I'd kept my fool mouth shut, he wouldn't have gone storming off alone."

"Don't torment yourself." Ruby's fingertips brushed his shoulder. "Sam knows every inch of this valley. If you can't find him, it's likely because he doesn't want to be found."

"I wish I could believe that. But if my own damn-fool arrogance has touched off a tragedy…" A shudder passed through his body. "All I can say is it wouldn't be the first time."

Ruby studied his rugged profile, aching for him. She'd felt all along that Ethan was holding something back—perhaps a secret as dark as her own. Maybe he was finally ready to share it.

"Tell me," she whispered.

He stared down at his hands. She sensed the pain in him, sensed the weight of the burden he carried. Part of her wanted to flee from what she was about to hear. But her heart knew better. If she loved him, she would listen, understand and accept what Ethan had to say.

"I wasn't always a lawman," he began. "Years ago I had a cattle ranch in Oklahoma. Ran a couple thousand head on it, and I'd built a nice house there, on a hill above a creek, for my wife and our two little girls."

Two little girls. Oh, Ethan! she thought.

"We weren't rich," he continued, "but we couldn't have been any happier. I'd have been content to spend the rest of our days there, on that blessed piece of land. But fate had different plans."

He paused to clear his throat, his gaze fixed on the window, as if he was watching the story unfold. "Some slick developers found oil on a property a few miles away. They started buying out every small ranch in the valley for less than the land was worth. For owners who didn't want to sell, they brought around some hired thugs to persuade them. Barns were burned, stock poisoned… It didn't take much more than that to get everybody spooked.

"I was for banding together against the bullies. I went around to my neighbors with a plan. We were going to meet in town, at the church, to discuss it. I talked a half-dozen men into coming. The rest were too scared. Or maybe too smart.

"The meeting was a waste of time. We couldn't agree on anything. I wanted to keep my land. The rest of them only wanted to hold out for a higher price." Ethan shook his head. "I called them all cowards. Lord, what a proud fool I was!"

Ethan's hands had gone slack between his knees. His voice deepened, roughened. "The meeting broke up with nothing resolved, and I left for home. As I neared the ranch, I saw my house ablaze. I rode like the devil, but the place was a torch by the time I reached it. Some neighbors were there ahead of me. They gave me the news. My wife and children had been trapped inside. It was too late to save them."

His shoulders had begun to quiver. Ruby fought the impulse to gather him into her arms. Ethan was reliving a nightmare. He might need comforting, but he wouldn't want it.

"I ran to the house and began bashing at the door. If I couldn't save my family I wanted to die with them. But the door was locked—I'd always told my wife to lock it when I was away. I grabbed the hot doorknob with my hands…"

"Oh, Ethan." Ruby ached to hold him, to cradle his head between her breasts and stroke his hair, but he was a wounded animal now. She knew better than to try.

"Somebody dragged me away," he said. "At some point I must've passed out. The next thing I knew, I was lying on the ground with my hands in wet bandages. By then the house was nothing but ashes."

"Did they ever catch the people who set the fire?" Ruby asked gently

He shook his head. "I had no doubt who'd done it. But when I went to the sheriff, he told me he couldn't make an arrest without evidence. Said that for all he knew, the fire could've been an accident. There was nothing I could do except bury the ashes and move on."

He related this last in a level voice, like someone reading a news article aloud. But Ruby could imagine what he'd suffered. Ethan must have been out of his mind with grief.

"I sold the ranch to a neighbor, who most likely sold it at a profit to the oilmen. Then I went on a drunken binge that lasted until I woke up in the gutter with no idea where I was or what I'd been doing for the past three months. After I cleaned up and got sober, I went to Colorado and signed up to train for the U.S. Marshals Service. Figured if I couldn't save my own family, at least I could help somebody else. That was four years ago."

He turned and looked directly at her for the first time since he'd started talking. His eyes were cloaked in shadow, his jaw hard set, as if he was about to deliver a blow.

Even before he spoke, Ruby knew it was over between them. All that remained was to discover the reason why.

"Ruby, there's something I need to say," he began. "If they'd lived, my two little girls, Missy and Ellie, would be about the same ages as your daughters." He exhaled brokenly. "Today, I willed myself to pretend everything was all right. But the truth is, every time I looked at those sweet children of yours, I saw my daughters' faces, and I relived that hellish night all over again. Being around your girls is like twisting a knife in my gut. You know how I feel about you, and how much I'd like to have more time together." He glanced down at his hands, then met her eyes again. "I'm sorry, Ruby."

And there it was. Overcome by a merciful numbness, Ruby gazed at him. She felt no anger, only a deep sense of hopelessness. Ethan could no more erase his past than she could give up her children.

"I suppose you'll be moving back to the hotel," she said.

"I considered it. But given what happened at Mabel's, I think I'd better sleep here for now. As long as Harper's on the loose, your place could be next."

"Fine. We'll do our best to stay out of your way." Ruby rose from the couch. The numbness was wearing off now, allowing the hurt to glimmer through. If she didn't leave now, she would end up saying things she was bound to regret. Ethan was a good man, and it would take her a long time to stop loving him. But some things couldn't be changed.

"Good night, Ethan." Eyes blurring, she turned and strode away, her exit marred by a stumble against an armchair. Righting herself, she plunged into the shadows of the hallway. She heard him speak her name, but she didn't turn around. There was no way she would let him see her cry.

Ruby woke at six to a quiet house. Mandy and Caro still slumbered, their little bodies warm and sweet on either side of her. Wriggling free, she rose, flung on her wrapper and padded out into the kitchen.

There was no sign of Ethan. A quick check of his upstairs room revealed that his clothes were still in the wardrobe, his books on the table. But his bed didn't look as if it had been slept in since the last time she'd checked. Maybe he'd spent the night searching for Sam. Or maybe he'd gone back to the scene of the fire.

She'd lain awake most of the night, yearning to be in his arms again. But now it was time to stop mooning and get on with her life. She would never stop loving Ethan Beaudry. But the chasm that divided them was too wide to breach. The sooner she accepted that fact, the better off she'd be.

She could only hope he was safe this morning, and that somehow, in the years ahead, he would find some happiness. If only it could be with her—but no, if she went down that path, she'd only make herself miserable. Ruby forced the thought from her mind.

In the kitchen once more, she fired up the stove and measured oatmeal, water and salt for breakfast. At least she'd learned to cook oatmeal. But the girls wouldn't love it. What a shame she couldn't just take them to Mabel's and treat them to flapjacks and homemade strawberry jam, their favorite. But Mabel's little café would be ashes this morning. Such a loss to the community. And the poor woman must be devastated. What was Mabel going to do now?

The flash of inspiration that struck Ruby was so brilliant, and so perfect, that she could scarcely credit herself for thinking of it. Yes, she thought. It was the answer to so many things. She glanced at the clock. It was early yet, and the girls needed their sleep. But as soon as everyone was up, dressed and fed, she would set out on her errand.

Her idea had to work. It just had to.

Ethan surveyed the ash heap that had been Mabel's café. The brown leather satchel he carried held a small camera loaded with film, paper envelopes, a magnifier, a jar of the red chalk powder he'd used earlier, a roll of bathroom tissue, a packet of plaster with water and a bowl for mixing it, a tiny tube of graphite, matches, a pencil and notebook, some fine brushes and an assortment of small tools. He'd assembled the kit himself over time, and it had served him well. A number of felons, who might otherwise have gone free, were behind bars because of the evidence he'd presented at their trials.

But before he could collect anything here, he would first have to find it.

He'd picked up the kit at the boardinghouse last night, after Ruby had gone to bed. Too worried to sleep, he'd spent most of the dark hours on Sam's front porch, waiting for the old man to show up. He never had.

The long wait had given Ethan far too much time to think about Ruby. He knew he'd hurt her, but she'd responded with the class of a true lady. It would have been easier if she'd railed at him, called him every dirty name in the book. He could have taken that, and worse. But that little catch in her voice as she'd said good-night before she walked away had damn near killed him.

At least he'd been honest with her. He hadn't strung her along or told her lies or made her promises he couldn't keep, like a lot of men might. But he felt like a rat all the same. And he couldn't shake the feeling that the one he'd hurt most was himself.

Ruby was one woman in a million. He would never forget her.

At the first flush of dawn, he'd checked the jail and stopped by Mabel's house. There was no sign of Sam at either place. Mabel had been worried, too. "I tried to talk him out of going after Harper," she'd told Ethan. "But the stubborn old fool wouldn't listen. Please, if you find him, let me know."

Now, with the sun just coming up, Ethan inspected what was left of the burned café. The faint whiff of gasoline told him the fire had been deliberately set. But he needed more proof than the smell. Where would a man stand if he wanted to start a fire without being seen? he asked himself. The most likely spot would be the rear of the building, away from the street.

Behind the building was an alleyway, marked by a high wire fence that bounded the neighbor's vegetable garden. Next to what had been the café's back door stood a half-burned trash barrel. If the fire had started here, it would have burned its way forward by the time the fire department arrived. Intent on saving the railway depot to the east, the firemen wouldn't have bothered to come back here.

Dropping to a crouch, he examined the damp earth. The smell of gasoline was stronger here. Coming from the doorway, were some small narrow-heeled tracks, almost certainly made by Mabel when she came out to empty the kitchen scraps. But there was more. Ethan's pulse leaped as he found the boot prints—long and worn around the edges, leading into the alley, stopping opposite the door and turning to go back out again. The pattern of the exiting tracks—deep at the toe, kicking up dirt behind—told Ethan that whoever made them had been running.

As was his habit, he played a game of devil's advocate with himself. A lawyer would argue that the tracks could have been made well before the fire, or even afterward. He needed a closer look.

The pair of boot prints that faced the door would be the most telling. With a spoon, Ethan scooped up a sample of the dirt between the toe prints and raised it to his nostrils. The gasoline smell was strong and unmistakable. Sealing the sample inside an envelope, he cleaned the spoon and lifted a second sample from one of the boot prints. The dirt was clean.

Only one explanation made sense. The arsonist had stood here to douse the back of the café with gasoline. In his haste, he'd spilled gasoline on the ground and on his boots. Only the ground *underneath* the boots was protected.

Pulse racing, Ethan found the magnifier and set out to examine every inch of every print. It took him less than a minute to find what he was looking for—a fleck of red chalk ground into the damp earth. There it was.

"Harper Wilton, you bastard," he muttered, "I've got you."

His one regret was that Sam Farley wasn't there to share the moment.

Chapter Fourteen

Ethan worked methodically but swiftly, hoping to finish up before the place got busy. First he photographed the prints, then took soil samples and sealed them in labeled envelopes. After, he'd dusted the most distinct pair of boot prints with talcum, mixed the fast-setting plaster and spooned a thin layer into the damp earth. While the casts set he wrote up his notes and inspected the rest of the site. The monsters who'd burned his house and murdered his wife and children had gone free for lack of evidence he hadn't known enough to collect. Harper Wilton would not.

The fire was still Sam Farley's case, he reminded himself. But the fleck of red chalk in the track made it his case, too. The only thing that made sense was for them to work together. But first he had some tall apologizing to do—when he found Sam. *If* he found Sam.

Worry gnawed at Ethan's gut. He'd grown genuinely

fond of the old lawman. If anything had happened to him…

But Ethan couldn't bring himself to finish the thought, as if imagining some tragedy might make it real.

Twenty minutes later he was done, the casts wrapped in cheesecloth and placed carefully in his valise. He'd found nothing else linking the fire to Harper, but plenty of evidence that it had been started with gasoline. What he really needed was to get his hands on Harper's boots. Then he could nail the bastard to the wall.

By now the town was beginning to stir. Light traffic was moving up and down Main Street—shopkeepers starting their day, travelers waiting for the morning train and curious idlers checking out the fire damage. Ethan had left his horse at the livery stable. Now that he'd finished collecting evidence from the fire, he would pick up the horse and go back to looking for Sam.

He'd just stepped out onto the sidewalk when a long black Packard pulled up alongside him. He didn't have to look twice to recognize the mayor's car.

"Good morning, Marshal." Thaddeus Wilton was at the wheel, Harper sitting in the passenger seat, both of them dressed in suits and slicked up cleaner than a couple of show dogs.

"Dirty shame, that fire last night," the mayor said. "Always sad losing a business that way. I don't suppose Mabel had insurance on the place."

"I wouldn't know," Ethan said. "You don't have any idea how it started, do you?"

Wilton toyed with a button on his coat. Harper stared at the dash, making no eye contact. "Plenty of things in a restaurant can start a fire," the mayor said. "Could be some grease spilled on the stove and flamed up after the place was closed. Not that I was in the neighborhood, mind you. Harper and I were home playing cards all evening. We retired at ten, and didn't even hear the fire bell. But then, we don't usually hear much out our way."

"And I don't suppose you've seen Sam Farley this morning, have you? I was planning to meet him here, but he hasn't shown up."

The mayor shook his head. "Sorry, haven't seen Sam since yesterday. If I run into him, I'll pass the word." He touched the brim of his hat. "Have a fine day, Marshal."

Ethan watched as the Packard rolled down the street. The morning was cool, but the top had been cranked back, displaying Harper in all his purported innocence. If Sam had tried to arrest the mayor's son, he hadn't succeeded.

Dread, cold, dark and ugly, tightened its grip around Ethan's throat as he strode down the street. He needed to find the old man. But before he continued the search, there was one more thing he had to do.

With Harper spruced up and parading down the street in his father's Packard, the Model T he usually drove would be left unattended. Wherever that vehicle was, Ethan need to locate it and get a look inside. The car and its contents could be the key to everything.

Daughters in tow, Ruby marched up the walk to Mabel's house. She'd promised the excited girls a trip to see Jace and Clara's baby in the next couple of days. But right now she had important business to take care of.

Mabel's was a tiny place, charmingly kept, with a gingerbread porch in front and blooming tulip beds lining the front walk. Poor dear Mabel. Ruby could only hope the good woman would be open to her idea.

"Ruby! What a surprise!" Mabel answered her knock. She was neatly dressed, her face fixed in a welcoming smile. But her damp, bloodshot eyes revealed her true state of mind. She'd put her heart, her soul and most of what she owned into that little café. Now it was gone.

"And are these your girls?" Mabel asked, then answered her own question. "But of course they are. I can see you in both of them. Have a seat. I'll put on some tea. And I do believe I have a few oatmeal cookies left in that jar."

"Oh, look!" Mandy forgot herself as she spotted Mabel's enormous yellow tabby cat in the kitchen doorway. "Please, may we pet him?"

"You certainly may. He loves attention."

As the girls scampered after the cat, Ruby settled onto the sofa. "Please don't bother with tea, Mabel," she said. "We just had breakfast. And I wanted to talk to you before you made other plans."

"Plans?" Mabel's plump hands fluttered as she took a seat in the rocker. "Heavens to Betsy, girl, I can't plan what I'm doing from one minute to the next. That little place, and the people who came in every day, that was my life." Her eyes welled. "The only thing I'm sure of is, I'll be damned if I'm going to work for that weasel Thaddeus Wilton. I'll starve first!"

"I know how you feel." Ruby laid a hand on her shoulder. "That's why I'm here. I have a business proposition for you. I'll tell you what it is, and you can take all the time you need to think it over."

She paused, seeing the guarded look in Mabel's eyes. "You know I'm setting up a boardinghouse. The furniture's in and I'm almost ready to open. But there's one problem. Nobody's going to move into the place if they have to eat my cooking. You can't imagine how awful it is. I can barely boil water. I bought a cookbook, but—"

"Stop right there, honey," Mabel said. "I know where you're going with this, and I appreciate the thought. But that little café was my piece of the world, and I loved being my own boss. I don't want a job working for somebody else, not even somebody as nice as you."

"I know you don't." Ruby leaned forward. "But my business can't make it without you, Mabel. I'm not offering you a job. I'm offering you a fifty-fifty partnership in my boardinghouse. I take care of the property, you take care of the food, and we split the profits. It might be a struggle at first, but people will come for your cooking. Once we get on our feet, you might even want to reopen your café there. Mabel and Ruby's. How does that sound to you?"

For a moment Mabel's expression didn't change. Then a twinkle appeared in her eyes, spreading to wreathe her face in a radiant smile. "It sounds perfect. I don't need time to think about it. Let's get to work!"

* * *

Ethan took the horse at a canter down the cemetery road toward the mayor's house. The hour was still early, the road empty of traffic. He'd picked up the warrant earlier, but since there was no telling how soon the mayor and his son would be back, he needed to make the most of his time.

Dropping the reins in the graveled side yard, he dismounted and circled the house. There appeared to be no one around the place—Wilton's hired help likely did double duty at the hotel, where the mayor and his son took their meals. The front and back entrances to the house were both locked.

Offset behind the house was a long shed with a corrugated-tin roof. The wide double doors were closed, but the web of wheel tracks leading in and out confirmed that this was a shed for vehicles. A padlock was looped through the hasp. But human nature being what it was, the person who'd closed the door might not have wanted to bother with a key.

Ethan yanked on the lock and felt a small rush of satisfaction when it released with a click. Opening the door just far enough to admit some light, he slipped into the shed.

Harper's Model T was parked in a far corner, its black chassis spattered with dried mud. Muddy boots had left a mosaic of prints on the floorboard. The size, shape and texture matched Ethan's castings from the site of the fire. Two jugs of moonshine were stuffed under the rumble seat. Crouching, Ethan collected some mud samples from the wheels. There was no sign of Harper's boots, but he had enough evidence to get a warrant for the seizure of the auto. He could only hope the judge wasn't in the mayor's pocket.

Damn it all, where was Sam? He was getting more worried by the minute.

He was just stepping out of the shed when his nostrils caught the faint, acrid smell of something burned. He hadn't noticed it earlier. Maybe the wind had changed in the last few minutes.

Seeing nothing at first, he made a cautious circle of the shed. About fifty paces back, next to the barbed-wire fence that marked the property line, stood a large metal barrel, the kind used for incinerating trash. A thread of smoke curled from the top. Trotting back across the weedy ground, Ethan reached the barrel and peered inside.

Atop the heaped ashes lay the smoldering remains of a canvas tarpaulin and a pair of high-topped work boots. They were more charred than burned, as if they'd been damp before they were doused with gasoline and set afire.

Using a handy stick to lift out the tarp and boots, Ethan dropped them on the ground and stomped out the few remaining sparks. Stripping off his jacket, he made a bundle of everything and returned to where he'd left the horse. Mounting up, he headed back toward town. For now, he would take his evidence back to the railroad depot and put it in a locker for safekeeping. Then he'd resume his search for Sam.

Maybe everything would be all right, Ethan told himself. Maybe, with luck, he'd return to town to find the old man back at his job. They could go over the evidence together and construct an airtight case against the Wiltons.

But he was grasping at straws. He knew it even before he saw the stranger galloping out from town to meet him. The man appeared to be a farmer, dressed in work-stained overalls, with his hat blown back. Ethan's heart dropped as he recognized the lathered horse the man was riding. It was Sam's gray gelding.

"Marshal Beaudry?" The man reined in alongside Ethan. His eyes were reddened, his straw-colored hair plastered against his damp forehead. "They told me at the livery stable you'd gone this way. I need you to come with me."

Ethan had gone cold. "That's Sam Farley's gray horse, isn't it? What's happened?"

The farmer took a moment, gulping air to bring his emotions under control. "You know that bog out past the Gustavson place? My boys were there this morning, catching minnows for bait. That's where they saw this horse wandering loose. They were trying to round it up when they spotted the buzzards and found Sam." The man's voice broke. "He was shot through the chest, Marshal. Shot dead."

Sam Farley was buried the next afternoon. The citizens of Dutchman's Creek closed their businesses and turned out en masse to honor the beloved lawman who'd served them for more than three decades. Mourners overflowed the small church and fanned out over the grounds to wait in silent tribute while the service proceeded.

Only one notable resident was missing. Harper Wilton was behind bars in the town jail, under arrest for arson and bootlegging, with murder charges pending. With no deputy to take over, Ethan had assumed the post of acting marshal until a replacement for Sam could be found. The entire community was in a state of shock. Things like this just didn't happen in Dutchman's Creek.

The arrest had been accomplished easily enough. Ethan had simply waited for Harper to come out of the hotel after dinner and taken him by surprise. By the time the mayor's son had recovered his wits, he was handcuffed and on his way to jail. So far, Harper had remained tight-lipped, refusing to say anything until the family lawyer arrived from Denver.

Ethan had contacted the sheriff in Ridgemont, the county seat, and arranged for Harper to be transferred to the larger, more secure facility there. But the paperwork would take a couple of days. Meanwhile, the prisoner was Ethan's sole responsibility.

Ethan was still sorting out the details of Sam's murder. Judging from the hoofprints on the driveway, it appeared the old lawman had paid a late-night visit to the Wilton place. When he'd tried to arrest Harper, the weapons had come out. Sam had been shot once through the heart. His own Colt .45, unfired and wiped clean of fingerprints, had been found on Sam's body, still in its holster. The undertaker, who also served as coroner, had recovered the bullet, but the gun was still missing.

Evidence told the rest of the story. Bundled in the tarpaulin, the body had been hauled out to the bog, with Sam's horse trailing Harper's Model T. Clearly the intent had been to make the shooting look like an ambush. The mud on Harper's auto and boots matched the mud around the bog. And there were bloodstains on what remained of the burned tarp. All in all, the case against Harper Wilton appeared to be wrapped and tied in a neat bow—except for one remaining question.

What part had Thaddeus Wilton played in all this?

The reedy notes of the old pump organ signaled the opening of a song. As the congregation broke into "Rock of Ages," Ethan scanned the crowded chapel. With every seat taken, he'd deliberately joined the standing crowd in the back. His place at the corner of the rear pew gave him a discreet vantage point.

Thaddeus was here, seated near the front with the members of the town council. Since his son's arrest, he'd made a point of showing himself in the best possible light, stoutly insisting that Harper was innocent of murder, and that neither he nor Harper knew anything about any other crimes. It was a good act, but the mayor appeared more intent on saving his own reputation than on supporting his son.

And Ethan was no nearer to unmasking him than he'd been before Harper's arrest.

The song had ended. Brandon Calhoun, who'd known Sam most of his life, stepped to the pulpit to give the eulogy. As his eloquent baritone rolled over the listeners, Ethan's gaze was drawn to Ruby.

She was seated a few rows in front of him, dressed in her dove-gray suit and trim little matching hat. Her glorious red-gold hair was fastened in a gleaming coil at the nape of her neck. Ethan's loins ached as he remembered that hair falling like water around his face, pooling on his chest as she leaned over him. Ruby had given herself to him with total abandon and trust—something she would never give him again. He deserved to be horsewhipped for the way he'd treated her. But he would remember their lovemaking, without regret, for as long as he lived.

Things had been strained between them since he'd walked away. His possessions were still at the boardinghouse, but he'd be sleeping at the jail until Harper's situation could be resolved. There was no way he dared leave the bastard alone overnight, and no one else he could depend on to watch him.

He'd been back to the boardinghouse on errands, but had seen little of Ruby and her girls. She was avoiding him, Ethan knew, and he couldn't blame her. The only time they'd spoken face-to-face was when he'd told her about Sam. The news had shaken her badly. Her eyes had teared up and her throat had jerked as she gulped back sobs. He'd been prepared for her to crumple in his arms, but she hadn't. She had simply sucked in her grief, thanked him for telling her and walked down the hall toward her room. She was a proud woman, his Ruby, and Ethan knew better than to think she'd ever give him a second chance.

Not that he'd take it, he reminded himself stonily. That bridge had gone up in smoke.

His gaze wandered along the pew. Mabel sat on Ruby's near right, dabbing at her eyes with a wadded handkerchief. Ethan had heard from Mabel that the two of them planned to be business partners—a first-rate idea, he thought. Between Mabel's loss of her property and Ruby's dearth of cooking skills, the partnership was a match made in heaven. Mabel and Ruby's Boarding-house was bound to be a success.

Ruby's daughters sat on her left, their silky little heads just visible over the back of the pew. Jace Denby, who'd left his wife and newborn son to attend the service, sat on the far side of his young nieces. The handsome, graying man beside him would be Judd Seavers, his powerful father-in-law. And the elderly woman at the row's end, her face a mask of stoic grief, would be Judd's widowed mother-in-law, Mary Gustavson.

In the short time Ethan had been here, he'd already begun to recognize names, faces and family connections. He'd grown downright fond of this mountain-sheltered valley and its good people. But life had taught him not to form close attachments. With this case winding down, he'd soon be transferred to his next assignment. Dutchman's Creek would be one more place to put behind him and forget.

But he would never forget the stunning, courageous widow who'd forged a path into his heart.

Mandy and Caro were growing restless. Ruby bent to quiet them, touching her lips with a cautioning finger. She was a perfect mother to her girls, Ethan thought.

Together, the three of them made a package any man would be proud to call his own. He remembered the afternoon they'd spent wallpapering the bedroom. The girls had been so excited, so happy and playful. It had been all Ethan could do to keep from warming to them. But he'd known better than to let it happen.

Now, as he stood watching, dark-eyed Caro turned around and looked at him. Her serious little face lit up in a melting smile. One hand rose above the back of the pew. Small fingers waggled in a furtive greeting.

Ethan felt the stab to his heart. But not wanting to rebuff the child, he returned her smile with a lift of his eyebrows and the slightest motion of his hand. For a fleeting moment he imagined what it might be like to be free of pain and guilt, free to give Ruby's girls the caring friendship they deserved. But then the feeling passed. The black door closed inside him, and he turned away.

Ruby would do all right here, he told himself. Her scandalous past would become old news in time. Meanwhile, she had the support of the two most respected families in the valley. She had Mabel's friendship and business acumen. And she had her own beauty, intelligence and charm. No doubt, when Ruby decided to marry again, she'd have suitors fighting their way to her door.

Ethan could only regret that he wouldn't be one of them.

The funeral procession stretched from one end of Main Street to the other. Since Sam had no immediate family, it was the mayor and town council who rode behind the hearse in Thaddeus Wilton's Packard. Ethan watched as the procession of autos and buggies filed out of the churchyard gate. Ruby and her daughters, along with Mabel, had joined the Seavers clan in their spacious buggy. Ethan kept his eyes on them as he mounted up and joined the long procession to the graveyard.

After a brief graveside prayer the coffin was lowered, laying Sam to rest next to his beloved wife. With the service done and the weather fair, many folks took advantage of the occasion to mill around and visit. Ethan was making his way toward Jace Denby, meaning to congratulate him on the new baby, when Thaddeus Wilton stepped into his path.

"I was hoping to catch you, Marshal," he said. "How's my boy holding up?"

"As well as could be expected," Ethan said. "Still not saying much, but that's bound to change once he realizes what he's facing."

"You know that murder charge is bull, don't you?" Wilton's eyes narrowed. "Anybody could've shot Sam out there by that bog. Hell, you don't even have the gun. All you've got is a pair of muddy old boots and the tarp we used to wrap a deer carcass last fall. And you got those by trespassing on our property. My lawyer is going to blow a mile-wide hole in your case."

"Could be." Ethan nodded, knowing the man was mostly bluff. "I agree that somebody else could've shot Sam. If you have any theories about who it was, I'm willing to listen."

"That's your job not mine," the mayor snorted. "So

as long as you don't have a solid case, why not let the boy go until trial. I'll put up his bail myself."

"You heard the judge. No bail. Remember, we do have enough evidence to make the other two charges stick. If Harper's innocent of the murder, as you say he is, he may at least know something about what really happened. If he can tell us, or shed some light on who's really running that bootleg-whiskey racket, the state's attorney may be willing to cut him a deal...."

Ethan studied Wilton's face. The mayor wasn't the only one who could bluff. So far, Harper had remained as tight as a clam, but his father didn't have to know that. If a half truth could crack the man's cold composure, even a little—

Snatches of conversation a few feet away distracted both men for a moment.

"Why not come home with us today, Ruby," Jace Denby was saying. "You and the girls could see the new baby, have a bite of dinner, and we could lend you the chaise to drive home. You'd have plenty of time to make it before dark."

"Please, Mama!" The girls were dancing with excitement. "Please say yes!"

The pause before Ruby answered was little more than a breath. "Of course! What a wonderful idea! Let's get going now, so we'll have plenty of time."

Thaddeus Wilton smiled as they hurried toward the buggy. "So life goes on, I see," he said. "What a blessing that is. Don't you agree, Marshal?"

Without waiting for Ethan's response, he turned and walked away.

* * *

Young Thomas Soren Denby, named after Clara's two grandfathers, was a tiny, dark-haired bundle of perfection. Although he had Jace's long hands and feet, Ruby thought he bore a stronger resemblance to his brown-eyed mother. When he grew older, and his features took on a more masculine cast, he would look very much like Clara's uncle, Quint Seavers, whose photograph hung in the entry hall with others of the family. For now, little Tom was just a sleepy pink sugar lump. Mandy and Caro were giddy over him. Ruby had to remind them more than once that their new cousin wasn't a doll to be played with.

Now, cradling her brother's son in her arms, Ruby soaked in his baby sweetness—the warm, milky smell of him, the innocent trust that almost brought tears to her eyes. Had it really been that long since her own girls were this small? At thirty, she would welcome having more babies to love. But there was the small matter of finding the right father. Ethan was the man she yearned for. But he'd made it clear that he couldn't abide children. He'd even told her the reason why.

The sooner she forgot him, the better.

The baby squirmed in her arms, wrinkled his tiny face and began to cry. Laughing, Clara reached up from the bed to take him. She looked tired but radiant. "Sounds like feeding time," she said. "The little mite has a man-size appetite already." Gathering the baby close, she opened the front of her nightgown and put him to her breast.

"We should be going," Ruby said. "I don't want to

be on that road after dark. Thank your mother for the lovely meal, and thank you, Clara, for taking my girls this past week. I can't tell you how grateful I am."

"Having them here was a pleasure," Clara said. "I'm so happy you agreed to move here, Ruby. Families should be together, especially the children."

"Doesn't your uncle Quint have a child, too?" Ruby asked, remembering what the girls had told her.

A faraway look crept into Clara's eyes. "He and Aunt Annie have a baby girl. Emily's her name. They were married a long time before she came. I'm really hoping they'll bring her for a visit soon. But San Francisco's their home. I don't think they'll ever move back to Colorado." Her pretty face brightened. "All the more reason to be grateful that you and your girls are close by."

Jace stepped into the bedroom doorway. "I've got the chaise hitched up for you, Ruby. Figured you'd be wanting it soon. Keep it for as long as you need. The livery stable can board the horse in town. We have an account there, so don't worry about paying."

"We'll be off, then." Ruby embraced her brother and sister-in-law and rounded up her daughters, who were playing with the kittens on the back porch. They'd already picked the one they wanted, a spunky little black female with white markings. But the small fur balls were still too young to leave their mother.

The placid bay horse stood waiting, hitched between the traces of the two-wheeled buggy. "I put the hood up for you," Jace said. "It's clouding in the west. Wouldn't want you ladies to get rained on."

"We'll be fine," Ruby said. "It's only an hour to town. Come on, girls."

Jace helped them onto the seat, and they started down the drive. Ruby handled the reins with easy confidence. Back in Missouri, her husband had owned a stable of fine horses. Riding them had been one of the few pastimes that brought her peace. Back in those dark days she'd felt more at ease with horses than with people. Horses didn't gossip. They didn't judge or ostracize.

Turning at the open gate, she flicked the reins, urging the bay to an easy trot. The late-afternoon sun was warm and the girls were tired. Soon their heads began to droop against her shoulders. A raspy little snore escaped Mandy's lips. Ruby slowed the gait of the horse, filling her senses with their muzzy warmth and the sound of their breathing.

They were infinitely precious, her daughters. She'd done her best to shield them from the signs of their father's abuse and from the horror of his death. Mandy and Caro had seen nothing on that terrible night. But there was no way they wouldn't have heard what was happening. There was no way they couldn't be fragile inside, no way they wouldn't be vulnerable for years to come.

She'd come here, to Dutchman's Creek, to find a peaceful haven for them, a place where they could heal, grow and discover their own strengths. She could only pray that she'd be wise enough to make that happen.

The clouds Jace had mentioned were pushing eastward to spill across the face of the sun. The shadows they cast drained the day of warmth and color. A chill on the breeze signaled a coming storm. Ruby urged the horse to a faster gait. The dirt road would be a muddy mess in the rain. But never mind, they were at least halfway back to town. Another thirty minutes or so, and they'd be safely home.

Would Ethan be there? But why was she even thinking of the wretched man? Now that Harper was in jail he had no reason to stay and protect her. He could move his things and sleep at the jail, or at the hotel, until time for him to leave. With luck, he would never have to face her, or her daughters, again.

Ruby blinked away a tear. Blast it, why did love have to hurt so much?

The road here skirted a line between the hay fields and the wooded foothills. It was an isolated stretch, with no houses in sight, although Ruby knew there were crude cabins tucked among the trees. Ethan had told her about the secret stills where bootleg liquor was distilled from fermented corn. Some of them might even be close by.

Thunder, still distant, rumbled from beyond the peaks. A flock of blackbirds rose from the trees in a twittering cloud, circled and swept out over the fields. In their wake, the eerie silence that descended over the road was broken only by the plodding hooves of the horse and the faint creak of wheels.

A vague sense of danger raised prickles on the back of Ruby's neck. Acting on instinct, she slapped the leathers hard on the horse's rump. The bay snorted and broke into a brisk trot.

The sudden lurch jarred the girls awake. "What

is it, Mama?" Mandy murmured. "Is something the matter?"

"Everything's fine, dear." Ruby braced for a bump in the road. "Just trying to get home before the rain, that's— Oh, dear God!"

She sawed at the reins, but couldn't stop the horse in time to avoid the heavy rope that was stretched across the road in front of them. Colliding with the rope, the startled animal reared in its traces, causing the chaise to tilt backward.

"Hang on!" As Ruby struggled to calm the horse, four men, their faces masked by hats and bandannas, swarmed out of the trees. One of them seized the horse by its harness. The other three came for Ruby and her daughters.

"No!" Ruby flung herself between her girls and their attackers, fists clawing and flailing. It was a losing battle. She had no weapon, not even a buggy whip. Mandy and Caro were yanked squealing and kicking out of the chaise and hauled toward the trees.

"No!" Ruby screamed. "Let them go! Take me!" She lunged after her daughters, but strong arms seized her from behind. A rough, smelly rag was clamped over her face.

Everything went black.

Chapter Fifteen

When Ruby opened her eyes it was raining. Water droned on the raised canvas hood of the chaise, pouring down the sides and dripping off the edge. Her clothes were damp, the air chilly enough to make her shiver.

For the space of a breath, she lay sprawled on the leather seat, her mind in a fog. Then the memory slammed into her with the impact of a gunshot—the rope, the rearing horse, her daughters screaming as the masked men carried them into the trees.

She jerked upright, struggling against the leaden response of her limbs. Her head ached with a dull throb. She remembered the smelly rag pressed over her face. Chloroform, she thought, or something like it. Why wasn't she with Mandy and Caro? Why hadn't their attackers taken her, too?

Every instinct urged her to leap out of the buggy and race off in the direction they'd gone. But that would be foolish. She had no idea where her daughters had been taken, and tracking them in the rain would be impossible. Her only chance of saving them lay in keeping her wits about her.

What time was it? She peered through the rain into the gathering twilight. Soon it would be dark. Lamps would be lit in the cabins among the trees, making them easier to spot. But finding her daughters would only be half the battle. She'd need some way to get them free—a serious weapon, like a gun or a knife. Right now she had nothing.

A nauseating fear washed over her as she imagined Caro and Mandy in the hands of those ruffians. Their terror lingered like a miasma in the air. The memory of their pitiful cries tore at her heart. Heaven help her, if those men had hurt them…

Ruby's stomach heaved. She fought for self-control. She had to stay clearheaded for her daughters. She needed to find out where they'd been taken and how to safely get them back. And she knew she couldn't do it alone.

She needed Ethan.

Only as she heard the breathy snort and felt the slight movement of the chaise did she remember the horse. The patient animal was standing in the traces, head lowered against the pelting rain. Strange, she thought, that the men who'd taken her children would ignore a valuable horse, leaving her with a way to go for help.

As Ruby shifted to grab for the reins, something rustled on the seat where her skirt had lain. Her shaking fingers found the folded paper and opened it. There was just enough light to read the crudely lettered message.

> *MARSHAL:*
> *IF YOU WANT THEM KIDS BACK ALIVE, BRING HARPER WILTON TONIGHT. HARP CAN TELL YOU WHERE. COME ALONE OR YOU WILL BE SORRY.*

Ethan finished checking on Harper and settled himself at Sam's battered desk. It still felt strange, sitting in the chair of the legendary lawman who, despite their differences, had been his friend. The fact that he'd offended the old man, and never gotten the chance to apologize, was something he'd regret for the rest of his life.

But then, there were plenty of things he'd come to regret—his own arrogance and stubbornness, saying too much at the wrong time, or not saying enough, acting too impulsively, or not acting at all, talking when he should have been listening. Over the years, he'd accumulated a mountain of regrets, and there wasn't a damn thing he could do about any of them.

The desk was cluttered with paperwork, which Sam had pretty much ignored. At least, Ethan thought, it would keep him busy until the sheriff arrived from Ridgemont to transfer Harper to the county jail. And maybe the work would keep him from thinking about Ruby—as if that were possible. Every time he closed his eyes to rest, he saw her haunting face. Every time he drifted into sleep, it was with the memory of their lovemaking.

Outside, rain was falling in a steady drizzle. The sound only added to Ethan's gloomy state of mind. He'd convinced himself that walking away from Ruby was the right thing to do. So why did he feel so miserable about it?

He'd just finished sorting the paper into stacks when he heard the frantic pounding. Remembering that he'd locked up for the night, he drew his .38 and eased toward the door. Harper had some unsavory friends. They could be taking advantage of the storm to break him out of jail.

"Who's there?" he asked cautiously.

"Ethan!" Ruby's distraught voice stopped his heart. "Open up! They've got my girls! They want Harper!"

He freed the bolt and yanked the door open. She stumbled over the threshold and fell into his arms, quaking violently. He tried to warm her, but she struggled against him like a trapped animal.

"Men on the road—they took Mandy and Caro!" she gasped. "And they left this! Look!" Pushing away from him she pulled a rumpled sheet of paper out from under her jacket. Ethan felt the blood drain from his face as he read the message.

"Here, Ruby." He reached for an old army blanket that was tossed over a chair. "Get warm while we decide what to do."

"No!" She gazed up at him, as fierce and wild-eyed as a lioness. "I already know what to do. Damn your rules and regulations, Ethan! Damn your justice! And damn Harper Wilton! I want my girls back! And if you won't give up your prisoner for them, so help me, I'll find a way to take him myself!"

Ethan gripped her shoulders. His eyes took in her wind-tossed hair and stricken face. Ruby was out of her head with worry. But she was right. This was no time for following procedure. Get Harper and get her children back—nothing else mattered.

"The buggy's outside," she said. "We can take that."

"Fine." The idea was as good as any. Even handcuffed, it wouldn't do to put Harper astride a horse, and the buggy would be better for bringing the girls back—assuming they could be found and recovered. But Ruby had to understand one thing.

"The note says to come alone," he growled. "That means you're staying here."

"No!" She flung the word at him. "I'll stay with the buggy while you take Harper in. But I need to be close to my daughters. They'll be scared to death, and they're going to need me. If you won't take me along I'll get a horse and follow you."

He knew her too well to doubt that she'd follow through on her threat. Better to give in, and keep her close enough to make sure she stayed out of danger. "All right. I know better than to argue. But you're to keep quiet and stay with the buggy. Understood?"

"We're wasting time," she said.

"Wrap yourself in that blanket before you catch your death. I'll get Harper." Snatching up the keys and a pair of handcuffs, Ethan flung on his leather jacket and strode down the hallway to the cells.

* * *

Ruby's teeth were chattering. She picked up the ragged brown blanket and wrapped it around her shoulders. The thick wool was itchy and smelled like horse, but at least it was warm. Mandy and Caro would be cold, too, she reminded herself. They could use the blanket on the way home.

Would they make it home? Dear heaven, they were her babies, so young and helpless. What if something went horribly wrong? What if she and Ethan couldn't save them?

From the hallway came the metallic clang of the cell door, the rumble of Ethan's voice and Harper's nasal twang. As Ruby turned toward the sound, her eyes caught the gleam of something on the desk. It was the small .22 revolver Ethan had offered her on the eve of the mayor's party. She'd turned it down then. She would take it now. With luck, Ethan would be too preoccupied to miss it.

She checked to make sure the gun was loaded, then slipped it into her pocket. An instant later Harper emerged from the hallway, pale and unshaven, his wrists cuffed behind his back. Ethan walked behind him. His face was grim, his .38 holstered. He carried a short, double-barreled shotgun, deadlier than a pistol at close range. "Let's go," he said.

They trooped out into the dark rain. Main Street was deserted except for the chaise, which stood where Ruby had left it. Ethan shoved Harper onto the seat and took a moment to bind his ankles with a length of rope. Then he went around the rig, climbed into the driver's place and pulled Ruby up beside him.

Crammed against Ethan on the crowded seat, with the shotgun across her knees, Ruby huddled into the army blanket. Ethan brought the reins down on the horse's back. Muddy water splashed from beneath the wheels as the chaise shot down Main Street and onto the road out of town. She clung to the seat, the pistol a cold weight against her side. Nobody could predict what would happen tonight. But one thing she knew for certain. Whatever she had to do, no force on earth would keep her from protecting her daughters.

Ethan took the rig as fast as he dared, given the darkness, the rain and the treacherous condition of the road. The need to get to Ruby's girls was urgent, but he couldn't risk a spill, a broken wheel or an injured horse.

Harper sat on his left, huddled in silence. Ethan had expected the mayor's son to gloat over his coming release. But what he sensed in the man was fear. Harper didn't seem to be at all happy about where he was being taken. All the more reason to be ready for the unanticipated.

Ruby sat on his right. Through the thick blanket, he could feel her quivering. Those two little girls were her life, flesh of her flesh. She had given birth to them, nurtured and reared them. She had killed to keep them safe. Losing them would utterly destroy her, Ethan knew. He knew it all too well.

The thought of what she must be suffering sent a jolt

of protective love through him. What a blind, narrow-minded fool he'd been. Ruby was his woman, and her precious daughters were part of the package, part of *her*. The three of them were a gift that life had offered him, a second chance at happiness—and he had turned his back on them. If he lost them now, he would pay the price forever.

"Stop." Ruby touched his arm as they rounded an isolated bend. "We were right here when they took the girls. I tied my hat to that post to mark the spot."

Ethan reined in the horse and followed her gaze. There, on the open side of the road, was a wire fence. Ruby's soaked hat hung from a rough cedar post. On the other side of the road, the wooded foothills rose into darkness. A hundred yards up the slope he saw—or thought he saw—a flicker of light among the trees.

"Is this the place, Harper?" he asked. "The message said you'd know it."

Harper shook his head.

"You're lying," Ethan snapped. "Tell me the truth or I'll beat it out of you!"

Harper shrank away from Ethan's threatening fist. "That's it," he muttered.

Ruby had climbed out of the buggy to give Ethan room. He jumped to the road and strode around the rig to untie Harper's ankles. Without being told, she held the shotgun on Harper until Ethan straightened and took it from her. "Get back in the buggy and stay put," he said. "No heroics, Ruby. If I know you're safe I can focus on doing my job."

Her eyes met his. The love he saw there ripped at

his heart. "Just get my girls back, Ethan. That's all I'm asking. Get them back."

I will, he wanted to say. But it was a promise he couldn't make. Anything could happen out there in the rainy dark. But if his life was the price of freedom for those blessed children, he would pay it in a heartbeat.

Turning away without an answer, Ethan jammed the shotgun against Harper's side. "Move," he growled. "No tricks. I'll be right behind you."

Wrapped in the blanket, Ruby watched as the two men crossed the road and vanished into the trees. Ethan was a brave man who knew his job. He would do everything in his power to get her daughters back. But would it be enough? Fear perched on her shoulders, clutching her with its talons. Something was about to go wrong. She could feel it in every screaming nerve of her body.

On the ride back here, she'd had time to think about what happened earlier. Now everything came together. The kidnappers had been waiting for her to arrive. They'd known about the visit to her brother's ranch and her plans to return with the girls. Since she hadn't discussed those plans with anyone but the family, somebody must have overheard their conversation after Sam's funeral.

That somebody, she remembered now, had been standing a few paces behind her. As she'd turned to head for the buggy, she'd seen the mayor walking away.

Where was Thaddeus Wilton now? That was the missing piece of the puzzle—the deadly piece. Why had the note demanded that Ethan bring Harper back here and that he come alone? Why, unless Ethan was walking into a death trap, with her daughters as the bait?

She'd been ordered to stay with the buggy. But her presence would give Ethan two more eyes, two more hands and another loaded gun. If she could make the difference between life and death for her girls and for the man she loved, nothing was going to keep her away.

Securing the horse, she took a moment to scan the wooded hillside. It was dark except for the faint spot of light that flickered with the movement of the trees. Ethan and Harper would have taken a direct route. Cutting wider to come in from behind would allow her to size up the situation before she made her move.

Ruby took a moment to lay the blanket on the buggy seat. Then, with a silent prayer, she crossed the road and started up the slope.

If there was a trail, Harper had neglected to find it. Ethan cursed as his boot stubbed a fallen aspen log. Rain drizzled off the leaves overhead, streaming down his hair and face. Ahead of him, Harper swayed and stumbled, struggling to balance without the aid of his handcuffed arms.

"Can't you move any faster?" Ethan snarled at his prisoner.

"Might could, if you'd take these cuffs off me."

"You know better than that, Harper. I don't trust you any farther than I can spit."

"Then take me back to jail. I'd rather be locked up than face what's waitin' for me in that cabin."

Ethan's pulse slammed. Stopping, he yanked Harper around to face him. "Is there something you need to tell me? There's not much I can do unless I know the truth."

"Then listen good, Marshal. You know I'm no angel. I'll admit to sellin' moonshine and to settin' that restaurant fire, on my pop's orders. But, swear to God on my mother's grave, I didn't kill that old lawman. It was my pop done it. He made me get rid of the body. Said if I got arrested, long as I didn't talk, he'd get me off, and we'd both be fine."

"And if you did talk?" Ethan had gone cold beneath his rain-soaked jacket. That very afternoon, he'd hinted to Thaddeus Wilton that Harper was on the verge of confessing. Was that why Ruby's daughters had been kidnapped, to silence Harper? Was he to blame for this whole mess?

"Pop said he'd see me dead before he'd let me rat him out to the law. I think his goons are waiting in that cabin to kill me, and kill you, too. Don't take me up there, Marshal. For God's sake—I'll tell you everything."

Ethan shook his head. "They've got Ruby's daughters. We have to go up there."

"Then at least take the cuffs off and give me a fighting chance. Maybe I can keep them busy while you get the kids."

Ethan swore under his breath. Harper was a lying bastard, but this time he could be telling the truth. Taking off the handcuffs would be a gamble. But under the circumstances, so would leaving them on.

"All right," he said. "But the cuffs stay on until we're within sight of the cabin. And I want to make one thing clear. I don't give a damn whether you live or die, Harper Wilton. All I want is to get those little girls back. You make one bad move, and I'll blow you to kingdom come without a second's thought. Understood?"

"Yup." Harper began to walk again, head down, feet plodding. "He's not really my pa, you know. He married Ma when I was seven. Never did treat me like his own blood. It was more like he'd bought me and got a bad bargain. I might've run off after Ma died, but he was all I had."

And that, Ethan thought, explained a great deal.

They toiled upward, winding through stands of white-trunked aspen and clumps of sumac and chokecherry. Last fall's layer of rotting leaves was a treacherous slick under their feet. By the time they spotted the ramshackle cabin through the rain, they were both soaked and muddy.

Lamplight flickered through the small front window, but the flour sack that hung over the opening prevented Ethan from seeing inside. There was no telling what lay behind the closed door. But if Ruby's children were there, he vowed, he would give his life to free them.

A stone's throw from the entrance he unlocked the handcuffs from Harper's wrists. "Remember, no tricks," he cautioned. "I'll have this gun on you, and I won't hesitate to pull the trigger. Now, get those hands up and get moving. You're going in ahead of me."

They mounted the stoop, Harper's hands raised,

Ethan's shotgun at his back. "U.S. marshal!" Ethan thundered. "I've got Harper Wilton, and I'm here for the children. Open up!"

The door creaked open to silence. At a lamplit table, three men sat smoking and playing cards. Unshaven and dressed in dirty work clothes, their bandannas pulled down around their necks, they matched Ruby's description of the men who'd attacked the chaise. But there was no sign of Ruby's daughters and no sign of Thaddeus Wilton.

Ethan kept the shotgun trained on Harper. "All I want is the girls," he said. "Let me take them and I'll go."

The biggest of the men grinned, showing rotten teeth. "Girls? Hell, man, I don't see no girls here, do you?"

Ethan gulped back the nausea of dread. "Tell me where they are, you bastard. Tell me now, or I start shooting."

"Wouldn't do that if I was you, Marshal. Not unless you want to be dead." A fourth man stepped out from behind the door. This one looked much like the others except that he was holding a Winchester deer rifle, cocked and aimed at Ethan's ribs. "You can put your hands down, Harp. And you, Marshal, lay that gun on the table. The pistol, too. Then maybe we'll talk. Or maybe we'll just have ourselves some fun."

Mud-spattered, rain-soaked and shivering, Ruby crept toward the rear of the cabin. So far, she'd had decent cover. Five horses were tethered in the lee of a clapboard shed. Standing in the rain, they created just enough sound and motion to mask her own.

Five horses. She pondered the number. Four men had attacked the chaise and taken the girls. They'd come out on foot, but they could've had horses waiting in the trees. Had the fifth horse been brought for Harper, or did it mean that someone else was here?

She'd checked the shed in the hope of finding her daughters. The cobwebby interior held what she guessed to be the apparatus for a still, some firewood and rusty tools and a plethora of dirty-looking jugs. But there was no sign of Mandy and Caro. She could only hope they'd be inside the cabin, and pray that they were still alive.

Now, crouching among the horses, she studied the cabin's back side. The shingled roof extended over a cluttered porch. Through the rain that streamed off the eave, she could make out one covered window. Light filtered around the edges of the closed back door—an uncommon feature for such a small cabin, but it might prove a handy way in and a fast escape.

Ruby's fists clenched. If only she could see inside. If only she knew where Ethan was and how to get her daughters out safely. As things stood, she might as well be blindfolded!

As she crept beyond the horses, something moved in the shadows of the porch. Holding her breath, Ruby slipped the .22 pistol out of her pocket, thumbed back the hammer and waited.

A match flared in the darkness. Ruby gasped as its fire illuminated a face she knew all too well. Thaddeus Wilton cupped his hand around the flame as he puffed on a long black cigar.

Ruby watched him drop the burned-out match in the mud. The cigar's burning tip glowed red as he stood smoking under the shelter of the eave. He didn't seem in any hurry to go back inside the cabin. But then, the mayor wasn't one to get his hands dirty. Maybe he was waiting for something to happen in there, something he didn't want to be a part of.

No time to think about what that might be, Ruby admonished herself. No time to be afraid. She had to get closer.

She was plotting out her next move when the mayor turned his back and walked to the far end of the porch. Clamping the cigar in his teeth, he reached down to fumble with the front of his trousers. This was her chance.

Picking up a few pebbles from the muddy ground, Ruby tossed them over the backs of the horses. The startled animals raised their heads, snorting, shifting and jerking at their tethers. Using the distraction, she sprinted the open distance to the near end of the porch and ducked behind a stack of wooden crates. Wilton waited a moment until the horses had settled down. Then, after more fumbling, he released a stream into the mud.

He was still pissing when Ruby jammed the muzzle of the .22 against his temple.

"Not a move till I say so, you monster," she hissed. "You know I've killed one man. I won't mind making it two. Where are my daughters?"

The cigar dropped from his mouth. He forced a nervous chuckle. "Ruby, my dear! I must say, you've taken me by surprise. You wouldn't really—"

"Where are they?" She pressed the muzzle into his flesh, hard enough to leave a welt. "You know, I don't have to kill you. I could shoot off your nose or your so-called manhood and enjoy watching you bleed. Now tell me!"

"In…there." His head twitched just perceptibly in the direction of the closed door.

"Go on." She lowered the gun to his back and shoved him toward the door. "Open it. We're going in."

The door swung inward, opening into the cabin's single room. Ruby followed the mayor inside, her chest so tight she could scarcely breathe.

The scene unfolded before her like a slow nightmare, detail by detail. First she saw Harper. He was standing on the braided rug in the middle of the floor with an uncertain, scared-rabbit expression on his face. Near the front door, a man held a rifle on Ethan. Ethan's hands were raised, his lips pressed into a grim line. His narrow-eyed gaze spoke volumes of surprise, pain and helpless fury.

A few paces to her left three men sat at a table with cards in their hands. On the tabletop, next to the kerosene lamp, lay Ethan's shotgun and his .38 pistol. Mandy and Caro were nowhere to be seen.

Weak-kneed with desperation, she jammed the gun harder against Wilton's coat. "Where are my daughters?" she rasped. "Tell me now or, so help me, I'll pull this trigger."

"Ruby, Ruby." He made a small *tsk-tsk* sound. "It appears, my dear, that you haven't fully grasped the situation. I must ask you to give me that little gun of yours. Do it now, or your friend the marshal will be a dead man."

Ethan's eyes blazed defiance, a signal that he was prepared for whatever she decided to do. But Ruby couldn't risk him against such overwhelming odds. Heartsick, she lowered the pistol. Taking it from her hand, the mayor slipped it into his pocket and motioned her to one side of the room. "Stay there," he snapped. "I want to keep an eye on you while I deal with this boy of mine." Turning, he fixed his gaze on his son. "What have you got to say for yourself, Harper?"

The words were spoken softly, almost affectionately. But Thaddeus Wilton's eyes were as cold as the eyes of a snake stalking its prey. Watching, Ruby could see Harper begin to crumble.

"I done everything you told me to, Pop," he blubbered. "I kept quiet. Didn't say a word about what you done."

The mayor gave him a contemptuous sneer. "Maybe not this time. But I can't spend the rest of my days wondering when you'll get in hot water and decide to talk. You've outlived your usefulness, boy. You're no kin of mine, and you know too much." His sneer broadened. "As do you, Marshal, and you, my dear Ruby." He shook his head. "What a waste of a beautiful woman. I'd have draped you in diamonds."

"I've had diamonds," Ruby said icily.

His gaze hardened. "I'll be leaving now," he said, glancing at his cohorts. "You men know what to do. Give me five minutes' head start. Then kill them—all three of them, along with the children, and burn this place to the ground. When it's done, you'll get your money the usual way." He touched his hat brim in a mock salute. "Gentlemen…Ruby…"

He was turning to go when Harper snapped.

"You yellow-bellied snake, you don't even have the guts to kill me yourself!" he screamed. "Damn you! Damn you to hell!"

He launched himself at the table where Ethan's weapons had been laid. Before anyone could react, Harper had his hands on the shotgun.

The roaring blast hit Thaddeus Wilton squarely in the chest, ripping through cloth, skin, bone and the vital organs beneath. Blown backward by the impact, the mayor of Dutchman's Creek slammed against the wall behind him and slid to the floor, leaving a crimson smear down the logs.

Stunned by the recoil, Harper was an easy target for the man with the deer rifle. A shot through the back dropped him where he stood. The rug slid out from under his boots as Harper crumpled to the floor.

"Get down, Ruby!" Ethan moved with the speed of a striking cougar. Ducking in close, he seized the deer rifle and wrenched it from the shooter. The man went for the pistol at his hip, but Ethan swung the rifle and caught him with a bullet to the chest. He toppled backward, dead before he hit the floor.

The three men playing cards had had enough. They leaped to their feet, upending the table as they bolted for the back door. The lamp shattered, spilling a stream of kerosene across the floorboards. Flame followed, licking along the trail of fuel. Within seconds the cabin's interior was ablaze.

Ruby had scrambled to her feet once more. She stared at Ethan through a wall of fire and smoke. "Get out the back!" he shouted. "Get out now!"

"No!" she screamed. "Wilton said to kill the children! Ethan, they're here, and they're alive! We've got to find them!"

"You go! I'll look! Ruby, I won't leave without them! I promise!"

Ruby's heart burst as she realized what Ethan was saying. He would die in the fire before he would leave without her daughters. He would make the ultimate sacrifice for her, for them.

But even if she survived, if she lost her children and the man she loved, she would have no life at all.

"No! I won't leave without you! We'll look together!" Frantic, she cast her smoke-stung eyes around the cabin, searching for anything that might hide two small bodies—a trunk, a cabinet...

Her toe stubbed a rough spot on the plank floor. She cried out, dropping to her knees. Next to Harper's feet, where the rug had been, was a hidden trapdoor.

"Ethan!" She clawed at the edge. "Come and help me! Hurry!"

Covering his face with his arms, he dived through the flames to reach her side. His hands found the recess, lifted the crude door.

There, in a shallow earthen pit, bound and gagged, lay two terrified little girls.

In an instant Ethan had them. Yanking off his leather jacket, he wrapped it around Mandy. Ruby stripped off her wet skirt—the most ample garment she had—and pulled it over Caro's head and body.

Silently she thanked Providence for the rain, which had soaked their clothes and hair. The dampness gave them some protection from the fire as they snatched up the girls, bolted out the back door and flung themselves off the porch, into the mud.

Too spent to rise, they knelt there in the drizzling rain. A few strokes of Ethan's pocketknife freed the girls. Sobbing, they tumbled into their mother's arms.

Without a moment's hesitation, Ethan reached out and enfolded the three of them, holding them fiercely close. They were so precious. He had come so close to losing them. Now he'd been given a second chance. He would never walk away again.

The heart was a mansion with infinite room inside, Ethan thought. Sarah and Missy and Ellie would live in his heart forever. But there would be a place for Ruby and her young daughters, as well. As their family grew, so would his capacity to surround them all with his protecting love.

A fresh breeze swept over the mountains, blowing the storm eastward. In the lee of the shed, the two horses left behind by the bootleggers nickered and stirred. Ethan pushed to his feet, pulling Ruby and the girls up with him.

"Let's go home," he said.

Epilogue

August 2, 1920

The wedding was a simple affair, with family and close friends filling the front pews of the church. Ethan was strikingly handsome in a suit of charcoal gray. Ruby wore a high-waisted gown of sky-blue silk organza. She carried a bouquet of dewy pink roses and baby's breath that Clara's mother, Hannah Seavers, had picked that morning in her front yard. Mandy and Caro, two little princesses in pink, accompanied their mother down the aisle.

Ruby trembled as Ethan slipped the ring on her finger. After the long nightmare of her first marriage, she'd believed she would never have enough trust to wed again. But nothing had ever felt more right than the idea of spending the rest of her life with this strong, gentle man.

They might have married sooner, but, as was his

nature, Ethan had insisted on doing things in proper order. After resigning from the U.S. Marshals Service, he'd accepted the town's offer to replace Sam Farley as permanent marshal of Dutchman's Creek. He was training a young deputy to assist with the job of keeping the peace. He'd also bought a ranch on the outskirts of town and remodeled the older home on the property for his new family. Only now that it was finished was he ready to carry his bride across the threshold.

The wedding buffet at Mabel and Ruby's Café and Boardinghouse was as lavish as the ceremony had been simple. Mabel had outdone herself with breads, tarts, glazed vegetables, sauces and a pit barbecue in the backyard where beef from the Seavers ranch had simmered to juicy, fall-apart tenderness. For dessert there was homemade ice cream and a wedding cake so exquisite that Ruby had to be talked into cutting the first piece. Friends from all over the valley came to wish the new couple well and sample a bit of the food that had made the establishment a rousing success.

It was well after dark when Ruby and Ethan drove home in their new Chevrolet touring car. The girls would be spending the weekend at Jace and Clara's, giving their parents a little time alone. It was honeymoon enough for Ruby. All she wanted was to be truly home, at last, with her family around her.

"Are you really going to carry me across the threshold?" she teased as he helped her out of the car. "I'm not a little woman, you know."

He brushed a kiss across her lips. "That's what

you said the first time we met. As I recall, I managed fine."

"Yes, I know." She took his arm as they mounted the steps to the wide front porch. "But this time's different. You'll be lifting me, not catching me…"

"So?" His gold-flecked eyes twinkled. Sweet heaven, how she loved him.

"There's more," she said. "Truth be told, I may be a bit more delicate than I was then. You'll want to be extra careful with me."

His eyes widened in wonder as her meaning sank home. "Ruby, you're not—"

"Yes, I am." She beamed up at him. "And don't scold me for not telling you sooner. I didn't want you to think you had an obligation to marry me."

"You silly, adorable woman! Wait till we tell our girls! They'll be over the moon—just like their father!" Pulling her close, he gave her a kiss that lingered, warmed and heated until she fell back in his arms, a bit breathless.

"I…think we need to go inside," she murmured.

"Good idea." He opened the door and scooped her off her feet. As Ruby had said, she wasn't a little woman, but Ethan was a very strong man.

He made it all the way to the bedroom.

* * * * *

COMING NEXT MONTH FROM

HARLEQUIN®
HISTORICAL

Available March 29, 2011

- **THE BRIDE RAFFLE**
  by **Lisa Plumley**
  (Western)

- **DELECTABLY UNDONE!**
  by **Elizabeth Rolls, Michelle Willingham, Marguerite Kaye,
  Ashley Radcliff, Bronwyn Scott**
  (Anthology: Various time periods)
  *Five sensual short stories specially selected from
  Harlequin Historical Undone! digital program.*

- **WANTED: MAIL-ORDER MISTRESS**
  by **Deborah Hale**
  (Regency)
  Gentlemen of Fortune

- **HIGHLAND HEIRESS**
  by **Margaret Moore**
  (Regency)

You can find more information on upcoming
Harlequin® titles, free excerpts and more at
www.HarlequinInsideRomance.com.

HHCNM0311R

REQUEST YOUR FREE BOOKS!

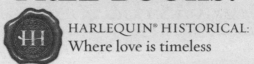

HARLEQUIN® HISTORICAL:
Where love is timeless

2 FREE NOVELS PLUS 2 FREE GIFTS!

YES! Please send me 2 FREE Harlequin® Historical novels and my 2 FREE gifts (gifts are worth about $10). After receiving them, if I don't wish to receive any more books, I can return the shipping statement marked "cancel." If I don't cancel, I will receive 6 brand-new novels every month and be billed just $4.94 per book in the U.S. or $5.49 per book in Canada. That's a savings of at least 18% off the cover price! It's quite a bargain! Shipping and handling is just 50¢ per book in the U.S. and 75¢ per book in Canada.* I understand that accepting the 2 free books and gifts places me under no obligation to buy anything. I can always return a shipment and cancel at any time. Even if I never buy another book from the Reader Service, the two free books and gifts are mine to keep forever.

246/349 HDN FC45

Name _____ (PLEASE PRINT)

Address _____ Apt. #

City _____ State/Prov. _____ Zip/Postal Code

Signature (if under 18, a parent or guardian must sign)

Mail to the **Reader Service:**
IN U.S.A.: P.O. Box 1867, Buffalo, NY 14240-1867
IN CANADA: P.O. Box 609, Fort Erie, Ontario L2A 5X3

Not valid for current subscribers to Harlequin Historical books.

Want to try two free books from another line?
Call 1-800-873-8635 or visit www.ReaderService.com.

* Terms and prices subject to change without notice. Prices do not include applicable taxes. N.Y. residents add applicable sales tax. Canadian residents will be charged applicable taxes. Offer not valid in Quebec. This offer is limited to one order per household. All orders subject to credit approval. Credit or debit balances in a customer's account(s) may be offset by any other outstanding balance owed by or to the customer. Please allow 4 to 6 weeks for delivery. Offer available while quantities last.

Your Privacy—The Reader Service is committed to protecting your privacy. Our Privacy Policy is available online at www.ReaderService.com or upon request from the Reader Service.

We make a portion of our mailing list available to reputable third parties that offer products we believe may interest you. If you prefer that we not exchange your name with third parties, or if you wish to clarify or modify your communication preferences, please visit us at www.ReaderService.com/consumerschoice or write to us at Reader Service Preference Service, P.O. Box 9062, Buffalo, NY 14269. Include your complete name and address.

Selene wanted nothing to do with the father of her son, Alex; but Aristedes had other plans...that included them.

Read on for an sneak peek from
THE SARANTOS SECRET BABY by Olivia Gates,
available April 2011, only from Harlequin Desire.

"You were right to turn my marriage offer down," Aristedes said.

And Selene found her voice at last, found the words that would not betray the blow he'd dealt her. "Thanks for letting me know. You didn't have to come all the way here, though. You could have just let it go. I left yesterday with the understanding that this case is closed."

Before the hot needles behind her eyes could dissolve into an unforgivable display of stupidity and weakness, she began to close the door.

The door stopped against an immovable object. His flat palm.

"I can't accept that." His voice was low, leashed.

What did her tormentor mean now? Was he ending one game only to start another?

She raised eyes as bruised as her self-respect to his, found nothing there but solemnity and determination.

Before she could voice her confusion, he elaborated. "I never let anything go unless I'm certain it's unworkable. I realize I made you an unworkable offer, and that's why I'm withdrawing it. I'm here to offer something else. A workability study."

She leaned against the door, thankful for its support and partial shield. "Your son and I are not a business venture you can test for feasibility."

His gaze grew deeper, made her feel as if he was trying to delve into her mind, take control of it. "It's actually the other way around. I'm the one who would be tested."

She shook her head. "Why bother? I know—and *you* know—you're not workable. Not with me."

His spectacular eyebrows lowered over eyes she felt were emitting silver hypnosis. "You're right again. Neither you nor I have any reason to believe that isn't the truth. The only truth. It might be best for both you and Alex to never hear from me again, to forget I exist. But then again, maybe not. I'm only asking for the chance for both of us to find out for certain. You believe I'm unworkable in any personal relationship. I've lived my life based on that belief about myself. I never really had reason to question it. But I have one now. In fact, I have two."

Find out what happens in
THE SARANTOS SECRET BABY by Olivia Gates,
available April 2011, only from Harlequin Desire.

Copyright © 2011 by Olivia Gates

SDEXP0411

HARLEQUIN® HISTORICAL:
Where love is timeless

USA TODAY
BESTSELLING AUTHOR
MARGARET MOORE
INTRODUCES
Highland Heiress

SUED FOR BREACH OF PROMISE!

No sooner does Lady Moira MacMurdaugh breathe a sigh
of relief for avoiding a disastrous marriage to Dunbrachie's
answer to Casanova than she is served with a lawsuit! By
the very man who saved her from a vicious dog attack, no
less: solicitor Gordon McHeath. Torn between loyalty for a
friend and this beautiful woman who stirs him to ridiculous
distraction, Gordon knows he can't have it both ways....

But when sinister forces threaten to upend Lady Moira's world,
Gordon simply can't stand idly by and watch her fall!

**Available from Harlequin Historical
April 2011**

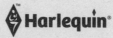

❖ Harlequin®

A *Romance* FOR EVERY MOOD™

www.eHarlequin.com

HH29638

Harlequin® *Blaze*™

red-hot reads

Sunny, sensual Hawaiian spring break…again!

Three best girlfriends are recapturing an amazing spring-break
vacation they had a decade ago.

First on the beach is former attorney and all-around good girl
Mia Butterfield. Meeting up with her boyfriend of old is a bust,
so she's shocked when her hero turns out to be someone she'd
never have expected…

Find out who it is in

SECOND TIME LUCKY

by acclaimed author

Debbi Rawlins

Available from Harlequin Blaze® April 2011

Part of the sensual miniseries,

Spring Break

Part 2: Delicious Do-Over (May)

Harlequin®

A *Romance* FOR EVERY MOOD™

www.eHarlequin.com

HB79607

MARGARET WAY

In the Australian Billionaire's Arms

Handsome billionaire David Wainwright isn't about to let his favorite uncle be taken for all he's worth by mysterious and undeniably attractive florist Sonya Erickson.

But David soon discovers that Sonya's no greedy gold digger. And as sparks sizzle between them, will the rugged Australian embrace the secrets of her past so they can have a chance at a future together?

Don't miss this incredible new tale,
available in April 2011
wherever books are sold!

www.eHarlequin.com

HR17722